D0341023

WHAT WE MAY BECOME

Also by Teresa Messineo

THE FIRE BY NIGHT

WHAT WE MAY BECOME

Teresa Messineo

SEVERN HOUSE

First world edition published in Great Britain and the USA in 2022
by Severn House, an imprint of Canongate Books Ltd,
14 High Street, Edinburgh EH1 1TE.

Trade paperback edition first published in Great Britain and the USA in 2022
by Severn House, an imprint of Canongate Books Ltd.

severnhouse.com

British Library Cataloguing-in-Publication Data
A CIP catalogue record for this title is available from the British Library.

ISBN-13: 978-1-4483-0867-5 (cased)
ISBN-13: 978-1-4483-0885-9 (trade paper)
ISBN-13: 978-1-4483-0886-6 (e-book)

All Severn House titles are printed on acid-free paper.

Typeset by Palimpsest Book Production Ltd.,
Falkirk, Stirlingshire, Scotland.
Printed and bound in Great Britain by
TJ Books, Padstow, Cornwall.

To Stephen Myers and Juilene Osborne-McKnight –

The truth is not always beautiful,
nor beautiful words the truth – Laozi

Ar scáth a chéile a mhaireann na daoine – Irish proverb

Beloved, now we are sons of God, and it doth not yet appear what we may become
– 1 John 3:2

*I*n her dream, she puts the baby down. She kneels down in the dark grass, wet and cool against her knees. She does not hold on to the heavy, warm bundle but, this time, lays it down next to the tree that is only half there, that is only half formed in her mind, its colossal branches reaching out sideways into the night sky, into nothingness. She knows if she looks up suddenly, if she turns around too quickly, the tree will be gone, the stars above her that are pouring down their light will not be there at all, her subconscious able to recreate one pattern, one sketchy constellation, maybe, but the rest remaining a dark sea of oblivion above her.

She smiles as she stands up, looking down at the child, at the pale, chubby leg that has escaped its shroud-like wrap, kicking silently in space. The baby coos and she smiles again, the curving half-smile of a madwoman, of a dreamer who knows it is a dream, who needs to prolong the illusion that what she does next is what she really did. She turns her back on the baby, still babbling happily to itself, as she starts down the hill towards the village. The village is glowing. She doesn't ask why, she doesn't need to ask, she saw it that night, but, for now, all she feels is relief. She has done it right, at last. Her arms are empty, light, and unencumbered. There is no screaming child in them, no thrashing monster throwing back its head and howling, drawing danger to itself, to the woman who carried it. No, the baby is at the top of the hill, far behind her now, she cannot see and yet she still sees its placid face, hears its happy gurgling. It has caught its foot in its tiny hands and is greedily sucking its toes.

She takes in a deep draft of night air and is content, is relieved, so relieved she hugs herself in her happiness, in her delusion that she knows by heart, she has dreamed it so many times before. The baby is safe, the baby is happy, she says without saying, without moving her lips, and the bodies on *the ground all around her do not disturb her, do not scare her as they did that night, because even they know she has gotten it right. They open their eyes and sit up slowly, nodding kindly towards her, good girl, brave girl, they tell her, you made the right choice, after all.*

She is barefoot, and she is walking towards the light, towards that yellow orange light, but it is only beautiful tonight, only a warm, welcoming glow in front of her, nothing else. There is no fire, the buildings are not burning, they are not exploding all around her. She can no longer hear the screams of the women, of the children trapped inside, or the smashing of bombs falling out of nowhere, out of nothingness, because nothing is falling and no one is calling out now. *It is perfectly still, perfectly lovely and still. She can hear the baby half a mile away, hear the sound of its sucking, of its contentedness. She has never felt so light, so carefree and young, like a child herself.* The baby is safe, safe without me, *and now she is standing right in front of the light, basking in the radiant, fiery glow and she laughs without sound in that vacuum, in that great silent space. But in the last seconds of her dream, all noise and sound come crashing back and with terror she looks behind her and the hill is on fire, the baby is gone, and she cannot look down, cannot force herself to look down, but now something terrible and heavy is back in her arms, dragging her down with its weight, and she screams.*

ONE

Montepulciano
Province of Siena
Tuscany
1945

She was screaming still when she woke up. The person lying next to her nudged her mechanically and another woman sleeping nearby rolled over and cursed under her breath and went back to a fitful sleep. But Diana was awake. She didn't want to go back to her dream, so she extricated herself from the tangled bedclothes, from the bed she shared with two other women. Her corner of the mattress had a hole in it the size of her fist and she looked away, automatically, as she always did, unwilling to think of what had made it. The room was quiet, except for the steady breathing of the women, piled three to a bed, two to a couch, lying pell-mell over the old wooden floorboards of the upstairs room. She stepped around outstretched arms, between piles of quilts thrown off in the night, the smooth outline of narrow hip bones, of voluptuous bellies showing through threadbare satin, tattered cotton, and gingham worn to a faded check. She heard the familiar shrill whistle near her ear, swatting vaguely in that direction, the *zanzara* moving off to feast on the sleeping women, joined by dozens of his compatriots swarming in through the open casement windows. The air was already hot, even though the sun was not yet up. When she reached the bathroom, the water was tepid coming out of the taps, the only coolness coming from the large square tiles beneath her feet. She caught sight of herself in the blistered mirror hung high on the wall. She could only see her face, her long neck, and dark hair. She stood on her toes to see her protruding collar bone, rubbing it slowly as if she could hide it, as if she could fix it, as if she could make herself look young and healthy and beautiful again.

There isn't much time, ran through her head. There isn't much time and there is too much time. In another moment, while it was still dark, Donna Lucia would come stomping up the stairs, yelling and cursing in Italian, using words Diana had come to recognize as *get up, you lazy bitches, time to work, I should throw you all out in the street*, followed by a diatribe that always ended in the same three names – gossiped to be former lovers, or the names of sons dead in the war – along with a swift kick to any late risers in her path. But now it was silent. The village outside had not yet risen, the old women – always up before anyone else – had not done their washing, were not outside tossing their basins into the street, the dirty water snaking its way around cobblestones, making long, dark lines that met and converged and ran down the sharply angled streets of a village built on top of a mountain. Diana rubbed her bare arms, not because she was cold but for reassurance, like a child comforting itself, as if to register the fact that she, Diana Bolsena, American Red Cross nurse, had come to this.

When the war broke out, Diana had been unstoppable. Serving as a nurse back home, then in England, North Africa, and Sicily, no one could touch Diana for her spirit or ingenuity or drive. Every night she had read and reread the page torn from her high school yearbook, covered with signatures and well-wishes from classmates and teachers alike, with one line standing out from the rest in a darker hand, its sentiment making up for any defects of penmanship or grammar. *To Dee, the cutest girl in class. I love you're smile. I know you will make your mark on the world. Never change. xoxo Jack.*

But Diana *had* changed. Anzio had changed her. Hell's Half-Acre, with its constant bombardment, with the nurses and doctors pinned down on the beach, unable to stand up straight for fear of being hit, moving around in a half-crouch – the Anzio Shuffle, they had called it. Their patients had complained they'd be safer in Germany than in those hospital tents in Italy, technically off-limits under the Geneva Conventions, but smack-dab up against the anti-aircraft batteries, ammunition dumps, airstrips, and food and mainten- ance depots that were legitimate – and frequent – targets.

Twenty-five thousand injured patients to care for. Another twenty thousand down with disease and five thousand more from accidents, teenagers staggering around in a world of metal shards and broken glass. Young men blowing up right in front of the nurses – Diana remembered four boys running towards the surf like students on summer holiday and then the shrill whistle and the explosion, and there had been nothing left to put back together. She saw again the hot shrapnel ripping through their surgical tents, the sun making bright spots against the dark canvas that glowed like stars at night. She could smell the dead awaiting identification, lined up in stifling hot tents swarming with flies. She could still feel the sensation of being trapped, all of them trapped together, sweltering on a sandspit of death for nearly half a year, with nothing but the ocean behind them. A front initially fifteen miles wide and seven miles deep with nowhere to retreat to. Caught between the devil and the deep blue sea. After Anzio, Allied troops had moved again, had finally begun to chase Jerry back through Italy, along the ancient *Via Appia*, towards Rome itself, which they took amid fanfare and carefully posed photo shoots that excluded any Allied officers but Americans, the MPs actually stopping British soldiers at checkpoints until the press had moved on. But, even with this victory, Diana had felt the loss, felt what she had left behind her until, one day, feeling she would never leave her mark on a world intent on tearing itself apart, she had thrown away the old scrap from her yearbook. It became just one more piece of litter left alongside the deep-rutted tracks the Allies were leaving all across Europe.

The Diana standing in the close, upstairs room shook herself all over to get out of her reverie. She stepped into her clothes and pulled on her shoes, scuffed and worn – the seam had come undone along her left instep, the stitches hanging loose. Anzio was a long time ago now, two hundred miles to the south, far from where she stood on this summer night in Tuscany. She could never go back there. She hadn't even been able to make contact with her army, separated as she was in this medieval town without telephone or mail service, in a place the retreating Germans had tried to destroy in their flight north. The war in Europe had ended, her side had won, but Diana Bolsena was lost.

Donna Lucia threw open the door at the foot of their stairway. They could hear her heavy-soled shoes thumping up the wooden steps. '*Alzatevi, puttane pigre, alzatevi, perché vi tengo qui?*' Get up, you lazy bitches, get up, why do I keep you here? she repeated by rote, like some bizarre perversion of *Good morning* other sleepers were receiving in kinder parts of the world. Diana was dressed, standing in the middle of the room now, as the other girls scurried for their clothing, for their shoes, for discolored cloth diapers used as sanitary napkins. Pushing hair back into buns, into hastily constructed braids, trying to dress and make up the beds and make a rush for the washroom all at once. A twelve-year-old child with thin, straw-colored braids was the last to get up and Donna Lucia kicked her as if she were a dog, with no more, with no less, emotion than she would kick an animal in her way, stamping and stomping and yelling at them in her deep man's voice.

'*Benedetto, Giuseppe, Giancarlo,*' she cried aloud, her litany of men's names rolling off her sharp tongue, and no one could tell from the way she said it if she had loved the men or hated them or both. The women, young and slender, old and shriveled, lined up as best they could, enduring the insults they no longer heard, starting to shuffle down the narrow staircase towards the smell of food, following the wide frame of Lucia and the indescribable pain her cruelty hid.

It was a question of work. When Diana was first separated from the American Army, she needed to find temporary work so she could eat, so she could stay alive long enough to re-establish contact. But there had been no work. The small medical clinic in town was run by religious, half-starved nuns who gave what little they had to their hungry patients. They apologized they had nothing to offer the American nurse, not even food, but begged her to stay on and help them. Only with great effort had Diana been able to walk away, to ignore the forlorn look in the elderly superior's and in the teenaged novice's eyes as Diana stepped out of the clinic's dark hallway into the blinding midday sun, in search of sustenance for herself. Most of the shops were still boarded up – against

Allied aerial raids and looters alike – and the ones that were
making a tentative reopening were already overstaffed with
relatives, with *cugini*, with second and third and fourth cousins
from the country, from the cities, unrelated refugees with the
same last name desperate for a place to stay. Diana spent her
last *lire* on bread, and her hunger had grown that first day,
then throughout the second, her desperation mounting as she
realized those few coins were all she had had in the world
and now they were gone and she had no way to get more. She
went to the churches – to the fourteen Catholic churches in
the same small town – with some vague Sunday-school picture
in her head, with a stained-glass image of well-groomed, well-
fed saints – royalty, mostly, Edmund of England and Elizabeth
of Hungary – opening their ermine-lined capes to reveal a
bounty, a cornucopia for a grateful populace. But instead, lined
up inside the churches' dark interiors, she had found crying
babies, sickly elderly, bandaged and splinted sufferers unable
to walk or move or even sit up. The priests and monks caring
for them saw Diana and assumed the able-bodied woman had
come to help, holding out basins of water for cleaning wounds
and small bottles of watered-down goats' milk for the orphaned
infants. When she explained in the broken Italian she had
picked up in Anzio that she was destitute, that she herself was
hungry, hadn't eaten for days, that she wanted to work, but
would at least need food, the busy men had looked confused,
as if her words hadn't quite translated, as if they required
further clarification. *She* was destitute, they asked? *She* was
starving? And they had motioned at the suffering humanity
all around them, many of the men, women, and children not
suffering from their first days of hunger, as Diana was, but
from their last. And the men had smiled sadly, shaking their
heads, making a quick sign of the cross over her as if wishing
her luck, and turned back to their flock.

There was no work. Try as she might, there was no work
in town, none far below in the fields, where she had picked
up the half-rumor that farm hands were needed. But that had
not been true. There were no seeds to put in that year – the
fields were burned out, anyway – and the farmhouses and
barns and any other buildings that might have housed the

non-existent harvest had been ransacked or burned down or both. By the time she had climbed back up into town, along paths so steep they had left her breathless, nearly doubling her over, she felt the seriousness of her situation. *You are the sum of your decisions*, the pink counted cross-stitch that hung above the icebox in the nursing students' lounge had read. She wondered now if that were true.

On the curving side street Diana had taken, when she returned from her futile search for work in the fields, she saw a truckload of girls getting off a dilapidated, canvas-backed truck. They were dressed in clean clothes, hair neatly groomed, not one of them over twenty years old. It was only sunset, not even twilight, and yet each of them was yawning widely, eyes red, and staring groggily ahead. Diana thought they would fall asleep on their feet. The girls got off the truck and filed into a small alleyway between buildings. The driver of the truck began to roll himself a cigarette and, before he had even finished, another line of girls, similarly dressed and aged, but looking much more alert, some even a little bit scared, had already climbed on to the truck bed. The driver pushed up the tailgate without even looking at his new passengers and, cigarette hanging from his mouth, thrust the truck into gear as it rattled towards one of the stone porticos leading out of the walled town.

Diana hesitated.

This is not me, she argued with herself. *Not what I was raised to accept as acceptable.* Back home in Oswego County, she hadn't even known the word for what these girls were doing, for what men called girls who did these things in order to survive. But – again, that sickening reality – what were her choices, really? She had tried for weeks to contact the Americans, the nearest outpost probably in Siena, maybe even Florence by now, several hours away by a train that no longer ran. Diana had scoured the town when she came to it, looking for a telephone, but the Germans had cut all the wires, toppling the telephone and telegraph poles from Rome to Trieste, in their flight north. As for available work, there would be no harvest that year, no employment on the overmanned farms, nor in the overstaffed shops in town, showcasing their pitiful wares in cracked-glass display cases. The church had seemed overwhelmed caring for even its most indigent members, those unable to work, or even beg, the poorest of the poor. Diana could not leave this town – not without provisions or transportation – and she certainly would not last long in this post-war village without money. To Diana, it seemed that the only thriving business in town – in any town with a surplus of hungry women to a glut of rationed men – lay at the end of the dark alleyway before her. Diana hesitated for another moment, trying to chide herself into acting reasonably, into being reasonable, into remembering the value of phrases she had learned growing up – like 'noble poor' and 'self-respect' and 'easy virtue.' Trying to remember the importance of who and what she was – that, whatever it was, it was not this. Then she caught herself trying to remember if she had last eaten two or three days ago – and couldn't – and, with that, she stopped thinking altogether. Diana clenched her fists and exhaled sharply, stepping forward quickly to join the line, following the last yawning girl as she disappeared into darkness.

The worst part was the laughter. Diana had gotten inside, sat down with the other women at wooden tables set up in a large, open room, been handed a bowl of plain pasta she devoured all at once. But one of the older women had looked at Diana, then looked again, then walked over to a large woman wearing man's shoes and stuck out her chin in the direction of the newcomer. Diana had thought there would be a scene, or even a scuffle, but Donna Lucia had only laughed. One or two of the older women who surrounded her joined in. Most of the young girls were too tired, or too intent on finishing their dinner, to seem to care. But one of Lucia's lackeys strode over to Diana, pulling her up to her feet with a grip surprisingly strong for her bird-like frame.

'*Chi sei?*' Who are you? the bird-woman asked her. '*Cosa vuoi?*' What do you want?

Diana knew enough Italian to answer.

'*Sono una americana.*' I'm an American, she replied. Then she added in a low voice, blushing to the roots of her hair,

'*Ho bisogno . . . ho bisogno di lavorare.*' I need . . . I need to work.

That's when the laughter had started in earnest. Diana had expected to be thrown out or, if accepted, to undergo some horrific ceremony, a branding or other painful initiation. But, somehow, she had simply become the butt of some incredible joke. Girls who at first had paid no attention to the new arrival now set their empty bowls down on the table and stared openly. Someone yelled something in a dialect unrecognizable as Italian, and a dozen more women leaned over the banister overlooking the dining room, pointing. From each girl there came a whisper, then a titter, and then everyone was talking at once and everyone – *everyone* – was laughing. Donna Lucia had tears in her eyes, she was having trouble breathing, clutching at her stomach as if in pain.

'An American!' the woman yelled the English words. 'An American she says, here, in my humble home,' and then she stepped up close to Diana, cocking her head and peering mockingly into Diana's eyes. 'She needs work, she says' – translating for the benefit of the room – '*Ha bisogno di lavorare.*' And everyone laughed again. Lucia poked Diana in the stomach, lifted her arms as if she were a rag doll, pulled back Diana's hairline, scrutinizing her scalp.

'How many years do you have?' Lucia bellowed the idiomatic expression.

'Thirty-two.' Now realizing the cause of their merriment, Diana could barely find her voice, the words catching in her throat.

'*Trentadue!*' the bird-woman held up her fingers to the room, translating for Lucia, who was pink from laughter, unable to speak, a thin line of drool shining on her chin.

'An old woman,' Lucia gasped at last, pointing at Diana. 'A grandmother. *Nonna.*' And the word, *nonna*, was taken up by everyone. Several young girls, not yet in their teens, took up the chant, *nonna, nonna, nonna*, banging their fists on the table in unison.

Diana's face was burning with shame, but a different type of shame than she had felt only moments before. She had sold herself to Satan, but now, incredibly, it seemed Satan didn't

want her. She had never even thought of doing something like
this before, not once during the war, no matter how bad it had
gotten. She had always felt she would be resourceful enough
to come up with a better, with a nobler, solution to any problem
life might throw at her. But now, from the women's reaction,
it seemed she had debased herself for nothing. Apparently, she
was much too old for this type of work, too old even to be
considered with so much – and so much younger – competi-
tion. She was a fool to have even tried, she realized, surrounded
by laughing, round-bottomed, firm-skinned young girls.
Diana's face burned again, but now in red-hot anger. *We all
take our sins seriously*, the words of Sister Karen came back
to her, suddenly, incongruously. *We all take a certain pride
in them, in their egregiousness and gravity*. Diana had taken
her sin seriously, with a deadly earnest in fact, as if she was
the first person to have ever had to make that type of awful
decision. But being poked, prodded, and ridiculed as a result,
turned into a general spectacle, like the last slave on an auction
block no one will bid on – that was intolerable to her, and her
hitherto unacknowledged sense of superiority. Diana knew she
should feel sympathy, should at least feel empathy for the
laughing women all around her, women who had been just as
desperate, just as hungry as she had been a moment before.
Women who had been through much worse, and much more
invasive forms of initiation. But Diana didn't. She just felt
angry. *They'd be lucky to have me*, she nearly said aloud before
the reality dawned on her that if this – the very last bastion,
her very last hope – had proved hopeless, then how on earth
would she survive? If not by this unthinkable, thinkable way,
then how?

Donna Lucia dried her eyes on the corner of her apron, a
curiously clean white expanse covering her wide belly.

'Stupid woman, I should throw you out. You are an old goat
that cannot turn a trick. But' – and here Diana was stunned
at the word *but* — 'I have not laughed so hard in longer than
I can say. I need someone to wash up, to clean the clothes for
these young bitches, they fetch a better price if they are clean,
on the outside, at least. I cannot do it all, and these *puttane*
are worthless at it – they are clumsy children. You stay one

day, I feed you one day, you clean the clothes or throw her out.' This last was directed to the bird-woman who looked angry she could not throw Diana out then and there.

Diana did not wait to give her a chance. Hurrying over to the rickety staircase the teenage girls were now ascending, tugging at their ribbons and undoing their long braids, Diana followed them and took a small corner of the bedroom floor as her own. The room quieted down quickly, no after lights-out chit-chat as there had been in her nursing dormitory back home or lying next to her own sister late at night. Diana exhaled. She had gotten in, she was safe for the night, she had eaten, that was the main thing. She felt the unskilled job of washerwoman might be taken from her at any moment, subject to the mercurial whims of her employer. So Diana decided that tomorrow she would tell them she was a nurse, could offer the girls valuable care. But she had gotten her foot in the door. That was enough for now.

After a few moments, a girl, the oldest among them – nineteen or even as old as twenty – came over to her and pointed at one of the beds that only had two girls in it. The girl stood there in her long, white nightdress, her golden-red hair hanging down loosely, her pale skin radiating from within, making her look like a Renaissance portrait of a saint or a virgin. She nodded at Diana, who crawled in and lay still as the girl went back to her own bed. In another moment, there was no sound at all but rhythmic breathing, and the high, shrill whistle of mosquitoes pouring in through the open windows. Diana's head was spinning from the jumbled sequence of the day's events, at the crazy, upside-down world she suddenly found herself in. She saw again the ugly face of Lucia, red and writhing with laughter, and the face of the girl who had pointed out her bed, as fair and beautiful as an angel's. Diana's stomach wasn't empty, it was no longer gnawing at her inside. She had made it through another day. But at what cost?

'Where am I?' Diana whispered aloud. But she knew no one was listening.

Diana was right about being thrown out. Halfway through that first morning, while she was hanging up the enormous piles of wet laundry, Donna Lucia came barreling into the small washroom, ripping a petticoat off the line and holding it menacingly in front of Diana's face.

'Do you call this clean?' she had shouted in her bellowing voice. The garment was worn thin from wear, the white cotton turned to a sickly grey. Diana had scrubbed it on the old metal washboard until her knuckles were raw, but its faded blood stains could not be completely removed, and small circles of discoloration marked the threadbare fabric.

'You think this is good enough? You go out. No food. Out, now, this moment,' and the woman had begun shooing Diana towards the front door. At that moment, the yawning queue of night girls was filing in from the canvas-backed truck, pushing past Diana and Donna Lucia as if not even registering their existence. At the end of the line, two of the women were supporting a staggering girl who seemed unable to walk on her own. Donna Lucia thrust her chin out in the girl's direction, making an interrogatory grunt. The two women holding the thin girl looked from Donna Lucia to Diana and back again, as if seeking permission to speak in front of an outsider.

'*Che cosa? Parlate,* mannaggia*! Cos'è successo qui?*' What? Speak, *goddamnit.* What happened here?

Although Donna Lucia was still hurrying her towards the door, Diana paused as she saw the young girl's lips go white, and her eyes start to roll back in her head.

'This girl needs help,' Diana said, instinctively taking a step forward. Donna Lucia grabbed on to her arm, but Diana pulled away.

'I can help her,' reaching for the words. '*Posso aiutarla.* I can help. I am a nurse, *un'infermiera,*' and she pointed violently to herself, her finger tapping again and again on her sternum.

'You lie. You only say this to stay here, to trick me . . .' Donna Lucia began in a low growl, but the girl collapsed at that moment and Diana sunk down by her side. She took the girl's wrist in her hand, feeling for her pulse.

All of a sudden, Diana was no longer a lost soul at war's end, desperate for food and shelter, at the mercy of some fool who had been about to cast her out. She was Diana Bolsena, and the competence born of caring for thousands of patients

– of kneeling over men with severed limbs, bleeding out, of snatching back boys from the brink of death – came back to her in an instant. Automatically, she took in the girl's breathing, her heartbeat, her coloring, the way she gripped defensively at her abdomen, even as she seemed to slip in and out of consciousness. Diana's own breathing was slow and steady, her eyes keenly focused, engulfed by a dead calm that cast aside everything but the patient in front of her. She could save this girl. She could save ten thousand girls like her.

'What do you have for medical supplies here?' Diana demanded, the power having shifted, the other women gathering around her now, looking to her for direction. Diana threw back her head in frustration. What was it the prisoners of war – the Italian doctors who had been captured on a Tuesday and, on Wednesday, had started working alongside their enemy counterparts, the American medical corps – called their medical kits?

'*Medici*,' she began, remembering the word for medicine, blanking on the rest. '*Kit medici?* Hell, you must have something here.'

Donna Lucia understood, barking an order to one of the women who ran into Donna Lucia's office, off-limits to everybody.

'And whisky,' Diana called after her, knowing the word needed no translation.

The woman came back after a moment, lugging a dull-green metal case with faded lettering, *Verbandkasten*, a German first-aid kit. Diana pulled one of the clean sheets she had folded earlier that day off a nearby counter, spreading it out on the floor and easing the girl on to it. She opened the kit, checking its contents, seeing what parts had already been cannibalized, noting mechanically that the gauze, bandages, surgical needles, and thread she needed were still there. Donna Lucia began pouring a glass of whisky for the girl to drink. Diana shook her head, 'No, *non per bere*, not for drinking,' and held out her hands. The Germans packed their medical kits, and all their surgical supplies, in Cosmolene to prevent them from rusting. The sticky stuff glistened on Diana's fingers from handling the equipment.

'Help me clean this off, the alcohol will cut it.'

Diana held up a surgical needle, letting the alcohol pour over it and cut through the grease, making it less slippery and easier to hold on to. She selected a glass ampoule stamped *Hartmann Steri-Seide*, a surgical catgut thread swimming in a sterile solution, and carefully began to thread the needle.

'Tell her it's all right, that I'm going to help her. That I'll try not to hurt her.'

Donna Lucia mumbled her translation in a low voice that sounded like a recited prayer. The girl moaned and tried to sit up, but the women were now half supporting, half holding her down. Diana reached down with her free hand and pulled up the girl's skirt. She could hear the women beside her suck in their breath, and then curse. On the inside of the girl's thigh was the raised purple imprint of a man's knee, where he had pinned her down. Diana rested her hand gently on the inside of her other leg, slowly moving her hand upward so the girl could feel where her hand was. The girl winced, and Diana spoke quietly but firmly.

'Tell her she is injured, there has been a . . . a tearing that must be repaired so she can begin to heal.'

'Will she work again?' Donna Lucia demanded. 'Tell me she can work again, and that this bastard has not cost me the price I pay for these girls.'

Diana fixed her with a stony look.

'Please translate.'

Donna Lucia hesitated another moment.

'These girls are worth nothing to me if they cannot work. This is not a charity I run here.'

Diana set her jaw.

'You will please translate, now. I need to suture her, to stop the bleeding. That is not comfortable, I can assure you, and I need to have her working with me, rather than against me. It cannot be done unless she stays very still. And she won't if she doesn't understand what I'm trying to do.'

Donna Lucia mumbled a few words to the girl who had regained full consciousness and was staring fixedly at Diana. She was young and thin and very pale. Little beads of sweat had broken out on her forehead. She remained still for another moment, then nodded her head quickly. The women on either side of her repositioned their grasp on the girl's arms, steadying themselves.

'She will work again? I need her to work,' Donna Lucia repeated, but in a lower voice this time.

'She will *heal* again,' Diana answered as she moved in closer. 'My job is to heal. What comes after that . . . well, we'll see. And, Donna Lucia' – it was the first time Diana had called her by name, and the woman shot her a surprised look – 'you can give her a little of that whisky, now.'

After that, Diana was never at a loss for work. She received double rations, which she split with the youngest girls, anemic, straggling pre-adolescents orphaned or sold for food during the war. Diana had treated hundreds of GIs with venereal disease – gonorrhea and syphilis, mostly – but each recruit had received the standard *Sex Hygiene and VD* pamphlet upon enlistment and had at least a general knowledge of how disease spreads and how they could reduce their risk of infection by using prophylaxis. But these girls were uneducated – well schooled in how to please a man and secure prompt payment – but woefully unaware of their own bodies or how to protect themselves. Laboring under old wives' tales and misconceptions outdated centuries before, they drank tinctures of holy wood, rubbed on ointments laced with mercury, or sat cooped up in sweltering hot rooms, windows shut and fire blazing in the middle of summer, trying to prevent or sweat out contagion. Diana showed them that the small, painless bumps the girls had assumed were pimples or ingrown hairs were really syphilis chancres, the rash on the palms of their hands and soles of their feet a more advanced stage of the disease. Once they knew what to look for, nearly all the women found signs of infection – mild fevers, sores on their lips, inflamed eyes and throat. Donna Lucia was all attention, taking stock of her inventory, eager to gain an advantage over her competitors' product.

'What can we do, to do better, to get more customers? They do not like to see these things, they will not pay the price for damaged goods,' she said as she pushed aside a young, pregnant woman with pus coming out of the corner of her eye.

You could stop this, Diana answered her, internally. *You could stop this madness, stop buying and selling women, children. Whatever your pain, whatever someone did to you once to make you this way, you are still a woman. Stop pretending they are not you and you are not them.* Instead, she asked, 'Where you send them, there is a black market? Don't answer. There is a black market, everywhere. Look for these things and buy them.' Diana wrote down the English words *penicillin* – the Americans' secret weapon during the war – and *prophylactic condoms*.

'What is this last one, *con-dom*?' Donna Lucia sounded out the unfamiliar word.

'The men might call them rubbers.'

'Ah, yes, no good. For the women, they are a luxury. And for the men, they do not prefer them.'

Diana looked at the girls ranged around her, half dressed, pointing out new rashes and sores they discovered on their neighbors or themselves. This was not right. With a little education, with even a little opportunity, these women could leave this life and start one on their own terms. Instead, poverty or circumstance or war had brought them here, helpless as babes, some of them – Gabriella, for instance – seemingly still innocent as babes, at the mercy of the next John and whatever infection he hid under his smooth exterior. Whatever her own beliefs were, Diana wanted to better the situation, the best she could. She searched for words that might influence Donna Lucia on terms she understood.

'Your girls will last longer, and will fetch a better price, if you use these things. Without them, your girls will get sick and diseased, and no one will want them. It's up to you. Men will come to your . . . your business if you can advertise you have clean, safe girls. Sick girls, no one wants.' *Especially you*, Diana thought as she watched the older woman rub her chin in thought.

Donna Lucia smashed her hand down on the table. 'We do it. We be the only business that does it. "Our girls are clean. Our girls are safe." Hah! We have our own American nurse.

No one can compete with us.' She stomped out of the room in the same thundering manner as always.

I wish I could do more for them, Diana mused. *This is not enough. This whole situation is wrong, what they're doing to these girls is wrong. They deserve so much more than a pill, and a piece of plastic, and a shove back out there to line their keeper's pockets.*

Then one of the girls, the one with straw-colored braids whom Lucia had kicked when she hadn't woken up fast enough, came up to Lucia, opening her mouth to show her a pustule on the inside of her lip that was raised and sore and angry. *It is not enough*, Diana thought again, *but it is enough for right now.*

When the girls went into the cities, Diana sent them with letters addressed to the nearest American outposts, giving them her name, rank, serial number, and location, explaining she had been separated from her unit but wanted to get back to the war, to her duty, to wherever the war was headed next. Diana asked the girls to send them from different post offices – one of them, surely, should be operational by now, should be able to get her letter out. Each time Diana walked to the ramshackle post office in town and asked if a letter had come for her, she expected to see the official emblem on the envelope, with directions on how she would be met and retrieved, like an article of clothing gone missing. But as the weeks went by and no word came, Diana became suspicious until, finally, she got Gabriella – innocent, angel-eyed Gabriella – to confess that Lucia searched them, coming and going, and had taken Diana's letters from them. They had never left the boarding house. So Diana knew that Donna Lucia – who had refused Diana's request to go into the cities herself – was intercepting her letters, was keeping her, would never let her go. Donna Lucia was using Diana to her own advantage, as a marketing gimmick for her customers, US Army–inspected prostitutes, stamped like they were grade-A beef. With no telephones or telegraphs, and with the village post office still in a shambles, there was no way for her to contact the outside world from where she was now. By now, both the army and her sister would have assumed she was dead. If she was ever going to leave this town, she would have to beat Donna Lucia at her own game.

The idea came to her while she was polishing shoes, the chestnut ones with the brass buckles. Diana had already hand-washed the green linen dress as a favor for one of the girls, ironing it carefully afterward; she had set aside the delicate underthings, laying them out flat to dry. The silk stockings had been an agony to wash, her rough hands catching at the flimsy material. But she had finished at last, neatly folding the outfit and patting it flat. She had picked up the left shoe and polished it; then halfway through the right she had paused, staring blankly into space, turning over an idea in her head that could change her life.

The thought was fully formed by the time she put down the second shoe. It had come to her nearly complete. As she rubbed the brush back and forth, back and forth meditatively, almost lovingly across the deep chestnut leather, she had filled in the last details of her plan. It really was the shoes that had given her the idea, they were exactly her size, like they had been made for her, made for this. She would take the shoes, the stockings, even the silk underthings, and finally the green dress itself, and leave this place. She had done all she could for the women there – a steady stream of black-market supplies came in with every canvas-backed load. Donna Lucia would never let her go if she could help it. Diana could not fix everything, or everyone. And, besides, that war in the Pacific was still going on – she assumed, with no newspapers to tell her differently – and she was still an army nurse with the duties that entailed. So she slowly pocketed first the right shoe, and then the left, and when no one was looking, she slid the thin green dress under her pillow and waited for her chance to escape.

The locals called it *la casa cattiva*, the bad house, although Diana couldn't find out why. It was a good way outside of town, a long walk, halfway again to Pienza, but in a more southernly direction, cropped out of a hillside overlooking the weird, almost lunar *sienese* rock fields that looked like grey lava flowing through the tall grass. Once a week, a load of laundry came in from the bad house. Donna Lucia had gotten two of the youngest girls to do the washing now, and Diana had noticed when they lugged it in that it included difficult things to wash – taffetas and silks, and long white runners for tables that must seat thirty people. Diana's Italian was improving daily, and she could tell the old man who delivered the bags was asking if Lucia could spare a girl to come live in at the house to help with either an invalid or a lunatic child – Diana couldn't be sure which. Donna Lucia would always wave him off, booming, no, none of her girls were for sale, at least not for that kind of work. She wouldn't send one of them out to the bad house, *non per niente*, not for anything. She didn't hate any of them enough for that. But one thing had become clear to Diana. There was some other kind of work out there, if she could get it, and maybe from there she could get word to the army. And even if the situation she was walking into was a bad one, could it be as bad as where she found herself now? Even if there was an unstable patient, she had completed a rotation in a psychiatric hospital, she felt ready. *I can handle anything*, she told herself, standing a little straighter. Then, her confidence waning for a moment, amended it, *I can handle* pretty much *anything*.

She had followed the old man, feigning a need to buy laundry soap for the girls as an excuse to leave the house, had seen where the road turned sharply left towards the southern slopes and their eerie rock formations. She got close enough to see the wrought-iron gate close behind the man, to see him lock it after himself. She had had to run back to the village, dripping with sweat, thankful Lucia had not been there to see her walk in late without a package in her arms. But that night, Gabriella, the angel-girl, had come up to Diana, as if she could sense she was leaving. The woman-child sat down gently on Diana's cot, Diana's eyes moving surreptitiously to the corner of the green dress that peeked out from under her pillowcase. But Gabriella had only looked at Diana and smiled, a wide, sorrowful smile like a Madonna's.

'*Non ci devi essere qui.*' You do not belong here. '*Vai altrove.*' You go elsewhere.

Diana nodded slowly, trusting the child not to betray her. She could understand more Italian each day, but still so many words were missing for Diana. She could not express herself, what she really thought, about God or love or the fate of these girls, or the meaning of life itself. She could not say what she wanted to say now: *I do not belong here, you do not belong here; you deserve, I deserve – we all deserve – so much more than this; we deserve life and liberty and the pursuit of a happiness of our own choosing, wherever and whatever that might be.* But all she could do was nod her head, cursing her empty vocabulary, frowning in consternation.

But the golden-haired child had smiled again, placing her tiny palm against Diana's cheek.

'*Dove vai, che gli angeli ti proteggano.*' Where you go, may the angels protect you.

And with that, Gabriella stood up, leaving Diana, blessing her and her flight.

Diana walked through the open gate. She had been afraid it would be locked, as she had seen it that day when she followed the old man out of town, but it was open now. For the hundredth time, she smoothed down the front of her dress, the green linen soft beneath her hands. She had hitched a ride on the back of a horse cart going out to the fields, bringing along the brush she used to keep up the nap on the woolen shawl Donna Lucia wore whenever she went out of the house. She had brushed herself off and then hidden the brush behind a stray olive tree that had grown up wild and straggly on the road's edge. She would retrieve it in a few moments if her interview did not go as planned.

As she started down the long drive, the white gravel crunched beneath the chestnut leather shoes. The driveway was meticulously raked, a sharp, edged line delineating stone from lawn. The grass on either side of the drive was thick, not the native *chaparral* growth – fire-resistant, olive-drab, growing short and close to the earth – but some blue-green turf imported from lusher climes. An enormous cedar rose in front of her, the drive dividing and running smoothly around its base, forming an island of green offset with spiky cacti, and a ring of small, perfectly matched stones painted white, running around it. Once Diana passed the dark tree, the house immediately came into view – she had not known it was so close. The house looked ancient, but that only added to its grandeur. The terracotta roof was splattered with lichen, not a single tile missing or cracked. The exterior walls were a weathered yellow, the tiny specks of stone giving it a softly raised texture Diana wanted to run her hand over. The muted color of the walls seemed intentionally understated, as if a splashier tint or smoother finish would have been in bad taste. As Diana approached the front door, dark and undersized for the greatness of the two and a half storys rising above it, she noticed a gold-flecked mural of Madonna and Child painted on to the house itself. It was just above eye level and to the left of the door. Half of the Virgin was worn away with age, but the baby was still visible, resting on his mother's one good hand, her lips brushing his curls still golden after all these years, the woman looking down on her son with her one remaining eye.

Diana pulled the bell cord and waited. There was no sound, not from within the house nor from the surrounding grounds nor from the rolling fields beyond. She noticed a reflecting pool to the left of the house where the impeccable drive swept around and out of sight. The surface of the water was unruffled, reflecting back the enormous white clouds that stood motionless above it. Two doves took flight, squabbling like old women as they erupted from the nearby shrubberies, causing Diana to start. Her nerves were on edge. She knew her very survival depended on the outcome of the next few minutes. She could hear the *swoosh-swoosh* of her pulse in her ears, then even that subsided, and all was still again. The door opened.

A woman stood in front of Diana, her thick hands still clutching the wood of the door. She was in her seventies, her hair cut short. She peered suspiciously at the newcomer, taking in Diana's clothing and her carefully polished shoes. The woman's dress was plain homespun; Diana could see the marks on the fabric near her hips where the woman had hurriedly dried her hands before coming to the door. So, not the woman of the house, Diana thought, but help – a housekeeper or cook, perhaps. Standing squarely in the doorframe now and squinting in the sun, blocking Diana's entrance. Diana felt helpless for a moment, and terribly foolish, as if she were about to try to sell this woman a set of encyclopedias. Then she exhaled and began in halting Italian.

'Good morning, I am here to apply for the position . . .'

The woman in the doorway remained immovable.

'Uh . . . for the position, for the child. The, uh, invalid. I am a nurse, *un'infermiera*,' pointing to herself.

The older woman shifted her weight from one weather-beaten shoe to the other; they were old, black leather bedroom slippers. There was a layer of silt on the wide stone threshold, and it made a sound like grating sandpaper as she shifted back and forth. She eyed Diana for another moment, taking her in from top to bottom. Then she grunted, turned, and walked back into the house. Diana hovered for another moment on the threshold before hearing the woman call out in Italian, 'Come inside, already. Do not stand stupidly in the sun.'

As Diana passed from light into darkness, her eyes needed a moment to adjust. Behind her, the sun still poured down on the reflecting pool, on the small white stones baking in the heat. But inside, everything was shut up like a tomb. Diana followed the slow-moving woman down a dim hallway, glistening with glossy wood and polished iron, the window at the far end covered in a thick curtain that made it glow a sickly red. They stopped at an interior door leading off the hall. The woman put her hand to the latch, spitting out ''*spetta*,' wait, as she stepped inside and hastily closed the door behind her. For a moment, there was the soft sound of muted conversation, the fast-flowing cadence of Italian reaching Diana's ears, the words themselves remaining indistinguishable. A tall grandfather clock stood next to her, and Diana listened to its *tick-tock, tick-tock* which seemed the only sound now in the silent hall, in that whole silent house. The hair on the back of her neck stood up, and she shook herself to ward off the inexplicable feeling of suffocation, of impending doom. 'Don't be silly, it's nothing,' she chided herself under her breath, wanting to break the silence with something, even the silly English phrase, saying aloud, 'Just a goose walking over my grave.'

The wrought-iron latch lifted on the door that swung halfway open before her. The woman didn't even give her a second look as she left the room, crossing the hallway towards the back of the house, mumbling to herself. Diana could see a little way into what appeared to be a crowded sitting room – she could see an upholstered ottoman, green tassels hanging from the quilted cushion; an ornate oil lamp atop a carved end table; small figurines dancing on a shelf, dark and shiny and twisted, pipes in hand, Pan and his followers balancing on hooved feet. Diana stepped inside.

The old woman rose with effort. She had been ensconced in a tall, wing-backed chair and Diana noticed her claw-like hand gripping the arm of it, trembling as she pushed herself up to standing while her other hand held on to a thick wooden cane. She was dressed in taffeta, in one of the black dresses Diana herself had cleaned on her first day, the stiff, shiny fabric overlaid with black lace and small onyx buttons at the wrist and neck. The woman was petite, standing just over five feet when she rose to her full height. But her eyes sought out Diana's and commanded them. Diana couldn't look away. As a nurse, Diana knew the white, hazy layer over the woman's cornea was a cataract, a vision impairment, nothing more. But, for some unknown reason, staring at her now, the hair on the back of Diana's neck beginning again to rise, she felt the woman's gaze was sinister, foreboding, a Gorgon's or a witch's, looking into Diana's clear eyes and seeing her soul, naked and exposed, already knowing all her secrets and every lie she had ever told. Diana forced herself to rally.

'*Buon giorno, signora.*'

The slightest inclination of the head. Diana swallowed with difficulty. She stumbled over the Italian words.

'I am here in response to the position, to the employment, of the child—'

'We will conduct this interview in English, as Italian is clearly not your *forte*. You may sit.'

Diana sat down on a nearby chair, sitting up straight, the carved wood uncomfortable and digging into her back. She was surprised to hear English spoken, and spoken so clearly. She had not heard it like that since the elocution classes her aunt had paid for one summer. Mrs Thromwaite, her teacher – 'a widowed gentlewoman of reduced circumstances,' her aunt had called her – had demonstrated articulation, and then inflection, and when Diana had proved herself completely useless at both, had, instead, taught Diana to cross the room with a book balanced on her head, 'so your aunt's money won't be completely wasted.'

The old woman retook her seat, but kept her grip on her cane, holding it out to one side like a scepter. She asked for Diana's name, and she gave it.

'I am Signora Bugari. Giuliana said, as far as she could make out, you were applying for a position here. But I have made no formal request, posted no notice of employment in the village. How did you happen to come here?'

The cloudy grey eye was staring right at her, as if the old woman were a sick cat about to pounce on a mouse she had unexpectedly trapped. How strangely she had phrased it – *How did you happen to come here?* – not confirming or denying a position existed, but cutting right to the chase. Diana's stomach turned over inside her. She needed this work.

'I am an American Red Cross nurse. I have been separated from my unit and have been unable to make contact with them.' She was grateful for being able to speak in English. Perhaps this woman's command of the language was not as good as it appeared, that something could be lost in translation, that Diana's feigned tone of confidence and indifference would gloss over the parts of herself she didn't want revealed. Like Donna Lucia and her washroom.

'There was an explosion, an accident of some kind, I don't remember. We – the nurses – were heading for Genoa. We were being shipped back home and then . . .' Diana's voice trailed off for a moment, before continuing, quickly, 'The next thing I remember is waking up here. A woman and her children down in the valley found me. They nursed me back to health.'

Signora Bugari made no sound, so Diana went on.

'I do not remember where I first heard of it,' Diana said, focusing on the oriental carpet at her feet, the complicated pattern doubling back on itself. 'But word of a young child reached me, and I thought I would apply as the child's nurse.

Until,' she hurried on, 'such time as I can resume my regular duties.'

The woman's incredible stillness unnerved Diana. She felt as if she was weighing and judging everything Diana said, holding her words up before her, making Diana see them for what they really were. *My regular duties.* What were they, exactly?

'You have only recently come to our town?'

The question was innocent enough, but Diana felt her face flush as she lied.

'Yes, quite recently.'

'And you have been unable to return to your . . . your work?'

The way the woman said that, Diana wondered if she could have somehow found out about the American woman in town, Donna Lucia's employee? Was she mistaken that the old man had not somehow seen her that day she followed him out of town? But Diana's thoughts were wandering. *Get yourself together. You need this work. You are not going back to Donna Lucia's. Sell her. Convince her. Make this work.*

Assuming a casual attitude that immediately felt false, she went on.

'Yes, the postal system has been unable to forward my letters. As you know, the telegraph poles are down all over the country. I have sent several letters to my superiors, as well as to my family back home. I have decided to remain here while awaiting their reply, it would be foolish to leave now that I've provided a forwarding address. I handled thousands of cases during the war, and when I heard about the child here, I decided to apply. I am a good nurse . . .'

She had meant to say more, but the last chance-phrase made her throat catch. *I am a good nurse. That's all I am. I am nothing else, anymore.*

'I see.'

A claw of a hand reached up and grabbed on to a gold locket that hung around the woman's neck. Diana saw her fingers were bent crazily with rheumatism, yet still covered in rings that shone dully as she stroked the locket. Diana fixed her gaze on the circle of gold, staring at it as she would at a conjurer's trick at the fair. She felt very tired, and deflated.

She had meant to impress this woman with her own force of will, to sell herself and her credentials, to come across as a wonder woman who would deign, out of the goodness of her heart, to take a position so clearly beneath her. But the old woman had unnerved her, showing Diana to herself – cut off from her world, at the end of a war she had lost even if her country and its allies had won it. She was nothing and nobody. She felt like a deserter from the army, someone who ought to be tried and shot and quickly forgotten. Why had she survived the explosion that killed the other nurses? Why was she still alive? She had not voiced her despair to the old woman, but she had said those words to herself. The utter emptiness they revealed to her, that made her unable to think or feel or be other than as an automaton that changed dressings, gave sponge baths, emptied bed pans, that was all she was now. She should have stayed at Donna Lucia's and drunk from the waters of oblivion. The stolen dress on her back, the stolen shoes on her feet, even the brush hidden under the olive tree at the edge of the lane accused her, showed her for the fake she was. She was still staring at the locket, she hadn't noticed the old woman had begun speaking until she was halfway through her sentence.

'. . . and you are clearly not telling the truth about how you heard about us, but that is your own affair. If you really are a nurse, if you are competent at what you do, we will find that out quickly, over the course of the next few days. I have a ward, a child of nine years. His condition is a tiresome one and, increasingly, it is more than Giuliana can handle on her own. She has other concerns, naturally, on the estate. What was your wage in the war?'

Diana was slowly coming back to reality. Was this woman negotiating terms? Could she be interested in her, after all?

'In the war?' she stammered. 'I made . . . I made a hundred and fifty-five dollars a week. A hundred and seventy-five dollars, once I made First Lieutenant.'

The figures seemed enormous to Diana now, they sounded unreal, as if she were reciting a favorite fairy tale, *I used to dress in French satin and eat five meals a day.*

The woman's expression remained unchanged.

'As your countrymen say, we will "split the difference." One hundred and sixty-five American dollars per week, plus meals and board. If you are satisfactory, that is. And if the work is satisfactory to you. The child is not difficult' – the old woman's gaze drifted for a moment before continuing – 'just tiring.'

The woman rose imperiously, and Diana found herself on her feet.

'I will send Giuliana to you, she will take you to your room. Good-day.'

With a rustle of taffeta she was gone.

What had just happened? Who had that kind of money now, after the war? And in *American* dollars, she had said? Diana had been hoping for room and board – room and board and a small stipend, perhaps, enough to save up for a passage home. At Lucia's, she had been slaving for her bowl of *pici* three times a day, with the occasional stewed tomato or gamey rabbit *ragù* thrown in. But here she was being offered her full officer's salary, for one small child. No matter how 'tiring,' who would pay that? Who could?

Then Diana looked around the sitting room, the shutters closed tightly against the sun, as if seeing it with new eyes. She realized this room looked like nowhere else in Europe she had seen. There was no broken glass here, no bombed-out walls. Not only had the grounds outside been immaculate, but the house, this room in particular, was flawless. Every set of figurines and miniatures – from the dark satyrs to the glass angels on the mantelpiece, to the delicate, hand-painted Russian eggs in the breakfront – was perfect, not a single one marred or cracked or mismatched. The thick carpets on the floor, the lavish, full-length curtains pulled back by gold cord, the remnants of cake on the sideboard with butter – actual fresh-cream butter – standing uneaten on a delicate china plate. What was this place? How had it remained untouched by a war that had ravaged not only Italy but Europe and Asia as well?

Giuliana came in, picking up the tray of cake and wasted butter, balancing it against her hip as she motioned with her head for Diana to follow her. The hair on the back of Diana's neck stood up yet again. Instead of congratulating herself on her good fortune, she instead felt an enormous reluctance to follow the servant who was already heading out of the room. Diana felt certain she was somehow walking into danger, and worse danger than she had ever known in the war.

'Do you come or do you not?' Giuliana called, impatiently, in Italian.

'*Vengo.*' I'm coming, and Diana quickly left the room.

TWO

Diana woke to sunlight streaming in through the open French windows. She lay motionless for a moment, the light hitting the left side of her face, catching at her eyelashes, unable to remember for a minute where she was. Her eyes wandered lazily over the ironwork of her bed, graceful circles bending up, and around, and back upon themselves. The clean white sheets were smooth and cool, the thread count pleasantly heavy against her skin. The room she was in was austere, except for the bed, which was its only luxury. The walls were whitewashed, naked but for two paintings; one of an old woman, abstract and grey, three red apples dominating the foreground; and another of a toddler-angel, lips puckered in a pout, arms crossed over its flat chest, colorful moth-wings curving delicately behind it. A bureau and a single wooden chair made up the remainder of the room. Diana sat up, slipping her legs out from under the sheets. She stood for a moment in front of the windows that led to the balcony. For miles, the landscape fell in front of her, undulating in a patchwork of fields and woods and small, chalklike dwellings too far away to be discerned, mere splotches of white or terra cotta on landscape squares of straw-yellow and olive-drab. She stepped on to her balcony, wrapping the sheet around her waist as she did so, but there were no prying eyes to see her bare legs, not a soul in sight, as far as the eye could see. Just the sharp darkness of cypress trees, cut like paint applied with the edge of a knife on to the soft, never-ending canvas of farm and field. The stone beneath her feet was rough, the errant, loose pebble smarting when she stepped on it. A lizard skittered away quickly at her approach and then sat motionless on the balcony ledge, mouth opened slightly, warming itself in the morning sunlight that was already strong and hot.

Diana sighed leisurely. *Breakfast is at nine,* Giuliana had told her that first night, nearly six weeks ago now, before closing Diana's bedroom door unceremoniously on her. *Breakfast is at nine, you work with the child at ten.* Diana compared her current routine to that at Donna Lucia's boarding house. Each morning there started in the dark and in a panic of shouts and threats, a mad scramble coming mere seconds after the first consciousness of day. She compared it to the routine she had known earlier in the military, the matrons clanging their bells before first light when the girls were still stateside, yawning widely as they made their beds and dressed and stood at attention. Or, later, waking in their tents to the sound of mortar shells, digging fox holes into the dirt floors of their tents, rolling off their cots into the dank coolness of soil, or the mess of cold puddles, so exhausted from work that they eventually learned to sleep there, undisturbed, until the bombing ended or the next shift began. But Diana didn't like to think of the war.

She re-entered her room now, casually throwing the sheet back on to the mattress – her own mattress, shared with no one, with no holes in it – and opened her bedroom door. Her room led out into a small hall. Giuliana had told her no one else lived in this hall; no one lived in this side of the house, as far as Diana could make out. There was a door immediately to her left, leading to a small, unused bedroom with a single window. Beyond this, further down the hall, was a sitting area for her use – a few chairs, a table set up for one, an oriental carpet worn to a comfortable nap. The sitting room had French windows, like her own, which led out on to the shared balcony. The drop from the balcony at the end nearest her room was sheer, dropping two stories to the packed earth below, but the ground climbed so steeply on the opposite side that anyone could straddle the wall there and have one foot on her balcony and one on the solid ground littered with dry leaves and cactus needles.

Diana left her room and turned right, into the small bathroom. She could not believe she had her own bath. She had never had one, not even at home where she had shared one with Marie. With her little sister living six thousand miles away who, by now, must be sure Diana was dead. Marie would have mourned and prayed for and, by now, begun the hard process of letting go of her only sister, a sister who wanted to be found again, and loved in the present tense. The hot water washed over her, over her thick coils of hair, and Diana closed her eyes against the pain that was Marie, that was America, that was her home, people and places that had forgotten her, that had moved on because they had to. It was the war that did that, she told herself. That could make people able to forget, able to shut down that part of their heart, this part of their soul, to be able to commiserate with someone at the market, the person next to you in queue – *did you lose someone, too? Ah, that's bad. I lost my brother, my son, my sister, my daughter* – and then smile sadly and shake your head and turn back to the pressing business of ordering a pork shoulder, *no, not that one, the bone's too skinny, it'll shatter before I can serve it, have you got something better in the back?*

The war had been hell. She had known it would be, before she even went; she had put on a brave show for her mother but she had read Remarque's book on the Western Front. She had cried over it in high school along with the other girls, looking wistfully at their fellow students, at Billy and Tommy and imagining them dead in the trenches, white-faced and still. But her war had been different from that young German's a generation before; there had been no battle for her, no offensives, just a constant influx of casualties coming in, a heavy flow that never ended, was never even staunched. She only knew the war by the injuries it created – the North African sand she could never get out of the boys' wounds; the deadly malaria from standing water left in the Germans' wake, aqueducts and artesian wells crushed with their tanks, leaving the Italians with no drinking water, with stagnant pools, ensuring their demise by the deadliest animal on the planet. Of course, Diana had heard the names of some battles, of some generals men said were brave, or courageous, or mad, but what did she know of them, personally? Boys came in and she saved them, or boys came in and they died, but they never stopped coming in. Boy after helpless, maimed boy. Boys younger than herself, younger than Marie, even, boys crying for their mothers or boys trying to be brave, gasping, *no, miss, it doesn't hurt much*, but biting their lips so hard to keep from screaming that their teeth sunk into their flesh. She hated herself now because she no longer cared about them, even though she played and replayed their deaths in her mind while she was washing her hair, while she was smoothing out the thick cotton sheets of her princess bed. She still saw the boys die as they always did, they never stopped dying in her head, but the difference was, now, she felt nothing. She had stopped feeling, she had had to. If you didn't, the older nurses had warned the girls when she got near the front, you couldn't bear it, you'd go mad. And they were right. There had been that one young nurse, Louisa, a sweet girl from Tennessee with a turned-up nose who had been talking to one of her ortho patients, been easing him gently on to his side, holding his left hand, while he flirted with her, *after the war, sweetie, you and me*, and she had laughed and he had smiled and then the ground had heaved, swollen up and exploded with the impact of the shell, showering them with bits of sod and splinters from the tent pole and she was still holding his hand, his dead eyes were still smiling at her, but his legs and lower torso were clear across the tent, hanging crookedly from a wire, and she had screamed and screamed and kept screaming until they had had to send her back, on convalescent leave, to a sanatorium, matron had said, or a rest home, or a mad house – they never learned which. That was what happened if you cared. Diana hadn't cared when Louisa went away because, by then, she had stopped caring about her or about anyone else. She had stopped that night with the fire and the baby and the tree on the hill. But she never thought about that when she was awake.

Her dreams were another matter. She couldn't control her dreams. Some days at *la casa cattiva* were good. The boy – upon examination a physically healthy boy, whose inability to sit still had been mistaken for illness or intransigence – was starting to thrive under her care, loving the new-found freedom she gave him to get up and go outside and play in the sun. Some days at the estate were not so good. She would get on Giuliana's bad side, inadvertently insulting her when Diana didn't realize the beer-battered zucchini flowers prepared for lunch were edible, pushing them surreptitiously to the edge of her plate. But whether the days were good or bad, whether she had efficiently discharged her duties or simply managed to aggravate one or both of the elderly women she lived with, the dreams still came. Sometimes Diana managed to wake up before the very end, struggling to a groggy consciousness before she reached the village, before it rained down fire. But, on most nights, it played out in a relentless sequence of inevitable events made all the more terrible because she knew it was a dream. She could not stop the dream, and she could not stop herself. Night after night, she saw herself put down the baby, turn her back on the helpless child, walk callously away, leaving it to certain death, and she knew she was right to do it and she knew she had been wrong, that night long ago, to take the baby with her but, right or wrong, it always ended now in death and her screaming into her pillow. She was glad she had the wing to herself.

Diana put on the neat striped dress that hung over the back of the chair, placed there the night before by Giuliana. Diana ran her hand over the smooth fabric, appreciating the light starch, the careful ironing that had not been done by her. She had not washed a single item since she'd left Lucia's. The dress – along with a dozen others in varying patterns and prints she had sewn for herself from the stockpile of fabrics Signora Bugari had placed at her disposal – would have made her Home Economics teacher proud. The first dress she had attempted, a lavender floral print with a high waist and ruching, had ended up with the hem two inches higher on one side. But by the time she had tackled the bold stripe print, with alternating lines of green and orange and cream, it had all come back to her, the careful darts hugging her bustline, the glossy amber buttons running neatly down the front in a row. She had asked Signora Bugari if she would rather Diana make herself nurses' uniforms, severe grey or blue duty outfits with high collars and stiff overlaid white aprons. But Signora had replied, practically, 'If the child is not sick, you need not dress as a nurse, if a nurse is not what he requires. You can sew, you say, so make yourself something decent, something respectable. I have a storeroom of fabric and you are dressed in nothing but rags, I can see right through your bodice it is worn so thin. Wear what a companion would wear, if a companion is what the child truly needs.'

Diana brushed her long hair, the copper hints in her brown coils brought out by the orange in her dress and the glint of the rising sun. She gave herself thick Dutch braids, wrapping them around her head. She had not noticed, in the war, how long her hair had gotten. When she had left home, her hair had been chemically waved and neatly bobbed just above the shoulder. She had kept it wrapped up in a towel or hidden away in a low bun for so many years now that, when she carefully washed it and brushed it and tilted her chin up in the mirror, her hair hung down her back to her waist. She slipped on her shoes and closed her door behind her. From downstairs, she could just make out the muffled chiming of the grandfather clock – seven o'clock. There would be two more hours until breakfast was laid out in the east drawing room – sweet jams and butter for the crusty bread, cream and white sugar for the coffee – and three hours until Giuliana had washed and dressed the boy in preparation for his *classe*, as she called them, Diana's 'lessons' with Paolo. Diana had tried to get Giuliana to allow her to help the boy in the mornings, but she had refused stubbornly, waving Diana away as an unwanted intruder. Diana now slipped down the back staircase that led to a small, rounded exterior door – she had to duck to get out without scraping her head. She set off, as she often did in the mornings when the great house was still silent, and headed for the fields. This alone – in her great, changed world – reminded her of home. The swifts and swallows darting overhead, diving for insects glistening in the sunlight. The squawk of startled pheasants. The cry of some mournful Italian bird that seemed to Diana to be calling out, again and again, *a-dess-o, a-dess-o*, the Italian word for *now*.

Diana walked until her shoes began to fill with grass seed, with tiny rocks or bits of soil, and then she would take them off and walk barefoot through the wild grass that was waist high, swirling around her like a living sea. She would walk until she was out of sight of the house, so far that the estate was hidden by the outcropping of boulders and she knew she would have to run to be back in time for breakfast. There she would stand alone, barefoot, in that great expanse. She would close her eyes and hold out her arms to her sides, like Christ on a beautiful cross, one made of sunlight and air instead of hard wood and nails. The wind would pull at her thick braids, little wisps escaping and whipping at her closed eyelids, and she would try to still her mind and think of nothing at all. She knew, one day, she would have to think of things, of the war, of the baby, of the terrible mistakes she had made. And she knew, if she didn't try with every ounce of her strength, the images that intruded unbidden into her mind – a thousand Louisas holding a thousand lifeless hands – would rush in upon her now, engulfing her completely. On some instinctual level, she realized if she was ever to get to a place inside herself where she could think again, where she could face what she had done and what she had failed to do – if she was ever going to own the space inside her head again, and let the dead rest in peace instead of replaying their deaths on an endless circuit – she would have to think of nothing. Clear her head and just *be*.

She could not pray. She had tried to utter the words she had learned by heart as a child, but they died on her lips. There was no connection between the soul trapped in the body with the bold striped dress and whatever deity she had once believed she could reach. Her only prayer, if she had one any longer, was a moan, an agonized moan that came from deep within her, sometimes rising like a funereal keen, sometimes inaudible to anyone but herself, a tortured groping in the dark, a desperate begging for help without any real hope that help would come.

She stood still now, and the images bombarded her consciousness, flying at her across the open fields, the pain shooting into her as if she were a practice dummy on a range. She clenched her eyes further shut, like a child blocking out something it will not see, her arms still outstretched and beginning to ache. She tried to slow her rapid breathing, stop the panicked shallow breath that went with her nightmare. Every once in a while, she could take a breath, a real breath. Today, she even smelled the crushed grass under her feet, and the faint sweetness of some wildflower hidden from sight. She noted this progress, impartially. The resurgence of even one sense – of smell, or taste, finding a wild strawberry one day and the taste bringing her back to her youth, to Marie, to a time before the numbness – these were things she acknowledged as a first step. As a needed purgative. As a precursor to a pain that would be awful and would, at this moment, be unendurable but could, one day, be the pain of rebirth. Of resurrection. Of allowing herself to be alive in a world where so many others had died.

The pain in her arms from holding them aloft Christ-like ceased as she slowly lowered them to her sides. She could no longer smell the crushed grass, but she had for a moment, and that was enough for today. She had healed so many wounded bodies, comforted so many broken souls, but now she faced her greatest test – the task of healing herself. It would be slow, she knew that much. It came to her, suddenly, that, maybe, the downed telegraph poles, the stopped mail service, the inaccessibility of this medieval place lost to the modern world was, in fact, where she needed to be right now. Would she have had these moments of quiet walking down Madison Avenue? Could she have stood and screamed unnoticed in the middle of Central Park? The momentary thought and its implications were too esoteric and she let it drift from her and float out over the waving grasses. This was where she was now, she thought practically, and she would make the most of it. Her duties were light, she had been granted a reprieve from the brutal struggle for survival. She could afford to heal, to re-piece herself together, as she had relearned to sew the cut-outs of fabric that made a dress that was new and whole. She had been silly, that first day here, to give in to that feeling of impending doom, of disaster and danger worse than any she had known. She must have been light-headed from hunger or heatstroke that day to have taken the feeling seriously, to think an old woman with a cataract was sinister, could somehow see into her soul. Signora was a rich woman, but there were still rich women in the world, it was not that unusual, certainly not ominous – perhaps she had had some friends who had advised her well, protecting her assets in Switzerland. There was a reasonable explanation for everything if you gave yourself enough time. Diana had come here thinking she would be taking care of a deranged patient, possibly even a dangerous one, and had gotten, instead, a sweet boy eager to greet each day. She had ascribed to Signora Bugari every malevolent intention, imbuing her with super-natural perception and hypnotic command, but she had turned out to be an old woman grateful to have the physical duties of nursemaid lifted from her and Giuliana's shoulders. Diana swung her shoes almost jauntily in her hand as she headed back for the house, for her hot rolls and coffee, momentarily missing the ham and eggs of a farm breakfast back home but knowing, in only a few hours, she would be stuffed by an enormous *pranzo*, the Italian midday meal of pasta, and meat, and cheese that rivaled Thanksgiving dinner for the sheer quantity – and quality – of food.

'I was a fool to worry about them all,' she said to herself lightly, almost gaily, thinking how wrong she had been. 'Save up your pay, girl, get yourself right in the head. You've landed on your feet here, and no mistake about it.'

She plucked a head off one of the tall grasses, placing it in her mouth and tasting its familiar sweetness.

'You're safe now. And nothing bad is ever going to happen to you again.'

When she got back to the house, it was in utter confusion. Everyone was awake, for one thing, which was unusual at that hour, and moving hurriedly from room to room – even Giorgio who usually kept to the grounds and outbuildings during the day. Boxes were being lifted, were being carried up from the cellar or down from the top floors. Giuliana was complaining about the dust being tracked everywhere, even as she blew a thick layer off the box in her hands and prized open the lid. Signora Bugari hadn't fastened the last of her buttons, as if she had been disturbed halfway through dressing, and the starched white camisole that showed beneath the dark fabric of her bodice looked indecent, as if she was walking around undressed, and oblivious to the fact.

'*Che cosa è successo?*' What has happened? Diana asked.

She got no reply. Signora took a small object, perhaps an ashtray or ornate bowl out of the box in front of her, scrutinized it, then slammed it against the kitchen butcher block in irritation. She looked up and saw Diana, but only paused long enough to interrupt the flow of Italian complaints and exclamations of frustration by switching to French. To Diana's surprise, the housekeeper and groundsman effortlessly followed her lead, and Diana was left with no idea of what they were saying. Giuliana dropped her box, coils of old wood shavings spilling out and littering the floor.

Giorgio grabbed his cap off the peg where it hung in the disordered kitchen, and made for the door.

'*Aller! Aller!* Go!' Signora Bugari was calling after him, shooing him with her hands as if the old man could not go fast enough.

'Where is he going? What's wrong? I insist on knowing what's happening.'

Diana surprised herself with the forcefulness in her voice. Signora seemed startled for a moment, as well. She tried to smooth down her shirtfront, her hands coming upon the undone buttons, her bent fingers fumbling with the closures as she spoke evenly in English.

'It is nothing.'

The lie was apparent, but she went on hurriedly.

'It is nothing that concerns you. We received a telegram this morning. It came by messenger, who has only recently left us. We will be having a . . . a visitor.' Here she shot a quick glance at Giuliana, who had opened her mouth to say something, then stopped. 'A gentleman whose presence requires a certain amount of preparation. Giorgio has just gone to the village. We will, temporarily, require additional staff.'

Giuliana slowly closed her mouth, frowning at her employer, then bent painfully to gather up the shavings.

'*Who* is coming?' Diana asked.

'That is no concern of yours.'

Signora snapped the words in her customary imperious manner, but with great surprise Diana also noted an undertone of fear. The old woman had finished with her buttons, and was now unconsciously wringing her hands, which were visibly shaking. Her voice had cracked when she spoke, not with the usual sharpness of a woman used to command, but with the throaty sound of someone beginning to lose control. She glared at Diana as if she would take back the moment of weakness, hide what she had revealed, but it was too late. Diana had seen and heard exactly what the old woman wished most to conceal. The young boy, Paolo, walked into the kitchen, drawn by the sound of voices. He was barefoot and still in his pajamas, his light-brown curls tousled and falling over one eye. His slight frame and pale skin made him look younger than his years, as he stood there rubbing his eyes.

'Giuliana, you didn't come,' he said simply, in Italian. 'I waited for you but I got so hungry and you didn't come.'

Signora Bugari turned on the child, her recent anger at betraying herself to Diana still stinging her. She lashed out in Italian, 'Stupid boy, get out of here, this is no place—'

'Signora.'

Diana only said the one word but said it in such a manner and with the same authority she had used on prisoners of war back when her bored patients had squabbled over card games played for packets of cigarettes, threatening to fight each other, *to kill you, you stupid bastard*, and she had shouted and given them the penicillin they had then taken obediently, like chided schoolboys. Now, Signora stood silent, aghast. Diana crossed the room and gently took the boy's hand in her own. He was staring at Signora and trembling, his lower lip starting to pucker.

'I'm sorry you were alone, Paolo,' Diana said soothingly in Italian, trying to stroke his recalcitrant curls back into place. 'But I'm here now.'

She walked over to the remnants of the chocolate *torta* Giuliana had served the night before, and cut off an enormous slice. She opened the icebox, removing one of the slim, white milk bottles that were delivered in the dark each morning.

'*Colazione fuori.*' Breakfast outside, she said as the boy's glance moved from the decadent dessert to Diana's eyes and back to the cake again. He broke out smiling, all memory of Signora's impatience blotted out. He was skipping happily as he reached the kitchen door, one hand still holding on lightly to Diana as she looked over her shoulder at the women who had already turned back to the crates, furiously digging through their contents as if their very lives depended upon finding whatever it was they were looking for.

Paolo stretched out on the lawn, green grass stains already appearing on the elbows and knees of his pajamas, sharing bits of cake and the bottle of milk with Diana, who smiled as she joined in the meal. But as soon as he moved off to pick flowers for Diana to weave into a garland for him to wear, she quickly produced the telegram from her pocket, where she had hidden it after snatching it off the sideboard table on her way out. Taking the telegram had been a sudden impulse, but one born from the fact there would be no other way to glean even a little insight into their visitor – and why his appearance was rattling even the implacable Signora Bugari. Diana couldn't make out every word, but the Italian words she did recognize were *returning*, *remaining*, *eagle*, and, repeated three times despite the added cost to the telegram, *my possession*. She could make no sense of the *eagle*, but the rest seemed to imply someone was coming back to the estate, was perhaps planning on remaining there until he had retrieved whatever possession he had left behind. Could that be what the two women were so desperately trying to find now, to give back to – or hide from – their guest? And what sort of man was he that this estate – untouched by the war, pristine and immaculate, with luxuries and appointments unrivaled in a pre-war, let alone a post-war, world – was not good enough for him? That his mere presence as a guest would necessitate a full staff, recruited from the nearby farms and village, most likely, hastily trained as houseboys, maidservants, and liveried chauffeurs for the gleaming automobiles Giorgio always kept in polish but never took out. Diana slowly folded the telegram and slipped it back into her pocket, taking the bunches of yellow and pink from Paolo's overladen arms and slowly beginning to weave them into a crown and necklace, as she had done with Marie when they were young. Paolo laughed as he waited, tucking in his arms and rolling down the embankment, laughing, running back up to the top, and rolling down again. Diana shook her head, incredulous how anyone, in a misguided attempt to care for this boy, had relegated him to a life of bedrest and dimmed upper rooms. He was growing stronger each day, life a seemingly never-ending series of joys and adventures. How wrong people could be. Then Diana thought how wrong she had been when she first met Signora Bugari. Back then, she would have sworn that nothing could have moved the old woman, that she went through her days completely in command of herself and of all she surveyed. And, here, a dozen words sent by telegraph, delivered by hand to this forgotten spot, had shattered the façade completely. Not just of this idyllic place, but of the woman who had seemed impervious to war, and misfortune, and life itself.

Diana and Paolo avoided the house for the rest of that day, sneaking in only for the boy's clothes and more substantial provisions from the icebox. Several hours later, Giorgio returned with a cartload of valises, trunks hastily tied shut with rope, and several chickens that, apparently, could not be left behind – the personal belongings of the dozen mismatched persons who now walked in his wake. One or two older men, perhaps friends of Giorgio, to help keep the others in line; some small village boys, already turning somersaults in the drive and throwing pebbles at each other; the rest, women – kitchen help, undoubtedly – heavy-set with strong, powerful limbs, along with some plain, timid adolescent girls thrown in to make up the pretense of housemaids. The men moved off slowly with the contents of the cart, gesturing and talking loudly. Giuliana came running out into the courtyard to commandeer the women and children for tasks that, from her frantic gesturing, they were already nearly too late to complete.

Meals that evening were a haphazard affair, the by-product of culinary mistakes discarded hastily – the ends of cheeses and salumi, hand-rolled linguini that had broken off into bite-sized pieces unsuitable for serving to their guest – whom, Diana learned, would be arriving in two days, or even as early as tomorrow afternoon, a discrepancy that only added to the general attitude of near-panic and despair. Diana settled Paolo in for bed, readily assuming the extra tasks she felt should have been hers from the start. Giuliana looked up from her preparations around midnight, as if suddenly remembering something, asked after the boy and, being told *la compagna*, the companion, had cared for him all that day and had helped him to sleep hours before, had grunted, *le cose sono come sono*, things are as they are, *non come dovrebbero essere*, not as they should be.

Diana had offered to help with the preparations after Paolo was in bed, but she had been shooed away by the old women who seemed to have redoubled their manic energy, intent to stay up all night, if need be, to have everything in readiness. That night, as the faint sound of voices and clanking pots found their way up to Diana's wing, she thought about the changes a day could bring. She had started that particular day in peace and sunshine, focusing on herself and her well-being, sure nothing adverse would ever touch her again. While she was glad she was finally being permitted to work more closely with her young charge, she couldn't help but wonder again about the upcoming days and what the arrival of their unwanted guest would do to their quiet lives. The last thing Diana remembered before drifting off to sleep, as the summer breeze stirred the curtains of her open window and ruffled her luxurious sheets, was Giuliana's enigmatic words. But she must have already fallen asleep because, this time, Signora was saying them, a much younger Signora, beautiful and helpless-looking, a young girl trapped in her old woman's clothes, the heavy rings encircling childlike fingers that were no longer crooked. She held her face in her delicate hands, the rings showing dark against the white skin, and she was weeping, saying the words over and over again. *Things are as they are, not as they should be.*

Diana rose early, but, already, sounds were coming from below – from the kitchen, from the dining *salon*, from outside the garages where the men had the cars out in the drive and were polishing them to a sheen that reflected the rising sun. Diana dressed hurriedly and went to Paolo's room where the boy was awake and watching the activity from his bedroom window. He was clapping his hands.

'So shiny! The automobiles,' he said, in Italian, pointing. 'Green and red and blue. And so many people. What are they doing? Will I play with them today?'

Paolo looked so eager, chatted so happily as Diana helped

him dress. She told him, in Italian, 'I will play with you today, if you like.'

'Yes, you are my friend. Giuliana is my friend, too, but she does not smile like you. And she brushes my hair so hard it hurts.'

They spent the morning playing ball on the lawn, exploring the streambed that ran through the lower field, picking flowers for Diana's hair. Every once in a while, there came the crash of glass, or crystal, from the house, a scream of anger or protest, but Diana imagined time would not allow Signora to dwell on the loss of this priceless goblet or that irreplaceable figurine. The shards would be swept up, thrown in the dustbin, another casualty of the war Signora was waging against time and her unwelcome guest. As the noon hour approached and, once again, the two vagabonds scavenged for their midday meal, the frenetic pace of preparation did not slacken. Not once, in her six weeks at the estate, had she ever known *riposo* not to be observed. Religiously, the household had gone back to their rooms and slumbered from noon to two while Diana sat idle. But here it was half past one, with no pause for a meal or even a rest, just Giuliana crying aloud *to put that here, place that there, no, you stupid girl, where have you lived all your life, in a pigsty*, and then Giuliana cutting off the girl's reply to yell out of the window at Giorgio *to move those cars, they're blocking the view of the pond, line them up by the cypresses and send one of those boys over to me, no, child, not through the lawn, take the path, stupid boy.*

Diana noticed a young girl by the gate, maybe nine or ten, holding a fat baby in her arms, and a younger child, perhaps six years old, grabbing on to the hem of the bigger girl's dress. Diana walked over to the trio slowly. The older girl looked as if she might dash away at any moment, eyeing suspiciously the large automobiles and the men who yelled directions at Giorgio as he pushed the cars slowly into place.

'*Buon giorno, posso aiutarti?*' Can I help you? Diana asked softly, as she came up to them. The girl started for a moment. She had hold of the baby across its chest with one arm – it was too heavy for her, and she tried to stick out her hip to take off some of the weight, as she had seen older women do, but she was too thin and little, and the gesture held a certain futility. She jutted out her chin towards the house, and the sound of women's voices coming from the kitchen.

'*Mia mamma.*'

'Oh, your mother works here,' Diana said in English, forgetting to translate.

'You are American,' the girl promptly responded. 'Mamma said there is an American woman at this place. You are the lady.'

'Yes, how did you know? And how do you learn to speak English out . . .' She had almost said *out in this backwater place* but had caught herself in time.

'My twin brothers. They studied it in school, and then taught me from their books. I could not go to school – the babies' – she gestured to her siblings – 'but my brothers taught me and they were very good. They are dead now, in the fighting.'

The simplicity with which she said it created an uncomfortable feeling in Diana's chest. She had not responded like that, she had not responded at all in longer than she could remember to news of death, or another's sadness or pain. With a feeling of hope, quickly replaced by a greater sense of fear, she recognized the knot in her chest. She was beginning to feel again. And she was not sure if she was ready.

'Mamma came here to work because there is no work in the village, there is nothing to buy food for Sarina or the baby with. But the man, the old man who came, said women with no children, or only women with boy children, could come. They had no use for girls. Mamma has three girls – me, and Sarina, and baby. So, she said to me to stay behind and follow her this day. To stay out of sight and maybe she could take us somewhere, get us some food and hide us from the man who does not want us here. But I see that man, there' – she pointed at Giorgio – 'and I do not want Mamma to lose the work if he sees me.'

The baby started to fuss and, automatically, the girl started bouncing it on her non-existent hip.

'What is your name?'

'Dorothea,' the girl answered, shifting the baby to her other arm.

'I'm Diana. How about you come with me? I take care of a little boy here, just about your age. He would be happy to have friends to play with. We can sit in the shade until your *mamma* is done, and I can tell her you are here so she doesn't worry, and I can get food for you and Sarina and the baby. Does the baby have a name?' Diana added, smiling.

'Her name is Evangelina Augusta Victoria, but we only call her *bambina*, baby. Sometimes *bambola*. How do you call it, doll?'

'Well, maybe one day she'll grow into her full name but, for now, *bambola* sounds fine to me.'

The two older girls hesitated for a moment when they met Paolo, not because they suspected any disability on his part but, Diana thought, from the fact they had not been allowed to act as children for so long, saddled with the responsibility of adults. Once Diana had shared some of their stolen hoard of food, and after she had offered to hold *bambola* so the children could play on the lawn in front of her, the girls quickly started a game of tag that delighted Paolo, who was almost immediately caught but cheered and applauded, as if being captured was the point of the game. Paolo showed them how he rolled down the embankment and they followed suit, scrambling up and down the hill until they eventually tired of that and started chasing white moths that hovered around the field's edge. The baby had fallen asleep in her arms, its large head slumped drunkenly to one side.

'You really are the most enormous baby, *bambola*,' Diana said, laughing to herself. She shifted the heavy, sweaty bundle on to the picnic blanket, but as she laid it down, there was a ringing in her ears. The bright sun above seemed to darken, she saw black spots as she stood up and took a jerky step backward. She swung her head around to the tree behind her, then to the baby she had just put down. Her breathing was coming fast, too fast and too high. Her chest was constricting. She knew she was safe, she knew it was daytime and this baby was not that baby, but it had come upon her so suddenly, she hadn't expected it, and now her nostrils flared and she swore she could smell burning flesh where, only a moment before, the smell of freshly baked loaves had been wafting on the air.

'This is not that baby. That baby is gone. That baby is—'

The baby on the picnic blanket started in its dream, a chubby arm flinging out and back again reflexively, a curled fist jamming against its mouth for comfort.

'That baby is . . . dead.'

As Diana said the words, she felt all energy leave her body. She sank to her knees, then put her arms out to steady herself, afraid she would faint. She knelt there, on all fours, and her breathing slowed because everything was slowing down: her breath, her heart, her mind. She was nearly dumb, unable to think. She felt as if she were drowning, slowly, or watching herself drown, but, somehow, she could not die.

The baby woke up and started to cry, and Diana moved her arms to soothe the baby, but her arms did not move. Diana sank on to her haunches, pushing herself slowly back up off the ground. The baby looked at her accusingly as it inhaled and then cried again, shutting its eyes tight and howling. Diana said *there, there baby, don't cry, don't let them hear you cry*, but her mouth wouldn't move so no words came out. Dorothea dropped down from a nearby tree she had been climbing, rushed over, and picked up the baby, bouncing it violently until it stopped crying. She handed her sister a cheese rind, which the baby alternately chewed and held up to its eyes for inspection. Sarina came up timidly and sat down at her older sister's feet, surreptitiously plucking at a half-eaten bunch of raisins.

Diana's breath was coming more regularly now, the constriction in her throat beginning to loosen its stranglehold. She looked at the girls, at Paolo who had walked over and was gently stroking Diana's head.

'You turned all white,' Dorothea said. 'Did you get sick? Are you faint?'

Diana shook her head dumbly, she did not trust herself to try speaking.

'Oh, well, maybe it's the baby.'

Diana shot the girl a startled look, as if Diana's thoughts – and guilt – were visible for all to see.

'The baby is not an easy thing, some silly people think it is, but it is not. Not everyone can handle a baby like me.'

The thin girl went on bouncing the heavy, gurgling child, its fingers slippery and wet now with saliva and wax and cheese, a look of pride on the older girl's face. She smiled indulgently at Diana.

'Don't worry. You will get better with the baby.'

'I hope so,' was all she could gasp.

The rest of the afternoon passed uneventfully. Dorothea continued her play, but had done so half carrying, half dragging her baby sister along with her, propping the child up against tree trunks or the sides of buildings, laughing at *bambola* as she tried to crawl or pull herself up to standing. Diana had snuck the girls into the kitchen when she was sure Giuliana and Signora were outside inspecting the automobiles. There had been a brief, but passionate, exchange of embraces, the huge frame of the mother engulfing her three daughters all at once. The woman had looked at Diana, nodding her head in silent thanks, then had sat down heavily on a kitchen bench, untucking her shirt and lifting it to nurse her baby, even as she automatically checked a scratch on Sarina's cheek and asked Dorothea a quiet and rapid succession of questions. Diana moved to get food for the young girls but she didn't need to. Before she had taken two steps, the woman was reaching into her pockets for small parcels of food – cheese and bread and salumi already cut into thin slices for the girls to eat. One of the women working nearby handed Dorothea a handful of olives, and another gave Sarina a shiny red apple which the girl took in wonder, clutching it to herself with both hands. The baby broke suction and the mother deftly flipped it around, switching sides quickly. Diana was mesmerized by the woman's efficiency, by how she fed her baby using only one hand, the other running through Sarina's thin hair, pulling at tangles, tugging down the hem of Dorothea's dress which remained stubbornly too short for the angular girl. The other women working at the busy table took little notice of them, except to pat the girls' heads, or laugh kindly, or say something Diana couldn't catch that made the girls smile. They worked around the nursing mother, doing her work for her while she fed her baby, not saying a word but taking hold of the dough she had been kneading a moment before and finishing the loaf themselves, forming it and slashing its top and throwing it into the brick oven with their own. Covering for the woman, pitching in as countless other women had pitched in for them and for their mothers and for all the keepers of the human race.

Dorothea nodded at her mother and stepped over to Diana.

'My mamma says thank you for helping us, and bringing us in. It is so busy here, she says, no one will mind us. The woman in charge only cares about the food; now that she knows how good my mamma is, she will let us stay if that means Mamma will stay, too.'

The girl looked proudly at her mother, who was already tucking in her shirt and holding the baby out to Dorothea.

'I have to go help Mamma now. But I had a good time today getting . . . getting to play again.'

'Come out and play anytime your mamma can spare you. Paolo would like it. So would I.'

'*Thea,*' her mother called, and the girl jumped to grab the squiggling baby, holding it above her head, kissing its toes and pretending to nibble on them. The baby laughed a hearty laugh, low and guttural, and the women around the table laughed in response, repositioning themselves to allow the girls to sit on the crowded bench, protecting them within their circle, tossing them pieces of dough to play with, including them in their work, mirroring for them the only life they had ever known.

Diana went back outside, walking slowly. In the distance, she saw Paolo with Giuliana and Giorgio. He had asked to see the cars and was jumping from foot to foot in his excitement, Giorgio letting him wear his cap or hold one of his wrenches and Giuliana fussing over him, pulling up his socks and trying vainly to subdue the boy's hair, which had grown into a mass of curls without her vigorous brushing. Diana was struck by how different the couple was with the boy. With anyone else, they were brusque, monosyllabic with anyone save Signora, with whom Diana suspected they shared some bond other than that of just employer and employee. But with Paolo, their eyes lost their set look. Their faces relaxed into smiles that softened the hard line of their jaws. Giorgio's eyes grew wet, Giuliana frowned with the deep pride of a grand-mother, the old couple bickered over what the boy could do, or wear, or how much he could eat, *no, not another candy, he will get sick, all right, then, well, just the one.* Diana walked up to the trio, her shoes making a crunching sound on the gravel that made Giuliana turn sharply in her direction. The woman's face closed quickly, putting back the mask she wore for everyone except the boy.

'We were just coming, we were finishing up here . . .' Giuliana stammered in Italian, as if caught in some wrong-doing, as if guilty of misconduct. Diana saw her look wistfully at the boy, brushing invisible flecks off his shirt. Diana had not realized how much Giuliana had missed the child, giving him his bath and combing out his thick hair, even one missed day had taken its toll on her. Diana had no argument with this old woman, had not meant to come between her and, seem-ingly, the only thing she loved. *Why do we hurt each other, without even trying?*

'If you're not too busy, Giuliana,' Diana began hesitatingly, not wanting to insult the proud woman, trying to choose the right Italian words to convey her meaning, 'would you mind taking Paolo up to bed tonight, for me? I . . . I have a slight headache,' she lied, pantomiming, pressing her palm to her forehead.

Giuliana was quick to accept.

'Of course, of course, we have done our preparations. Paolo, come, child,' and she had happily led the boy off, holding him gently by the wrist as he cavorted and danced, waving Giorgio's cap with his free hand and singing. Giorgio looked at Diana for a minute, not smiling, not showing any expression at all, then inclined his head quickly, almost imperceptibly. But Diana had seen and understood. He was thanking her.

Giorgio walked off to smoke a cigarette with the other men, hidden out of sight behind the garage. The sounds from the kitchen grew less. The women were done with their labors, tucking pies under clean dish towels, setting enormous cast-iron pots of sauce on the stove to simmer, checking and rechecking everything was in readiness before heading to the back rooms that had been set aside for them, a wing at odd angles to and far off from the main living areas where there would be no sight or sound of them until they were needed. Diana walked around the house, taking the steep steps down into the garden, circling around the hedge maze, its sides twelve feet high, thickly set and ingrown. Once inside, you could not see through the greenery to gauge your location. It made her feel claustrophobic, just to look at it now in the growing twilight. She hurried past it, walking through the western gate and setting out once more for the open fields. The sun had long since been hidden by a dense bank of clouds, but the sky was still a riot of color, pink and salmon and a deep, rich purple. The breeze came to her across the plain, rustling the grass which was beginning to dry out – they would harvest it soon, rolling it into enormous round bales too heavy for one man to move unaided. She walked out into the living, breathing expanse, the wind through her hair, the sky directly above her a dome of royal blue, one star bravely competing with the undying sunset. Everything seemed at peace, after the rush and bustle of the day, after the hours of preparation. An expectancy hung in the air but, out here, surrounded by beauty, she could convince herself what she was waiting for was the arrival not just of a stranger but of the next phase in her life. A time where she could be whole and entire and forget the dirtiness of what she had done, of what she had had to do to survive an unwinnable war. The soft summer air seemed to be waiting for her to say something, expecting something from her, so she whispered, 'Come now, I'm ready, I'm whole enough, I'm healed enough. Whatever comes next, let it come now,' and the sun broke through a line of bushes far down on the horizon, swathing her for a moment in its light, in a warm, fiery glow.

She woke up suddenly, sitting up in bed and breathing hard. She looked around her room in confusion, coming back to reality with difficulty. Her dream had seemed so real. She had been outside, in the fields again, but the sun had been rising this time, not setting. She was experiencing everything again, in full detail. The feel of the grass seeds between her toes, the chirping of the birds circling above her, the malty smell of the fields and the warm, damp earth. She had been wearing her duty uniform, not the hospital issue from back home, or even the white dresses they had packed when they first went to war, but the drab overalls they had scavenged from utility closets and mechanic shops so they could straddle stretchers, and lift patients on to trucks, and save men's lives without worrying about their undergarments showing. She had been barefoot in her dream, the jumpsuit unbuttoned at the neck as they had done when it was hot, when they were sweltering in North Africa. She had been in the field and then the field had become an open *piazza*, an enormous stone square bigger than any they had seen in Rome. A girl had come hurrying across the square, directly towards Diana but not seeming to see her, a young woman pulling up the skirts of a heavy dress far too big for her. She stumbled twice on her hem, looking worriedly over her shoulder, as if something was after her. As she got closer, Diana could hear the girl was crying, gasping for air and crying, repeating something to herself over and over that could have been a prayer or a plea or a form of self-assurance, that whatever was chasing her would not catch her, that she would make the shelter of the far side of the *piazza* before it came, before it swallowed her whole. Diana reached out to grab the girl as she came close. She wanted to help her, to stop her, to force her to see her and realize she wasn't alone. But as the girl struggled past Diana, wrestling out of her grasp and hurrying onward, Diana could see it was the same woman she had dreamed of the other night, the same pale, luminous skin, the same dull, dark rings on her fingers. It was Signora, Diana knew that for a certainty, youthful and slender, but there were dark circles under her frightened eyes that hadn't been there before. She looked at Diana without seeing her, disheveled hair falling from the high, teased style of another era, the ill-fitting clothing made for another woman impeding her flight as she raced across the open space. Diana could hear the click of her heels receding in the distance, she was sure the younger version of Signora would be safe, would make it in time. But then, from over her own right shoulder, Diana could feel a presence. Cold and dark and malevolent. She could feel its breath on her bare skin and the terror rose in her as she reached behind her without looking, and felt something wet and damp and clinging, a hand of a corpse lifeless one minute, then crushing her in its grip the next.

It was then Diana had woken up. She was in her own bed, but she felt a sense of urgency, as if she must get out of it, get up at once. She felt she had been awoken by something more than just the terror of her dream. She felt that something – some sound – had awoken her a moment before. She thought, if she could concentrate hard enough, she would remember what it was. She hastily tied the belt of her robe, stepping out on to the balcony, but all was silent there except the far-off barking of a dog. She walked back through her room, into the hallway, down the hall, and out into the long landing that overlooked the lower floors. From here, she thought she could hear something – voices, perhaps – but far off and muffled. She tiptoed to Paolo's room, opening his door silently and looking in – the boy slept peacefully, moonlight illuminating the foot of his bed. She closed the door and continued to the head of the stairs. The voices were louder here; she could make out Signora's voice and another's that might have been Giorgio's. She didn't know what urged her to start down the main stairway, holding on carefully to the banister; she noticed, with increased perception, the feel of the wood under her hand – it had never had this much polish. The runner, too, under her feet had been taken out and beaten, and it felt new and stiff under her bare feet. At the foot of the stair, in that great, sleeping house, she paused. The same grandfather clock she had seen on her first day stood by, counting out the seconds, *tick-tock, tick-tock.* Diana held her breath, as if unwilling to break the great silence all around her that seemed a living thing in itself.

Suddenly, she heard raised voices – a man's she did not recognize, and Signora's. Without conscious volition, as if still half in her nightmare, she ran across the hall and threw open the door to the study. She stood gaping for a moment. The same fawns danced motionlessly on the mantle, the same glass figurines posed in frozen perfection on the tables. The thick curtains were loosed from their gold cord, the oriental carpet had been repositioned to hide the thin spot in its middle. But Diana saw none of these things. What she saw was Signora, still dressed for the evening, in the same formal black taffeta she wore with the regularity of a nun's habit. She was in the center of the room – the colored glass of the hanging chandelier illuminated her face and caught at the shiny, onyx buttons at her cuffs. But Signora was not looking at Diana. Her eyes, one clouded, one clear, were transfixed on the man in front of her. The two were standing so close their bodies met and merged into a solid black mass against the red velvet of the far wall. He was a full eighteen inches taller than Signora, straight-backed and broad-shouldered. He was clutching Signora's high-necked collar, crushing the white lace at her throat, choking her. 'Stop!' Diana called out, even as she charged forward, channeling her momentum into her right shoulder, which she rammed into the stranger's back as she had seen cornerbacks do back home on a Friday night. The man lost his grip and stumbled a few paces.

Signora crumpled to the floor, coughing feebly. Diana helped the old woman on to the same highbacked chair she had sat in that first day when Diana had imagined her cane a scepter. Diana poured water into a crystal goblet she had never seen before; the table was set for two, and the remains of a dinner were still visible. Signora gulped painfully as Diana turned to face the intruder. He had looked momentarily surprised when he first saw his assailant. Now a leisurely smile spread across his face.

'Aren't you going to introduce us, *Frau* Bugari?' the man asked in stilted English, smiling insolently at Diana. 'Really, your manners are not what they once were.'

'Are you all right, Signora?' Diana asked, not taking her eyes off the man. 'Do you need me to fetch Giorgio, or a doctor?'

'No,' came the strangled reply, Signora clutching at her throat. Then, in a much lower voice, 'No, I do not wish for you to send for anyone. I will be all right, in time.'

'That is correct,' the man continued for her. 'You came upon us at an . . . inconvenient moment, shall we say? We were just discussing how much time we have – all the time in the world, really. I, for one, am not going anywhere. Not until Signora and I complete our business transaction. But enough of this. There are more important things than business,' and as the man said the last word, his eyes took Diana in, from head to toe, grinning. His military bearing and short-cropped hair made his age difficult to determine – over fifty, certainly, but how much older Diana could not tell. He sauntered over to the table and poured himself a glass of amber-colored liquid – he downed it in one gulp, staring at Diana all the while, as if proving something to her, or to himself.

'And now that you've had your drink, get out,' Diana ordered, and the forcefulness in her voice made the man raise his eyebrows in mock alarm as he slowly refilled his glass.

'Oh, an American. How fresh. How new for you, *Frau* Bugari, what a welcome change from the eternal Giuliana and her even more ancient husband. Are they still with you? I cannot imagine one of you without the other.' Then, the smile deepening, he addressed Diana, 'But, *Fräulein*, you and I have – how do you Americans say it? – started off on the wrong foot. Isn't that the expression? *Frau* Bugari and I are old friends – *very* old friends – and appearances can be deceiving. You seem under the impression I am unwelcomed here, that I am here against the wishes of my gracious host—'

'Since you seem to know a little of my language, let's see if you know this one. Shut up.'

The man broke out laughing.

'Again, I must congratulate you on your choice of companion. This one is delicious. I might have to steal her from you.'

Diana stepped towards the man as if to slap him, then checked herself. He looked momentarily disappointed, but only for a moment. The next he was smiling down on her and, although he did not touch her, she felt almost trapped by the intensity of his gaze.

'*Frau* Bugari, you do not wish me to leave, do you?'

Signora was silent for a moment before replying.

'No. There are reasons you must stay. For now.'

'See?' the man asked in a silky voice and, at that same

moment, Diana imagined a spell being cast by that voice, and by the icy blue eyes that held her. 'I am not unwelcome here. I am Signora's friend. I am your friend.'

He held his glass in one hand, slowly swirling the richly colored liquid which seemed to dance in the light of the chandelier. Diana heard the ticking of the grandfather clock grow louder and, somehow, slower – distorted, as if she had water in her ears. There must be something in the air, Diana thought desperately, some drug or powder thrown on to the fire, as she had seen in movies back home, things that made you powerless to resist, or think clearly. Then she remembered that it was summer, that no fire had been laid in the grate, that it was hot and that she had on only the old silk robe Signora had given her out of pity and her own thin nightslip underneath. She wondered why she should think of that now, think about what she was wearing at a time like this, but she gave it up. It was becoming harder to concentrate. The man had hold of her wrist now, she hadn't noticed when he took it. He kept pressing firmly on the inside of her wrist, as if it meant something, as if it were a code she could decipher. Her heart lurched in her chest, at first, she assumed, in alarm, but then with a slow, stupid kind of realization she knew it was something else. *This man is evil*, she told herself, *he must be evil, he was choking Signora*, but even as she formed the words in her mind, she knew there was something emanating from this man that negated her thought, that dispelled all reason. She felt as though she was looking into a flame, a single, burning flame she could not turn away from. There was a magnetic pull coming from him, an inexorable current as if in a river. After mere moments in his presence, she could barely resist it. In another moment she forgot what resistance was, forgot herself, forgot the boy sleeping upstairs. She forgot Giorgio and Giuliana, and the three girls tucked into bed somewhere with their mother, the baby nursing in its sleep, dreaming as Diana was beginning to dream now, standing still in front of this man. She blinked her eyes slowly, as if the effort to reopen them was becoming too much for her. She remembered the young girls in the canvas-backed truck who had looked as though they would fall asleep on their feet. She felt that way now.

'What is your name?'

Diana heard the words but they came from a long way off. She didn't answer and only after a long pause did she realize they might have been meant for her.

'Diana.'

'Like the goddess,' he said so softly she barely registered the words, the image of a huntress tracking a stag flickering for a moment in her mind before vanishing.

'Diana Bolsena.'

She didn't know what had prompted her to offer her last name. Maybe she had sensed he wanted her to.

'Like the lake these Italians so love. Goddess of the Lake.'

He must have put down his glass because he held both her wrists now, continuing his steady *tap*, *tap*. Pulsating, it was a pattern, she was sure of that – maybe morse, or something else. He was telling her something with his hands. With his eyes.

'I am Herr Adler.'

She had never heard a voice like that before, low but commanding. Mesmerizing. Shutting out all other sounds. He was smiling now but not with his mouth. He seemed to have gained the control he wanted. The woman in front of him, wearing only a castoff shift, a slip made out of nothing, was staring up at him, transfixed, her body limp and receptive, awaiting his command. His hands moved slowly up her arms, taking hold of her elbows, drawing her closer to himself. The woman did not resist.

At that moment, there was a tremendous crash. Diana was startled by the sound, stepping back and out of Adler's arms, snapping out of her trance. Signora had risen to her feet but was unsteady, swaying dangerously before catching herself on the armchair. In another moment, Diana realized why Signora had almost fallen. She was missing her cane, something the old woman was never without. Diana turned her head, disbelieving at first glance. The cane rested now on the top of the mantle, where the old woman had thrown it a second before. The shattered pieces of china and glass lay scattered on the floor. A moment later, Giorgio came staggering in, wearing a nightdress like those Diana had seen in illustrated copies of *The Night Before Christmas*. Giorgio took a step towards Adler, but Signora stopped him with her voice.

'All is well, Giorgio.'

Giorgio continued to glare at the newcomer.

'Would you please see Herr Adler to his room? He arrived later than expected and has eaten an informal *repas* with me here.'

Signora Bugari made no mention of Diana in her night-clothes, of the smashed figurines, of her thick cane thrown halfway across the room. Giorgio looked as if he would say something to her, but her eyes warned him not to. He glanced again at the broken pieces on the rug, then at Signora, then, without uttering a word, stepped aside and stood deferentially by the door.

Adler smiled his perpetual smile.

'Now this is more like it. A proper valet,' Adler mocked, straightening his cufflinks and walking towards the door. 'Thank you for your hospitality, *Frau* Bugari. If this is what I have to look forward to' – here he looked directly at Diana – 'I will enjoy my stay here even more than I had anticipated.'

Adler stepped carefully around the sharp shards on the carpet, exiting the room as Giorgio closed the door behind them. Once he had gone, Signora Bugari sunk back into her chair. Diana rushed over to her, kneeling down on the hard wood. Signora had her head in her hands. Diana was struck by the resemblance to the young girl in her dreams.

'Signora, let me get you help. You need a doctor.'

Bugari simply shook her head without lifting it.

'You cannot mean to allow that man to stay here. Who – *what* is that man?'

Diana received no reply, so she continued.

'Signora, why are you so afraid of him?'

Bugari sat up straight.

'Can *you* ask that? After what you saw? Did you not feel it?'

'Feel . . . feel what?' Diana stammered.

'You know what I mean. Listen, child.' Bugari had never called her *child* before, never used one term of familiarity in all her weeks with her. Now she grabbed hold of both of Diana's hands, her thin, bony fingers clutching them tightly. 'You have no idea what that man is capable of. He is pure evil. I don't believe in good or evil any longer, except in regard to that particular person. The things he has done – the things he has caused others to do. It is unspeakable.'

Diana had never seen Signora look more frail or more fiercely alive than she did at that moment. She was glad the old woman had broken the spell, had pulled her out of the dizzy, chloroformed state Adler's words had reduced her to. She knew deep inside that, even in her daze, some part of her had been crying out not to trust him, not to touch him, that whatever paralysis he had induced in her mind and body, some essence of herself had still rebelled, had still wanted to escape the void she had found herself falling into. Giuliana came into the room in a stiff nightgown. She took one look at the mantlepiece, another at the two huddled women, and walked directly to them. She winced as a broken satyr pressed against the worn sole of her slipper, but she grabbed on to Signora's arm and eased her to her feet.

'Giuliana, Adler was choking Signora when I walked in—'

The two elderly women exchanged furtive glances and started slowly for the door.

'Do you hear what I'm saying, Giuliana? The man is dangerous, he cannot stay here—'

'*Basta.*' Enough, Giuliana said, waving her off, putting an arm protectively around Bugari. But her voice had cracked. 'Signora knows what she is doing,' she mumbled in Italian.

'I don't think she does – she is allowing this man in her home and—'

'Enough.'

Signora, leaning heavily on Giuliana and Giorgio, who had re-entered the room, turned towards Diana. Something of her old command had returned to her voice.

'You will go to your room, Miss Bolsena, and stay there. Lock the door to your wing, lock your windows. Let no one in, under any pretense. Giuliana will sleep in Paolo's room tonight, so you need not concern yourself with him while Adler remains. *Stay out of his way.*' She emphasized the last words, her voice dropping to a hoarse whisper. 'Do not confront him, or cross his path, or exchange words with him, for any reason. He is . . . he is not natural.'

'What do you mean, "not natural"?' Diana asked, following alongside the trio who were making their steady ascent up the stair. Signora remained silent until they had gained the top and accompanied Diana back to the door leading to her wing.

'Show me your key,' Signora commanded as Diana fetched it from her pocket and held it up to her. 'You will lock this door as soon as it is closed upon you, do you understand me?'

Diana nodded her head.

'You will promise not to unlock it until morning. Under no pretense will you permit anyone to enter, until Giuliana or myself come for you.'

'All right, but . . .'

For the first time, Signora seemed to relax by an infinitesimal degree.

'Very well, then. You asked me what I meant when I said the man is unnatural. I have only this to say.'

Signora motioned for Diana to enter her own hallway, partially closing the door on her.

'I pray you never find out.'

With that, the door was shut to firmly and Diana was alone on the other side. She turned the key in the lock, hurrying down the hall, switching on lights, locking the tall French windows, the small window in the unused bedroom, shutting the skylight in her bathroom that even Sarina would not be able to crawl through. She pulled every curtain shut, then looked through her wardrobe and under her bed, under the bed in the room next to hers. She searched her bare apartment where no one could hide, where nothing hidden could remain unseen. Then she sat down on the edge of her bed, her robe still wrapped tightly around her, every electric light blazing. She looked at herself in the mirror, a stranger sitting on a strange bed, a woman she did not recognize, someone who had been hypno-tized by half a dozen words spoken by a man she had first seen attempting murder. Who was this man, she wondered again, and what was his power? And then a more frightening thought took hold of her, as she remembered the rhythmic tapping on her wrists, the way all thought had left her as she melted into him, the way she had felt herself at the edge of a cliff, with this man about to push her off, and done nothing to keep herself from falling into the black void of his nothingness.

Who was she?

Diana woke in the morning not to memories but to a blank slate. She had had no dreams, as if the events of the previous night had been more than enough for her subconscious, had filled the quota for the bizarre and the strange. Diana's body felt heavy, she was not used to solid rest, certainly not to a dead sleep that now left her right ear numb – she must not have moved once her head hit the pillow. She had sat up in bed the night before for as long as she could, listening for sounds, for a rattle at the door, for the sound of someone fumbling at the French window latch. But no sound had come and, somewhere, she must have fallen asleep on top of her blankets, the knot in her robe still tied and uncomfortable, pressed up under her ribs. Diana got out of bed, the room stuffy with no ventilation, going from room to room switching off the lights that must have burned all night like a beacon. Diana turned on the shower and stepped in, watching the water circle down the drain, and all of a sudden she was back in the war. But not a part she often remembered. It was hard to believe, now that it was all over for her, that there had ever been a time when she and the other nurses had been happy, had laughed and played pranks on one another, had sat in the open-topped convoy trucks and sang *Don't Sit Under the Apple Tree* at the top of their lungs. It was hard, after all the death and carnage, after the inhumanity they had witnessed, to recall the pleasant times, but those times had existed, too. In Tunisia, where they had been stationed further back from the line, when there had been a lull between each battle and the influx of patients, the nurses had decorated their barracks, or hung streamers in the mess hall to denote Thanksgiving, Christmas, New Year's Day. They had organized crowded dances with the officers, the female lieutenants prohibited from fraternizing with enlisted men, although Diana remembered Louisa, back before it had gotten bad for her, sneaking outside the mess tent and dancing with her boyfriend from the maintenance depot. Diana had kept watch for the two lovers as the muffled music reached them, as they swung happily around the trash cans and rubbish heaps, their smiles bright in the dark African night. The nurses had come from all over, and from all walks of life. There were country girls from out West who had never left their county seat, and big-city girls who had gone to finishing schools in Paris and used their French now to negotiate deals on the black market. Girls who had lived like nuns back home learned to swear, and smoke, and flirt with pilots. And girls who had been trapped in the shallow world of debutante balls and female backbiting learned – some for the first time – the depth of friendship and human loyalty. Their camaraderie grew with their shared experience. They shared hair pins, shoelaces, and bar soap. They helped each other pack when the order to move out came down. They covered each other's shifts when someone fell in love, when someone's beau got leave, they lied and said *yes, Katie got in before curfew, yes, I'm sure, I was with her the whole time.* There had been one wedding. Hastily thrown together on no notice, they had grabbed the company chaplain and stood inside a half-bombed-out church and made cream puffs for the reception afterward that had made everyone sick when the raw milk they used had turned. But weddings were a rarity because, by army regulations, no two spouses were allowed to serve within the same theater of war. That bride, still clutching her stomach two days later, had been sent to the Pacific, to a nightmare she knew nothing about and could not even imagine, while her surgeon husband had stood by glumly as she boarded the transport truck. So, rather than send the person they loved to the Pacific Rim, or into the even more remote China–Burma–India campaign, secret engagements became the norm, with many couples who would rather have been celebrating their first or second wedding anniversary having to settle instead for a three-day pass – and friends who would cover for them. The later events of the war all but erased the memory of these happier times. The injured civilians, the women lost in childbirth, the children blown apart by booby-traps or poisoned by chocolates left behind by the Germans, these were the images burned into the nurses' minds; this is what they'd take with them, along with the memory of the thousands, the unending thousands, of American injured. Teenage boys. Captains of their track teams. Presidents of their Senior class. Mowed down by the relentless, senseless machine of war. But the fact remained that there had once been good times, times of companionship and deep love – for many, the deepest love they would ever know – and, if they lived long enough, one day, maybe, they'd remember it.

Diana toweled off, got dressed, and had just combed out her hair when she heard a knock coming from far off down the long hall. She ran.

'It is I, Signora Bugari,' came the voice on the other side of the door. 'You may open this door now.'

Diana quickly unlocked the door, stepping out on to the landing and locking the door behind her. Her hair was dripping wet, soaking the back of her lavender dress, the one with the uneven hem.

'Signora, I have so many questions for you this morning—'

Bugari cut her off.

'Allow me to make one point clear. While Herr Adler is our . . . our *guest*, he will be my primary concern. I amend that statement. He will be my *only* concern. It will take all of my ability, as well as that of Giuliana and Giorgio, to do what needs to be done before he can leave us. That being said, any questions you might have are irrelevant, for the time being. Your duties will be light – Giuliana will have charge of the boy, for the present – no, no arguments. That is decided. You will have to take care of yourself the best you can and stay out of Adler's way, as I told you. We cannot be everywhere at once, and the estate is extensive. Do not go anywhere where you might be alone with him or have him come upon you suddenly. I will not answer for that.'

'Signora, I am not a child. I can take care of myself. In the war—'

'I can assure you I understand what war is more than you. I have lived through . . . more than one of them.' Bugari held a far-off look for a moment before continuing. 'But, by and large, you were dealing with men, I believe. This is different.'

Bugari had reached the end of the landing and was working her way down the stair. Diana noticed she had her cane again. In fact, everything about Bugari's appearance – the stiff black dress, the perfectly starched lace that covered any bruises left on her throat the night before, the gold locket, the polished onyx buttons – seemed as normal, as if last night had left no mark on her. But Diana knew it had. She reached out and stopped the old woman, placing her hand on the delicate, bony arm.

'Signora, I will take care of myself, I promise. But you cannot mean Adler is something other than human, any different from any other man. You are not talking about ghosts or monsters or demons, are you? Because, if you are, I must tell you I don't believe in those things. They are not real.' *We create enough of those for ourselves, without their help*, she added mentally.

Bugari looked down at Diana's hand, then up at her face.

'I don't know how you expect me to answer that. I cannot, not without going into the type of detail I just said I have neither the time nor the energy to expend now. If you do not believe in monsters, then your war ended too soon for you. If nothing haunts you, you have learned nothing.'

Diana stood still at the base of the stair as Signora walked into the study and closed the door behind her. Signora's words rang in her ears. *If nothing haunts you.* But what was the baby and the tree and the hill, the nightmare that came unbidden, if not a haunting? She was haunted, she wanted to scream at the closed door, she was haunted but what had she learned? What had it all been for? If for nothing, then nothing held any meaning. But if there was some awful, terrible meaning to life, could she possibly discover it? Would she be strong enough to endure it if she found out the secret? Or would the answer destroy her as completely as the Allied bombs had destroyed that baby, had destroyed the villagers in that town that fateful night?

The dining-room door was closed and Diana, unwilling to come upon Adler having a late, solitary breakfast, passed by it quickly on her way to the kitchen. There she found the usual frenzy of activity, everyone, except *bambola*, hard at work.

Sarina was dicing onions with a dull knife, and Dorothea was carrying heavy plates and bowls from one woman to the next, stopping by the open-topped crate they had turned into a makeshift crib to toss the baby some shiny object – a spoon or a tea-strainer – to teethe on. Dorothea smiled at Diana in welcome and seemed about to speak but was immediately called upon to peel an enormous pile of potatoes. Diana took a small roll, poured some coffee out of the enamel pot on the stove, and stepped outside. There was no sign of Adler, or of whatever conveyance he had used to reach the remote spot the night before. Diana walked over to the garage, standing on tiptoe to look inside the paned-glass windows, but the only vehicles were the red and the green and the blue automobiles she had seen the day before. Diana turned to survey the house. She knew, from the preparations that had been made, that they had given Adler a ground-floor apartment at the back of the house, one that overlooked the extensive gardens and the hedge maze. From this side of the house, Diana could make out the windows of the study where Signora had ensconced herself, but the windows were shut tight, despite the growing heat of the day, and the curtains were closed. She could learn nothing there.

Diana loitered around the grounds. Giorgio was using the presence of the extra help to work on a wall that had tumbled down in one spot, where they were pulling off thick vines and replacing the missing stones. Diana walked around the back, waving at one of the women who was hanging kitchen towels out to dry on the line. The woman waved in reply, hanging the cheerful white and yellow rectangles that snapped in the rising wind like signal flags. From her vantage point, she could see Paolo's open window, hear snippets of the song Giuliana was singing to him. This was to be their plan, then, to keep the boy under house arrest, to lock him in his room until the danger had lifted. Diana shrugged her shoulders. Perhaps they knew best.

The day was hot. Diana had not even gone halfway around the building and already she was thirsty. She walked for a few more minutes, coming upon the manual hand pump by the side kitchen garden. It was rarely used since electricity had been laid in the house, but she had seen Giorgio use it to fill a watering can, or drink from it himself when a trip inside was inconvenient. It was cooler on this side of the house. Large trees cast their shade on the pump, on an odd semi-circle of stones that had once been something – a dais or a stone porch – but was now more a dry spot of lawn than anything else, the flat stones showing through the parched grass that would not grow. Diana thought again about how ancient everything was in Italy. Back home, the historic buildings had been the town hall, and Mrs Claymore's house, which had been built two hundred years before. But here, this small circle of stones could have been laid by the previous owners, or by Romans in the time of Christ, or by the ancient Etruscans who pre-dated the Roman Empire itself. The china cup Diana had drunk her coffee from still dangled, empty, from her pinky finger. She placed it down, carefully, as she primed the pump. Just like back home, at the pump she had used to water their livestock, she moved the iron bar up and down. Slowly at first, with the resistance of the weight of the water and the depth of well fighting her, then more easily as the cloudy water began to rise, coughing and spitting as it first came out, then running clear and cold, a white-gold glistening stream of ice. Diana bent as she pumped, drinking in deeply, the water splashing on to her face, and down her neck. She drank until she was satisfied, letting go while the momentum still moved the handle up and down for another moment, splashing the water over her arms and her legs, as she had done as a girl. When the pump stopped moving and the sound of water hitting stone had ceased, it was then that she heard the voices. One was Adler's and not far off – perhaps just on the other side of the row of cypress trees lining the old farm path that ran from the house to the fields. Diana stepped towards the trees, growing so close together she had to press her way in between them. She had not forgotten Signora's warnings, or her promise to her, or the mindless state the man had reduced her to with such seeming ease. Diana had not forgotten these things, but she was acting on instinct – not the instinct of a senseless creature seeking its own destruction but, rather, a deeper instinct, wedded to her innermost self and her identity as a woman. She pushed past the trees and found herself on the farm path, dusty but smooth. Adler was in front of her, but he was not alone. In front of him was the reason she had broken her promise and was putting herself directly in the path of danger. The other voice had come from a child.

It was one of the houseboys, a village child no older than Dorothea, Diana had seen throwing stones into the manicured lawn on his first day there. He was thin and frail and stood digging the toe of his shoe into the dust of the lane. Adler had his hand extended, handing the boy a sweet which the child popped greedily into his mouth. Adler raised his eyes to look at Diana, her wet arms and legs glistening in the sun. The man turned back towards the boy, keeping his eyes on Diana. He continued his conversation with the child. Diana felt that, in his mouth, even the lilting sweetness of Italian seemed suddenly sinister.

'And do you like sweets?'

'Yes, sir, of course.'

'You did not receive many, during the war.' It was a statement.

'No, sir, not any. Not any half as good as these.'

Diana noticed the boy's mouth was crammed with candy, it was hard for him to speak. She wondered how long they had been out here, and under what pretense Adler had gotten him to this remote spot where no one could see them.

'I have many more of these, delicious ones,' Adler went on, smiling. The child turned the hard candies over in his mouth, running his tongue over the sticky sweetness.

Diana stepped forward quickly, yanking the boy by the elbow.

'You are wanted in the kitchen,' she said sternly in English, forgetting to translate. Then, as the boy hesitated, looking wistful as the man dug deep into his pocket for another candy, she ordered, '*Subito.*' At once.

The child could hear the rustle of candy wrappers.

'And if I ever see you with this man again,' she continued, pointing at Adler, her voice rising, '*ti frusterò la tua pelle.*'

The boy's eyes opened wide in fear, and he ran for the

house. *Ti frusterò la tua pelle.* Donna Lucia had always been
threatening it, it had been her favorite expression when she
thought a girl lazy or found any recalcitrance in her. *Ti frusterò
la tua pelle.* I will whip your hide, she had said, in the exact
way Diana had said it to the boy. It was a horrible thing to
say to anyone, let alone a child starved for sweetness after the
bitterness of war, but it was the only thing she had been able
to think of to protect the boy from Adler. And she would not
trust the boy's self-control when it came to candy. She would
warn the mothers in the kitchen, let Giuliana and Signora
know, too, that there was more than one child in their care
that needed protection from Adler. The boy would be all right.
Diana turned to go.

Adler gently placed his hand on Diana's arm, as if to detain
her, but she whipped it away.

'Don't touch me,' she snarled.

Adler took several paces backward, raising his hands
placatingly.

'I was only going to say' – his voice calm as ever, a hint
of a smile behind it – 'it is not wise to come between me and
my . . . prey.'

Diana stared at him. In the dappled sunlight that came in
through the double row of trees, she could see little lines of
silver running through his hair, glistening in the light. His face
was smooth and pink and so closely shaven she wondered,
incongruently, if he had used a straight razor. She did not
speak, or take her eyes off him, but she had begun to walk
backwards, slowly, towards the gap in the trees.

'Your *prey*?' Diana asked accusingly. 'Is that what you call
a child?'

'Perhaps I have chosen the wrong English word. Perhaps
subject is what I meant. Or *object.*'

The man's clear blue eyes seemed to bore into her.

'But you are fascinating, my dear, absolutely fascinating,
and you know that.'

The way he said the words made her face flush with a guilt
she knew she did not have.

'You are American, which is always novel to work with. I
have had far too many Europeans.'

Diana had no idea what he was talking about – had too many Europeans for what?

'Coupled with your spirit,' he chuckled reminiscently, 'your tackling me last night when you felt your employer was in danger – really, I couldn't be more pleased. I mean, certainly, I have encountered resistance before in my work. There were those, surely, that put up a fight, at first . . .'

His voice trailed off as he took a step towards her. Diana noticed the fine silt of the cart path had settled on the polished black of his boots, in the cuffs of his carefully pressed suit pants. His smile disappeared as he searched her face, almost clinically, for something he could not find there. Diana reached a hand behind her, feeling for the trees. She was at the gap, she did not need to listen to this man any longer – a straight shot past the well and she would be back in sight of the woman hanging out the washing, of Giorgio and the men sweating to set the wall to rights. But what had he meant about his 'work'? Who had put up a fight?

'You are a challenge, my dear. An enigma.'

He took another step, into full shade this time, and the youthful flush the morning sun had given his skin was gone. He looked cadaverous now, an old man with sunken eyes. His closely shaven skin bulged above his tight, buttoned collar. His hands clenched and released spasmodically, before suddenly stopping.

'But do not count too much on that. You have interrupted me, here, on a pleasurable errand. And I do not like to be interrupted. As I said, you came between me and my prey, which is not advisable. Do you know why?'

Diana was breathing quickly now, she could feel her heart thumping in her chest. She was not mesmerized – his voice held none of the soothing power it had the night before, or only moments ago, with the boy and his candies. She had the feeling she was looking into something dark, an abyss that was black and unknowable, except for the danger it held. She stepped between the trees, dried twigs crunching under her feet. Then she was running, past the well, past the blue-patterned teacup abandoned in the grass. She was past the flapping towels, and the men rolling cigarettes as they rested, she was in the house and up the stairs and in her room, the door locked securely behind her. But she still heard his words, low and menacing, the answer to his own question, as the first twig snapped and she broke into her run.

'Because now you become the prey.'

THREE

Adler had had enough. Bugari tried to dissuade him, tried to distract him with Caribbean cigars and fortified Portuguese wine. But he cast them aside untried, kicking over side tables and yelling at her in German, English, and Italian.

'You know what I have come for. Now give it to me.'

As Diana passed by the closed library doors – Bugari's voice a steady monotone, Adler's loud, barking commands – she wondered why the old woman didn't just acquiesce. She would have to give in to him, in time. She could not hold out forever with this German stalking around her home, emptying drawers, throwing their contents out on to the floor. Pushing over armoires, knocking on paneled walls for the sound of hollow spaces behind them. Yelling at the servants, storming through the kitchen and looking in the pantry, in the larder, thrusting his arm into the barrel of farina, up to his elbow, searching every nook and cranny for whatever it was he had come for. *She should just give it to him*, Diana mused, surveying the wreckage the man left behind him, the extra house servants righting tables and lamps and picking up broken crockery in his wake. *Whatever it is, it can't be worth this.*

But, apparently, resistance was worthwhile to Bugari, even if only for a short time. In the few moments Diana caught sight of her – walking with the aid of her cane, moving as swiftly as possible from one room to another, fingering the keys she kept deep in her pockets, only taking them out to hastily open and then lock a door behind her – Bugari's face looked set. Grim. Determined. Diana couldn't get her to stop and talk with her even briefly, and Giuliana spent all her time locked up with Paolo, out of Adler's reach. The only one Diana could talk to at all about what was happening was Giorgio, who was reticent in any language.

'Giorgio,' Diana pleaded. 'Please tell me something. Give

me one reason why Signora puts up with this man, doesn't either throw him out or give him what he wants or—'

'Give him? *Give*, to him?' Giorgio looked truly puzzled, shaking his head almost imperceptibly. 'You do not give to men such as this. It is like in church, when they read the *vangelo*, how do you say it? The gospel.'

Giorgio's face held a sad, hard look as he recited from memory, more to himself than to Diana, '*Poiché a chiunque ha, sarà dato ed egli sovrabbonderà; ma a chi non ha, sarà tolto anche quello che ha.*' Seeing the blank expression on Diana's face, he repeated, haltingly, 'For to everyone who has will more be given, but from him who has not, even what he has will be taken away.' Then he walked out of the room, ending their conversation.

The women in the kitchen had been warned – in a mixture of half-words and gestures – about Adler, about his proclivities and the threat he posed to their children. They nodded their heads sagely, as if not surprised by what lay hidden in men. They organized their day and their tasks to allow for a lookout, a scout, someone who would always know where the children were and where the threat was and to keep one from the other. Diana marveled at their matter-of-factness, at the seeming absence of any emotion or outrage. To Diana, there seemed to be some ancient knowing at work here, some primal directive that did not permit the expression of anger in the face of evil, but a simple, searing, focused energy, directed to keeping an extant evil away from the ones they loved.

As for Diana, and the threat Adler had leveled towards her, he had not yet acted upon it, at least not in any way Diana could ascertain. She checked and rechecked the lock on her bedroom door, on the slim French windows that led to her balcony. She learned from the women where Adler was, and kept to other parts of the house and estate. After she had fled from him, for the rest of that day she had gone from room to room, from floor to floor, avoiding the man who bellowed below stairs, demanding the return of what belonged to him. Diana listened at the top of the stairway or hung her head out of the window to try to catch his words. Praying Bugari would give in, despite Giorgio's prophesizing, would give the devil his due and get him out of the house that had – before Adler's arrival – begun to feel like a home to her.

Diana ate a hasty, largely silent dinner that night with the women in the kitchen. Food had been left out on the sideboard for Signora and her guest, but neither entered the dining room, the sound of falling boxes and crates echoing up from the doorway leading to the cellar. At first, both their voices could be heard. Then, after a brief silence, Bugari appeared in the kitchen, her black dress smudged, thin spider webs clinging to her cuffs and hemline. The women offered her food, but she shook her head, taking only a small glass of port, ordering the women to go to their rooms as soon as they had cleared up, and to lock their bedroom doors and the door to their wing.

'Signora . . .' Diana began, as the women put away their dishes and began to hang up their aprons. 'Signora, I must speak with you. I must . . . I must *help* you,' Diana said, surprising herself. She had not meant to say those words, but seeing the woman – old, and frail beyond reckoning, blue-veined, fragile hands, thin, bony neck encircled by a swath of faded lace – elicited a surge of protectiveness in Diana. 'Let me help you, Signora, please. This man, whatever hold he has over you, whatever he wants. Please, give it to him. Give it to him and let him leave us in peace.'

Bugari put the delicate crystal glass down on the thick butcher block of the table. The women were checking the pilot light in the oven, covering the dough rising on the countertops with striped kitchen towels, switching off lights and heading for their rooms. For a moment, Signora seemed to regard Diana as if she had not been there a moment before, as if she had not noticed her or the words she had been saying for a long time, as if the sounds Diana made were thin and hard to hear and coming from a long way off. Then she smoothed down her black shirtfront and her stiff, black, taffeta skirt that reminded Diana of the color of starlings.

'Help me?' Bugari asked, her voice cracking slightly. 'You cannot help me, child. You can only help yourself. By keeping safe. By not letting him add one more injury to this world.'

Bugari turned to go, but Diana rose hurriedly from her seat and followed her.

'Signora, don't let him do this to you. He is ruining you. He is ruining your beautiful house, looking for—' Bugari shot her a sharp glace. 'For whatever he is looking for. Send him away.'

Diana had not realized she had grabbed the old woman's arm, had not realized her voice had risen and she was holding on to Bugari as if she would force the old woman to yield to her, to Adler. Bugari raised a single eyebrow.

'You will release me. You will release me and you will retire to your room.'

Diana let go, surprised by the command Bugari's quiet voice held, by the stiffness and strength in the old woman's arm, the small muscles firm and taut, like those of a crouching cat, ready to pounce.

'I have my reasons for what I do and when I do it. And if you do not understand me' – here she paused for a moment before continuing – 'I do not care in the least.'

Diana took a step backward, staring at Bugari's dark, unfathomable eyes. She opened her mouth to speak but could not find the words. Bugari sighed, then continued quickly, in her most businesslike manner.

'I will bid you goodnight and remind you again, and with all possible urgency' – Signora switched off the last kitchen light, leaving them in darkness save for the soft glow coming in from the hall – 'lock your door.'

Diana sat upright in bed. She was sure she had heard it before her eyes were open, before she even knew where she was, what bed or room or even time or place she was in. Her heart was thumping hard in her chest behind the clothes she still wore; she had not changed for bed but had lain down fully dressed, shoes on, hair still tightly braided. She had not meant to fall asleep, but she must have, for an instant. And it was in that instant that the noise had come. Diana lay still another moment, listening to her own breathing, straining to hear over the rushing pulse in her ears. Then it came again, soft but unmistakable. The sound of the handle turning on the door at the end of the hall. Diana did not wait to check her watch, to see what time it was. She stood up and pulled back the thick curtains that covered her French windows. Immediately, moonlight flooded the room, and in her heightened state of awareness, Diana took in the play of moonlight on the curved iron of the bedstead, on the wooden leg of the chair, on a chip in the floor that stood out now as a sharp, dark shadow against a relief of pure white. The sound came again, still quiet but more urgent now, as if someone was also pushing against the wood of the door to get it to open. As silently as possible, Diana undid the latch of the long, paned windows, stepping out quickly on to the stone balcony, cool now and no longer hot, no longer host to the orange and red and blue-green lizards that played on it by day. She closed the door behind her and, crouching low, hurried across the balcony, past the small window of the spare bedroom, past the curtained doors of her living room. Careful not to upset the rickety drying rack at the far end where she hung out her underwear during the day, she lifted one leg over the stone brickwork where the ground rose up to meet the balcony, straddling the low wall for an instant. Then she was over, taking cover in the laurels, moving as quickly as she dared through their prickly thickness, past the crumbling outdoor oven, forsaken now amid the overgrown bushes and cacti. She kept her head down as she half climbed, half slid down the embankment, crossing the packed-earth driveway to the estate, showing white now in the moonlight. Then she was running, through the olive groves that grew from here to the high road and from there – half running, half jogging, her breath tearing at her throat – all the long way back into town. Past the church of San Biagio, nearly to the *cimetero* itself, to the wayside shrine of Santa Anna where she could crawl into the small, circular structure, lying down in the dark beneath the dried flowers hung in bunches on the wall, a promise of protection, tokens of prayers answered by the mother of the mother of God.

Diana stepped out of the shrine into full daylight. She had not imagined she could sleep so long on that hard, stone floor beneath the circular wooden bench, but the tension she had been living under since Adler's arrival had taken its toll until, finding herself in the safety of an obscure and unfrequented spot, her body had taken advantage of the opportunity to sleep. She rubbed her eyes, looking up towards the town, and then down the long hill towards the church and the way she had come in the night. Suddenly, she was overcome with revulsion for what she had left behind her at the bad house, a house that was beginning to earn its name – an insatiable Nazi, taciturn co-workers who revealed nothing, an employer who had told her to her face that she didn't care what Diana thought or felt. It was all nonsense. And she decided it was no longer her nonsense. The trials and tribulations of one old lady, the petty secrets of her past, and the (most likely) unimportant mystery she preferred to keep hidden were irrelevant in the grander scheme of things. The war in Europe was over, but there was still the Pacific campaign and she was still an active service member, bound by her duty, even if those in command had written her off as dead and buried by now. Diana took a step forward and then paused. An idea came to her that she had never had before, had never thought she'd entertain, even for a moment. But it came to her now, suddenly, in full force and she stood there, unmoving, in the middle of the long path that led from the church of San Francesco at the top of the hill, all the way down to San Biagio at the bottom, with its ornate well and incongruously manicured lawns.

She could disappear.

Diana Bolsena could disappear. The US Army thought she was dead, her sister, too. Marie wouldn't even recognize her sister, recognize what she had become, if Diana walked into her tiny bungalow in San Diego. There was no need to go back to Signora Bugari's, but there was equally no reason to go back to the war, to the killing and fighting and tearing that had brutalized her and made its mark on her soul these past three years. For whatever it was worth, her life was completely her own. She held it in her hands on that summer morning, as the birds chirped and dove above her head, singing a sweet song to the lavender-blue of the Italian sky, as if the war had never happened. She could go wherever she wanted, and the incredible freedom that brought to her made her catch her breath, actually caused her chest to hurt a little as if she had been physically struck. *I'm free*, she thought as tears rolled down her unwashed face. A rooster crowed nearby and a child – shielded from Diana's vision by a thick row of trees except for the bright pink of her dress – whistled to her chickens as she threw them grain. They squawked in approval, flapping their wings in excitement.

Diana looked down the hill again but, suddenly, it was no longer a dusty cart path, bright in the summer sunlight, but another path and another hill. Instantly, she knew this was her nightmare pressing in on her again, but now it was coming in broad daylight, no longer waiting for the night and the solitude of her iron bed. Her breathing came faster as she stared, wide-eyed, as the valley grew dark below her, illuminated only by explosions and the fire at the bottom of the hill. Diana could feel the wet tears on her face, even as she had felt them that night. Her chest constricted. She felt threatened by the dark-ness in the valley, a darkness that would not lift because the baby was dead and she had killed him. She had killed him by doing the wrong thing, and it was her fault, and her fault would follow her around forever, wherever she went. She was sure she would never be free if she ran now, even if she left the army and started a new life. With a cold certainty she knew, this time, she would have to see it through, watch the nightmare play out in its entirety, in all its terror. She would have to face up to what she had done or the baby would follow her everywhere because everywhere Diana went she found herself. And it was from herself that she was running.

A thin veil of clouds above her covered the sun – or maybe it wasn't clouds. As the light dimmed, Diana felt cold. A wind ran low along the ground, rushing past her and on up the hill, turning the leaves of the trees upside down, showing their white undersides. Diana stood still as the encroaching darkness drew close and then engulfed her, the sounds from that far-off night filling her ears. It was not the silent vacuum in which she usually relived her nightmare, but as it had actually been. A cacophony of sounds. Falling bombs. The roar of the airplanes. The brittle crash of glass as windows blew out. The sickening thud of stone falling on stone, the screech of metal being torn from its hinges. And above – beyond – all those sounds, the sound of screaming, of crying, the women and children and old people trapped in their homes, crushed under rubble, begging for help in the universal language of pain. And the baby – now back in her arms along that old cart road by the shrine of Saint Anne – looking up at her, the fire and explosions reflecting in its wide baby eyes, looking to her to protect him. Diana turned around, knowing what she would see, knowing the whitewashed building with its flowers would be gone and, in its place, the huge tree, stretching its ancient arms out into nothingness. The wind picked up, and Diana smelled the smoke coming from the village. She looked up, and as the Allied planes moved over in formation, they blotted out the stars. She wanted to call to them to stop, that she was an American, that they were her countrymen and killing her, killing the baby. They could not know what they did on the ground, she thought, these flyers; they must not know, must never see it. She tried to cry but now the tears would not come. The baby fussed in her arms, struggling to be put down, to be laid at the base of the tree where he would be safe. But Diana only clutched the baby tighter to herself.

She started down the hill, not towards the manicured lawn of the church but towards the burning village. The baby was screaming now, with a wild energy, much stronger than any baby could muster, as if it knew its survival lay behind him at the base of the tree. Diana crossed her arms in front of her, holding the baby close to her chest. *I can't leave you here*, she said again, as she had that night. *I will not leave you here to die.* The baby bumped its head against her collar bone, screaming in pain, but Diana kept stomping down the hill in jerky, unnatural motions until they were in among the buildings. Bodies lined the street, but they did not move or call out to her. They were dead, their bodies smashed. *If I abandon you, you will die, like them*, she told the baby, said again to herself, but the baby kept struggling – it was almost out of her grasp. She hoisted him up to reposition him, and the blanket she had wrapped him in fell to the ground into water and blood. *I found you along the roadside and I will not leave you along the roadside to die all alone*, she said, but her voice broke from dry heaving, from gasping for air. *You cannot die alone*, she pleaded with the child insensible now with rage, as if he was not screaming just for himself and his mother – who was dead miles back along the road, whose arms had been stiff and whose fingers Diana had had to pry back, she had held on so strongly to her child, even in death – but screaming now for everyone destroyed by war. *Do not ask me to leave you, back there by the tree, although you would have lived, although that tree was the only thing that was spared, I did not know that then, I could not know that then. I'm taking you with me, to save you, not kill you. I didn't mean to kill you. Forgive me, forgive me.*

And, for a moment, everything stopped. The wind and the smoke and even the steady rumble of the plane engines overhead were stilled. The fires still burned, but Diana only saw them dancing in the baby's eyes, which were no longer shut tight but looking up at her now, calmly, in a kind of wonder. *Forgive me*, Diana whispered, and in that whisper was all the pain, all the loss, all the horror of what she had seen and what she had been unable to prevent. She looked down on the baby, now relaxed in her arms, his downy head resting gently against her heart. The corner of the baby's mouth twitched in a reflexive smile, lasting only an instant, but it was enough to make Diana smile in return, as she would have if it were her own baby, as a thousand thousand mothers had before her, gazing down and losing themselves in their baby's face. The baby blinked slowly, its tiny eyelashes still clumped together by the tears that no longer fell. Then, knowing what would happen next, holding on to and stretching out the memory for as long as she dared, tracing the outline of the soft baby features one last time with her eyes, Diana said, *I forgive myself*, even as the building to her right exploded. Diana was thrown to the ground, glass falling on to her like a shower of red-hot pain. She was dazed for a moment, shaking her head, feeling herself all over instinctively for broken bones, struggling to her feet to see if she could bear her own weight, if she could walk. Then she noticed her arms were empty. Amid the dust and the debris that were still settling around her, she coughed and staggered forward, moving aside rocks and rubble until she found him, until she held him, kneeling in the sunshine as the birds flew overhead, the baby bleeding out in her arms,

the young girl in the pink dress whistling again to her hens
before throwing them her last fistful of grain.

Diana walked slowly into town. She felt numb after her
experience and looked to the solidity of the ancient town for
groundedness. There again was the *duomo* that dominated the
piazza grande, doors left open in the balmy air, cats sneaking
into the cavernous church to sleep on the upholstered chairs
designed for monsignors and cardinals. She walked aimlessly
down the winding side alleys of the town, mechanically stopping at the post office, the old ladies behind the barred windows
shaking their heads at her arrival, indicating they had nothing
for the lost American. She wandered by the churches – *chiese
di San Bernardo, di Sant' Agostino, di Santa Lucia, del Gesù,
di Santa Maria dei Servi* – but she stopped inside none of
them. She was unable to pray or, rather, she felt she had just
prayed so deeply she was left empty inside, unable to speak.
Unthinkingly, her feet led her towards the twisting side street
of Donna Lucia's boarding house. She pulled up sharp as she
saw Donna Lucia herself walk out to the truck and talk to the
man inside the cab. Even from the distance of half a street
away, Diana could make out the man's whining voice, and
Lucia's angry response, as both gesticulated wildly. There
would be some disagreement, Diana thought, there always
was. The rations for gasoline would not be enough, or the risk
the man was taking in transporting the girls would be too
great, or there would be suspicion on one – or both – of their
parts that they were cheating the other, making money on the
side, not being completely honest. Diana smiled wryly at
the thought of honesty, at their outrage that one might be
deceiving the other. *But what do you trade in but deception?*
Diana thought. *It's all deception.* Deception that the girls love
the Johns, deception that there is no risk or danger in what
they're doing, deception that buying and selling human beings
is OK, is all right, is permitted under made-up circumstances
Lucia and the driver were only too eager to make up in order
to make an extra *lira*. And here they were fighting over honesty,
and integrity, and treating each other as they would like to be
treated. Lucia pounded her fist against the dull paint of the

truck door and stomped back inside. The man continued his conversation with the woman after she left, the words obviously flowing more freely without her intimidating presence. In another minute, Diana knew, the girls would start filing out, hair neatly parted and braided, faces made up carefully to hide any bruises or sores or marks left by men hardened by the violence of war, expressing their violence through sex now that the fighting had ended. Diana had only a minute to approach the man in the truck, to pay him to take her to the nearest city. She had her wages in her dress pocket, she had kept them with her after Adler's arrival in case he gained entrance to her room. She had more than enough, she thought, to bribe this man, no matter how fearful he was of Lucia, no matter how many times she had forbidden him to speak to the American nurse. She would catch him while he was still arguing with his invisible opponent, while he was still angry enough at Lucia to defy her. Diana put her hand in her pocket, fingering the thick wad of cash. It would be enough. It would have to be.

She took a step forward before she caught something out of the corner of her eye. She had only seen it for a second, but she could have sworn it was the little boy she had snatched away from Adler. *It couldn't be*, Diana told herself, mechanically starting forward again, forcing herself not to follow the fleeting vision down the side street where it had flashed. But then a boy's voice rang out (*it could have been anyone's*, she chided herself), and the sound of running footsteps, and someone knocked over a display of needlework propped up against a shop door to her right. The careening boy pulled up short, surprised, staring open-mouthed as he recognized Diana, and panting hard. Diana stood stock still for another moment. The man in the truck had finished rolling up his cigarette, had thrown the match away with a curse and ended his conversation. He exited the truck, walking around the back and lowering the tailgate in anticipation of the girls' arrival.

'Miss America,' the boy said in between gasps, using the name the children on the estate had adopted for her. His hands were on his knees as he struggled to catch his breath.

Diana looked at him, and then anxiously back as the first

of the girls walked out to the vehicle, the smaller ones reaching up their hands to the older girls to help them up into the truck bed. They would leave in another minute, Diana thought. There was no sign of Donna Lucia, who personally oversaw every departure and arrival. Diana might not get this chance again.

'Miss America,' the boy said again, standing up straight and wincing at a side stitch, rubbing his belly quickly. '*È morto.*'

'Chi *è morto?*' Diana snapped. *Who* is dead?

The last girl got on to the truck, disappearing under the canvas top. The driver slammed the tailgate into place and got into the cab, but Diana didn't see them. Her head was spinning. Who had died on the estate? It couldn't have been Paolo, she told herself, her stomach turning over at the thought. Giuliana would have kept him safe. One of the other children, perhaps. Diana could feel her pulse in her neck, see spots in front of her eyes. Dorothea, or Sarina, getting away from the tiresome gaze of the women who would only allow them to play in the lawn outside the kitchen window. Playing hide and seek. Getting back into the house or sneaking into the garage. Fitting through an opening in the stone wall, or in between wooden slats in the wellhouse door. Discovering the hedge maze and getting lost in it. In her mind's eye, Diana saw the dark form of Adler enter the maze, never quickening his stride but pursuing the child with a relentless, unnatural sense of direction that would lead him directly to his prey. Rage boiled inside her now. She was trembling and felt she would be sick. The truck pulled away, rattling noisily over the cobble-stone streets. Diana knelt down shakily in front of the boy, gently taking him by both arms, not wanting to scare him. Sweat soaked through his shirt. *He must have run all the way from the estate*, she thought disjointedly, before opening her mouth to speak.

'*Piacere.*' Please. '*Cos'è successo?*' What happened? '*Chi è morto?*' Who has died?

The boy looked at her, and then away. Whatever he had to tell her, he was struggling with how to say it. He tried to dig the toe of his shoe into the ground as he had on the dusty path, but the stone was hard and unyielding. Finally, he looked up and met her eyes. *God, don't let it be Sarina*, Diana prayed.

Don't let it be a child. And then, her pulse quickening, *Oh, God. Not Signora, either. Don't let him have hurt Signora.* Her breath couldn't come, her chest tight with the realization of how much the old lady had suddenly come to mean to her.

'They sent me for the police. I ran all the way.'

Diana focused intently on the boy, staring at his lips now instead of his eyes, following so closely as he formed the Italian words that she hadn't even noticed she was translating.

'He drowned in the pool. He's dead. The bad man.'

Diana felt dazed as they walked to the *commissariato di polizia.* When the boy had told her Adler was dead, she had taken his hand in her own, as if he were much younger, a toddler who needed her protection and guidance. Instead, the boy was now leading her, tugging at her to hurry, not because of the seriousness of what they had to report, but because Diana had promised they'd stop at the town's tiny *farmacia* on their way back to get him a cool, sweet drink. The police station, when they arrived, was unrecognizable as such. A door was propped open along a row of identical houses close to the church of San Bernardo. Four men in their shirtsleeves sat around a table set up in the courtyard in front of the open door, as if being in close proximity to it counted as actually being inside their place of work. A little distance away, there was a pile of broken terra-cotta shingles. An old woman, dressed all in black and poking at the rubble with her cane, rooted among the debris. Diana looked around helplessly for a signboard or any indication they had come to the right place, but the boy walked confidently up to the table. The men were playing cards, but with a type of deck Diana had never seen before. Three of the men were old, bald or wiry-haired, and pot-bellied; two had let their suspenders fall off their shoulders. The fourth man raised his eyes to Diana, obviously surprised at her approach. He was younger, about Diana's age, and did not seem to match the rest of the group. He, too, was in his shirtsleeves, but his jacket was folded and hung neatly on the back of his chair. Diana noticed he had been sitting a little forward to avoid creasing the material.

'*Signori*,' the boy began.

There was no response as the game continued, the older men arguing over a point.

'*Signori*,' the boy piped up again.

One of the men with fallen suspenders tried shooing the boy away, but he only dodged a little and persisted.

'*Signori, ecco una donna americana.*' Sirs, here is an American woman.

The men turned around at that, slipping their suspenders back over their shoulders. One of the men, who was absolutely bald, ran his hands over his scalp as if smoothing down stray hairs. The largest and fattest of the men pushed back his chair and tried standing up simultaneously, disturbing the cards and eliciting shouts of reproval from his peers.

'*Piacere, signori.*' Please, sirs, the boy called over the shouting in his high, shrill voice. '*La donna americana è della casa della Signora Bugari – dove un uomo è stato ucciso.*' The American woman is from the house of Signora Bugari – where a man has been killed.

The boy's words did not have the effect Diana imagined they would. The shouting over the card game died down, but the coins on the table were simply redistributed and the deck reshuffled. One of the older men ogled her waistline a minute longer, before turning his attention back to the game, complaining loudly when one of his dealt cards landed face up.

'*Mi scusino*,' Diana said, using the formal grammatical form in the hope of gaining their attention. 'Excuse me, but a man has been killed.'

The young man put his cards face down on the table and indicated Diana with his eyes to the rest of the group. The other men begrudgingly turned towards her again, but kept their cards clutched tightly to their chests.

'Who?' the large man asked shortly, obviously proud to know the English word.

'A German—' Diana began, but the old men spat and went back to their game, putting down cards in turn. Diana continued. 'Please, there must have been some accident, a drowning, in water, *in acqua—*'

'*Scopa!*' the bald man cried, grabbing the pile of coins and pulling it towards himself.

There was a collective groan from the table, but as the next hand was being dealt out, the young man smiled, shook his head, and stood up. He spoke quickly to the older men, so quickly Diana could not catch what he said. He took out his wallet, showing them an identification card they hardly glanced at. The men nodded their heads impatiently and waved it aside, intent on getting back to their game.

'If you will allow the intrusion,' the man began as he slipped on his coat, buttoning it despite the heat. 'I will accompany you and the child.'

'You speak English,' Diana said, surprised, even as the boy turned and started off in the direction of the pharmacy.

'A stilted and a formal English, I am told, but, yes, I can converse.'

'Are you a policeman?' Diana asked, eyeing the disheveled old men already arguing over their game.

'From here? No, miss. I was passing through on my way, making . . . how do you say it? *Making inquiries*, I believe, is the phrase.'

The boy was at the end of the alleyway where it met the main street, hopping from foot to foot in his excitement. The man came up to Diana and pulled out his wallet again. She looked down at an embossed identity card with a black-and-white image of a much younger man with a small mustache, although the man in front of her was clean-shaven. The photograph was overexposed, but she could just make out the resemblance.

'Permit me to introduce myself. I am Giacomo Travere. Detective Inspector Giacomo Travere. These good men' – here he smiled as voices were once again raised over the game – 'have been so kind as to *delegate*' – he said the word slowly, smiling at his success – 'me to act on their behalf. I will look into this affair and provide them with a thorough accounting.'

Diana looked from the man in front of her, to the boy waiting for her at the end of the alley, back to the old men seated at the table. She hesitated. She didn't want to get anyone in trouble back at the estate. Surely, Signora had been counting

on the boy bringing back one of these local men to carry out
a cursory investigation, not a detective inspector. But she would
have to go along with it now. There was nothing for it.

'*Signorina*,' the boy wailed, jumping up and down. She started
down the alley, even as Travere said goodbye to the old men.

'*Buona fortuna*. Good luck,' the fat man called after
him. 'If German no dead when you arrive,' he said haltingly,
translating for Diana's benefit, 'kill him for me.'

The men at the table roared with laughter and went back
to their game.

The boy danced in front of the couple as they trudged along
under the Tuscan sun. Diana watched as the boy skipped and
twirled down the dirt road, his feet kicking up plumes of
dust that turned white in the sunlight. In his hand, he held
the wooden Pinocchio she had bought him on impulse at the
pharmacy. His eyes had gone wide when she handed it to him,
as if he could not believe the small, painted man was really
for him. He had started talking to it in the store and, even now
as the grownups wilted on their long trek back to the estate,
the boy kept chattering, swinging the doll high above him, its
jointed wooden limbs flailing wildly.

'He has much energy, the boy,' Travere commented, wiping
his forehead with the back of his hand. He had removed his
jacket and held it carefully folded over his forearm. Perspiration
marks showed under the arms of his white cotton dress shirt.
Diana looked at him again. His dark hair, which had been
combed straight back when they had set out an hour ago, was
starting to show its curl. Shadowed under his thick brows, his
eyes seemed hazel and there was a hint of a smile in them
when he spoke.

'Yes,' Diana replied. 'These children have seen so much of
war, so much death, I think they are inured to it.' The man
looked puzzled, and she went on quickly. 'I'm sorry. I mean,
they are *used* to it by now.' Travere nodded his head in understanding. 'But even a little thing, a tiny thing, really, and they
seem able to forget all about it. Lose themselves in their
happiness . . .' Diana's voice trailed off, and they were silent
as they walked on for a few yards together.

'That is not something many of us can do,' Travere ventured. 'Forget the war.'

'No,' Diana said quietly, thinking of the baby on the hill and wondering, even if she lived to be an old woman, whether she could ever fully forget that night. 'No. War is not something you forget.'

The boy turned off the main road and headed downhill, making a sound like an airplane as Pinocchio swooped down upon some unsuspecting rabbits that darted away across the path. In the distance, Diana could just make out the sienese rocks that marked the boundary of the estate.

'It's not much farther,' she said, indicating the valley below them, trees beginning to dot the scorched landscape and offer some dark spots of relief. 'Soon we'll be out of this heat.' Diana saw black spots swim in front of her eyes for a moment, then blinked hard and shook her head to clear it. She rubbed the back of her neck and the hair that had fallen loose from her braids was wet and stuck to her skin.

'Tell me some more of yourself,' Travere prompted, shifting his jacket to the other arm.

'You know pretty much all there is to know about me,' Diana replied, wryly. Maybe it was his polite manner coming after the coarseness of war, maybe it was his overly formal English that seemed better suited for a drawing room than for a dirt road surrounded by burned-out fields, but Travere had, somehow, gotten the reticent Diana to talk about herself. Her childhood back home. Her training as a nurse. What she could remember from before the accident that had landed her in this remote spot on the map. Her failed attempts to reconnect with her army. Being hired by Bugari to care for her ward. Diana had not mentioned Adler, other than to say he had been a guest at the estate, and her employer would be better able to answer Travere's many questions about him. She imagined Bugari would want that opportunity – to spin Adler and his presence at her home in whatever way she thought best.

'And why shouldn't she?' Diana asked aloud, startled by the sound of her own voice, her head snapping forward as if she had just caught herself falling asleep.

'What?' Travere asked, inclining his head towards her.

'It's nothing, just the heat.' Her breathing became shallow and quick, and there was a rushing sound in her ears.

'You have gone all white,' he said solicitously, taking hold of her elbow and gently guiding her to the shade next to an enormous laurel bush. 'Sit for a moment. Here, boy!' he yelled after the child, who glanced back, and then sat down in the middle of the deserted road, standing Pinocchio on its head. Diana's knees buckled and she sat down hard, misjudging where the ground was. Travere sat down beside her.

'I know you are the nurse and I do not wish to intrude with my suggestions. But if you feel faint, I recommend putting your head between your knees. It has always assisted me,' he added, almost apologetically.

Diana sat still for a moment. It was a relief to be in the shade, after their walk in the heat. And not moving helped. She focused on a cypress tree across the valley, a dark line in a field of yellow scrub. She focused on it and slowed her breathing until it became deep and regular again. After a few minutes, she spoke.

'Thank you. I'm feeling much better now. In another moment, I'll be ready to walk again.'

Travere looked skeptically at her pale face.

'In a few other moments, perhaps. Is there anything I can do to help you?'

'You can distract me, until I get my legs back. I mean, until I'm feeling well enough to walk. I've told you all about myself, but I know next to nothing about you, other than you're a detective. If you're not police, you must be army. But whose army?'

'My good woman – it is right, that I call you that, *my good woman*, it is not forward of me? No? Very well. My good woman, you have presented me with a question for which no one can answer. Do you not know that Italy, she has had four governments during this war? A king, Badoglio, no one can keep count any longer, who is in charge. We are allies with Germany, we are allies with your army. Villagers are rounded up and shot if they are fascists, and then other villagers are rounded up and shot if they are not fascist enough. Even Mussolini, one day he is the *duce*, ruling with the fist of iron, the next they hang him and his lover upside down on meat hooks for anyone to spit and laugh at their corpses. It is a very long and a very sad story, what Italy has been through these past years. Too sad to tell on this bright, sunny day.' He wiped his forehead again, then clasped his wrist in front of him as he rested his elbows on his knees. 'I am an inspector, a detective. And I look for men, mostly bad men, and I follow the orders of those I think best in all of this. But do not ask me to explain further.' He shook his head. 'No one can.'

A disjointed thought came to Diana.

'Your army. Or armies. Do you come in contact with the Americans?'

Travere laughed. 'But of course. Have you not heard the war here in Europe has ended? There are Americans at every port city. They go to the Pacific next, to do in Japan what they have done here.'

'So, if I gave you my letters, you could get them to the Americans?'

'Better yet, my little lost nurse, after I finish my inquires here, I can get *you* to the Americans. What do you say to that?'

Diana put her hand on Travere's shoulder and slowly pushed herself up to standing. Colors blurred before her eyes for a moment, then she blinked and the landscape came back into focus.

'I will need to make sure first that Paolo – the little boy I help – and my other friends are all right. I was not here last night, and I don't know what happened. But, after that' – Travere stood up and took her arm as Diana made a first, tentative step – 'after that, detective, I'd say you've got yourself a deal.'

When they arrived at the estate, Bugari and her staff were gathered by the reflecting pool in the drive. To Diana, it seemed as if they must have been waiting there like that for hours, rooted to the spot. Someone had fetched a kitchen chair for Bugari, who still managed to appear imperious, seated upon her rickety wooden perch. The rest of the servants – Giorgio and Giuliana among them – stood at a respectful distance from the corpse, which was a dark, sodden heap at the edge of the pool.

As soon as they stepped on to the white stone of the driveway, the boy darted ahead of Diana and Travere, whistling to the other children to follow him. Even if they had not seen the new toy he brandished aloft, they would have welcomed the chance to get away from their dreary watch with the adults. The children disappeared around the side of the house and Diana realized, with a sudden, almost guilty surge of joy that, with Adler gone, they were finally free to run off and be children without fear or threat. She looked back at the husky women gathered behind Bugari, their thick hands clasped in front of them, their eyes cast modestly downward, and wondered if one of them could have taken it upon herself to guarantee her child that safety.

Her thoughts were interrupted by Travere walking quickly past her towards the body. He did not acknowledge Bugari or act as if anyone else was present. Ignoring the perimeter that had been left undisturbed all around it, Travere walked right up to the pool, stepping into the little puddles of water that had formed in depressions in the gravel. He grabbed the back of Adler's collar with both hands and heaved the body over, until it lay face up in the sun. Water poured from a mouth and nose that were discolored and swollen. Diana, who had followed Travere for a few steps, recoiled. She had thought Adler's face ugly while he was alive, although it had betrayed a vibrant, almost mesmerizing vitality. Now, after being submerged in the stagnant water, the blue-grey features were grotesque, almost unrecognizable to her. Travere brought his own face within inches of Adler's, scrutinizing it carefully. He went through Adler's pockets, turning them out and then dropping the body unceremoniously on to the hard stonework of the pool, where it slumped down into a half-sitting, half-lying position on the driveway, like a man shot or drunk. For the first time, Travere looked around him, taking in the group of people who stood staring at him.

'Has anything been disturbed here? Have any of you taken anything?'

There was no immediate reply, and he repeated his questions impatiently, in Italian.

Signora Bugari folded her hands on her knee before replying in English.

'I assure you, nothing has been disturbed – until your arrival. We have kept things exactly as we found them.'

Diana looked at the man's face as he ran his fingers through his hair. His eyes darted back and forth, as if he was reading something very quickly. He took a step towards the house, then stopped short, the gravel beneath his leather shoe making a harsh, grating sound. The thought came to Diana suddenly that he looked like a cornered animal. In another moment, though, he had regained his composure, taking a deep breath and turning a somber but composed face towards Bugari.

'You must forgive me for my manners. I am Detective Inspector Travere, and I am here to gather information regarding this incident,' he said, waving a hand in the direction of the body.

Diana thought it strange he did not say he had come to 'solve this crime,' or 'find the murderer,' or use any of the phrases she had read in mystery novels or seen in the movies back home. Maybe it was just his difficulty with English, she thought, his way of choosing the wrong word. But it seemed to Diana he was acting much differently from the man she had trusted so readily (too readily?) with stories from her past, both distant and quite recent. With a sinking feeling, she tried to remember if she had told him anything about Donna Lucia, or the baby, or if she had inadvertently let slip any information that would be unsafe to pass on to a stranger she had just met in what was, for all intents and purposes, still wartime in a foreign country. What did she know about him, really? Only what he had told her, which was very little. She had seen an identification card but couldn't remember now who had issued it. There had been an ornate seal at the top, but she couldn't remember the Italian words that had been inscribed beneath it. And what if he wasn't even an Italian, but an agent from some other army, a German, perhaps, a confederate of Adler, come not to investigate, but avenge his death?

Diana's thoughts were interrupted by Bugari repeating her name.

'As I said, Miss Bolsena will show you to Herr Adler's

room, where you will be at perfect liberty to take an inventory
of his belongings. He has been our house guest, and this is a
terrible accident, and we will do everything within our power
to assist the authorities.'

Diana looked from the bloated corpse, back to her employer
who had just made the claim that a man had knelt down in
front of a shallow pool and then held his own head underwater
until he died. She was waiting for Travere to challenge the
outlandish statement, but he just walked to Diana's side and
took hold of her arm, as if he would guide her to the room in
question, instead of the other way around.

'Yes, thank you, Signora. I will be as prompt as
thoroughness allows me.'

He was gently pulling at Diana now, who seemed rooted to
the spot. In the awkward silence that followed, Travere said
he would want to speak to each person in turn, to which Bugari
acquiesced with a nod of her head. Diana felt the two of them
were acting out parts in a play, not actually speaking to one
another here, in front of her, in front of Adler's disfigured
corpse.

'Miss Bolsena was overcome by the sun on our journey
here,' Travere offered delicately, letting go of Diana's arm and
taking another step towards the house. 'Perhaps someone else
could . . .' He left the phrase hanging in a silence broken only
by the heavy drone of insects.

'Oh, yes, of course. Giorgio . . .' and then the two men
were off, Giuliana giving orders to the staff who quickly
dispersed towards the direction of the kitchen. Only Bugari
remained, impervious to the activity around her, sitting in her
chair in the middle of the drive long after they had gone,
looking neither at Diana nor at the body of the man who had
tried to kill her only days before. At length, Bugari spoke.

'That man you brought here—'

'Signora, I found him at the police station, but he isn't
police. He says he's army, but I don't know which army and,
Signora—'

Bugari raised her hand, commanding silence.

'He did not conduct himself like an officer of the law – at
least, not an officer interested in solving a crime. No, perhaps

he has come here exactly for the reason he states. To gather information.'

'But if he's not army, if he's not Italian army, he could be German, like Adler . . .'

'Whether he is German or English or Japanese, it is all the same to me.'

Bugari got up slowly, leaning heavily on her cane. She took a few unsteady steps towards the splayed body and stood, meditatively, looking down on it.

'There is only one way to deal with men who deal in secrets.'

Again, Diana looked at her employer and wondered if she could be referring to killing Adler herself. Certainly, he had come prying into Bugari's past, into her secrets. He was a threat to her, and she most certainly had wanted him gone. But Diana saw how much frailer the old woman looked out in the sunshine (she realized, then, she had only ever seen Bugari indoors). Her pinched, heeled shoes sunk into the thick gravel; she had difficultly retaining her balance, even with her cane. No, there was no way Bugari could have overpowered her virile guest. Looking at her now, Diana saw the old woman as a wraith, a shadowy ghost looking down, without pity, on the recently departed.

'You said there's only one way to deal with this,' Diana prompted, her head still dull from sunstroke. 'One way to deal with these men. To give them what they want, so they leave quickly?'

Bugari gave an infinitesimally small smile.

'That's one way to deal with them, perhaps. A young person's way.'

Diana rubbed her eyes, and they felt dry and raw. 'Then, how?' she demanded.

'By making sure they never find what they're looking for.'

And, with that, Bugari hobbled painfully back to the house, closing the door behind her.

Diana waited with the rest of the staff in the hallway. As it had on her first day at the estate and for countless years before, the old grandfather clock loudly ticked out the seconds. After Travere had looked through the few belongings in Adler's room – an engraved toiletry set, six changes of nearly identical clothing, German-issued identity papers, two letters dated in March of that year – and then searched, unsuccessfully, for any hidden compartments or concealed panels, he had begun his formal interviews. Bugari had gone first, her set face betraying no emotion, either when entering or exiting her own sitting room, which had been converted into a makeshift inter-rogation center. Giorgio and Giuliana had gone, separately, since then, and one or two of the additional staff that had been hired for Adler's visit. The old man now leaning against the wall next to Diana was nervously turning his woolen cap around and around in his ancient fingers, staring at the closed sitting-room door in front of him. Two of the kitchen staff, rotund women who had tired of standing and sat down heavily on the last two steps of the grand staircase, had tried starting up a conversation, but the oppressive silence had been too much for them. They sat now with their red dishpan hands lying listlessly on their aprons, shifting their weight uncom-fortably from time to time on the hard wood as the hours dragged on. No sound could be heard from behind the solid mahogany door. No raised voice, or even soft rumble of conver-sation. To Diana, it reminded her of being a little girl and waiting in line for confession, to tell her sins to a faceless voice in the dark. She had been taught it was a sin to listen in on another's confession; that if she accidentally overheard even a snippet of conversation, she would be bound by the same sacred oath that prevented priests from divulging the secrets they heard. Her catechism had illustrated this by showing a padlock running through a priest's upper and lower lips, and the thought had thrilled the young Diana with its seriousness and its weight, but not enough to keep her from straining her ears to catch a stray word. As she was doing now.

The long silence continued, the clock's ticking being, at first, the only thing Diana could focus on before even that became a droning, mesmerizing sound she didn't notice. The thoughts of her childhood confessions – *bless me, Father, for I have sinned, I pushed my sister, I was greedy, I forgot to say my prayers* – led her to thoughts of the chaplains she had met in the military. Catholic priests saying hasty masses with the sound of gunfire growing closer. Protestant ministers sitting up with the dying, reading psalms by lantern light in soft, comforting tones. Overworked Jewish rabbis – two hundred chaplains to minister to the entire armed forces – flying from the Azores to Greenland, from the Gold Coast to India; she had once met a man who had been the only Jewish military chaplain, at the time, for all of China. Diana thought of the plucky Canadian chaplain assigned to a paratrooper unit, downed and recovering in one of the American field hospitals, who told her he would consecrate his wine while still on the plane, pour it into his canteen, and screw on the top before jumping because 'it gets a bit pricklish when we land.' Diana remembered staring open-mouthed – the incongruity hitting her as she and the other nurses cleared out debris from an abandoned German camp, to set up their own wounded – when she found a priest's stole, worn during confession, a thin strip of shiny cloth with its tassels worn off by long use, emblazoned with swastikas at both ends.

Diana's reverie was interrupted by the door suddenly opening and one of the kitchen staff hurrying out. The woman was covering her mouth with her apron as if upset, as if she would have liked to have covered her whole face instead. Travere's voice could be heard from inside the room, calling out sonorously, 'Alfredo Luigi Sebastiano.' The old man next to Diana started, looking around miserably as he fingered his hat, and shuffled forward. He didn't close the door all the way behind him as he entered the room. There was a mumbled exchange of voices, and then a silence, and then the sound of shuffling feet returning before the door shut to with a little bang. Diana wondered, for the hundredth time, why Signora had even bothered to report Adler's death. Of course, she had had no way of knowing a detective inspector would be in town at just that moment. But even so, why had she bothered? With all the death, with the literal millions of German bodies strewn from Poland to North Africa to the now liberated France, why had she bothered to report it? Diana's only thought was that Bugari had not wanted any loose ends, not wanted any further inquiries down the road. That the old woman had been hoping for one of the men from the *scopa* table to come, prod the waterlogged body with the toe of his shoe, say the man was dead, and then come inside for a drink. If her regular servants, Giorgio and Giuliana, had been the only ones with her, Diana was certain no more trouble would have been taken over it than Giorgio fetching the shovel from the garden shed to dispose of their unwanted guest himself. But the presence of strangers, the extra help that had been hired to create a façade for Adler's benefit, was the unknown variable. People Bugari could not be sure would not later turn against her, testify that a man had died without inquiry or investigation, hastily – even suspiciously – buried without her even calling the police. Yes, that was the only thing Diana could think of that would have made Bugari bring yet another stranger into her home to question her and her staff, and, potentially, bring her secrets to light. Diana thought how bitterly Bugari must be regretting her decision now.

The door opened quickly, and Alfredo strode down the hallway and out of the front door with an alacrity Diana would not have thought possible. The two women stirred, exchanging wide-eyed glances, craning their necks to catch a glimpse of the sitting room beyond the door that had been left ajar. Travere called out Diana's full name, including her middle name, which she hated and never used. The women on the steps visibly relaxed, rounding their backs and settling in for another long wait. To Diana, the ticking of the grandfather clock seemed suddenly much louder, and somehow ominous. For the second time in her life, she walked towards the sitting room with what seemed her entire future hanging in the balance. Diana had not known, before her interview on that first day, what lay in store for her. That she would meet Bugari and become, despite herself, involved not just in the successful running of the old woman's home but with the old woman herself. That she would come to care for Bugari, who would visit her in her dreams as a sorrowful young woman, and had – as an old woman – stood, as if at some inexplicable crossroads, between Adler and the destruction he would have wrought. Diana reached for the embossed brass doorknob, remembering not to touch the wood paneling of the door. Giuliana had instructed her, those first few weeks, not to leave smudges on the carefully polished woodwork throughout the house. Diana wondered again that Bugari, who ran such a strict household, who bristled at the slightest stain or imperfection or even a fingerprint left behind, had allowed Adler to ransack her entire house in an effort to keep him from retrieving whatever it was he had come for. And she had succeeded. But at what cost? Travere seemed intent on gathering information, if nothing else; and what if his search inadvertently uncovered the one thing Bugari had already sacrificed so much to conceal? What more was the old woman capable of?

Travere repeated Diana's name, the middle name sounding foreign and jarring to Diana's ears. She exhaled, then slid quietly into the room, carefully closing the door behind her, never once touching the wood.

FOUR

S lowly, the house began to heal itself. The extra staff were kept on, on a temporary basis, to set the place to rights. Broken crockery was swept up and discarded behind the garage, the debris raked in carefully among the compost and kitchen scraps, the piles kept at a respectable distance and out of the line of sight of the house. The linen from all the bedrooms – even rooms that hadn't been used in years – was gathered up and washed, and left out to air in the bright sunshine, as if to erase any memory of unwelcome guests, past or present. The heavy draperies and oriental rugs were hauled outside and beaten with rattan carpet whips, the children running in and out of the colorful hangings, laughing as their mothers scolded them to get out of their way. Giorgio and the other men argued with each other as they moved heavy armoires and chests of drawers from where they had been left standing in the middle of rooms, repositioning them carefully against ornate panel molding. The tiny slivers of crystal that had fallen into the crevices of the parquet flooring were painstakingly removed with a toothbrush, Francesca going along on all fours. Windows were thrown open, plumbing fixtures polished, the great clawfoot tubs and enameled sinks scrubbed until they shined. Fruit was ripening on the estate's orchard, and the old men and children harvested it while the women busied themselves preserving, putting up beveled glass jars of jams and jellies, sliced peaches in syrup, apricot preserves, tying them up with matching red and yellow and orange ribbons. The women could also sew, and from Bugari's vast, unused storeroom they replaced the worn kitchen towels and aprons, and added new sheets and duvet covers to the well-stocked linen cupboards. Francesca asked and, without even consulting Bugari, Giuliana herself gave permission for the women to fashion shorts and shirts and dresses for their threadbare children who now ran about the estate in bright colors, prints, and stripes instead of their usual homespun drab, matching hair ribbons trailing behind the girls as laughter re-entered the old house.

Of course, the first of all these chores had been disposing of Adler's body. Travere had asked to borrow one of the luxury automobiles to drive into town, only to be told by Giorgio – in a whispered side conversation out of earshot of the rest of the household – that they no longer worked, their engines having run down years ago. Frustrated, Travere had walked the long way into town by himself, returning with the report that the local police refused to come out for the death of one more German, telling Travere to deal with it himself. In the end, he had had to pay a local farmer for the use of his horse cart – the detective inspector riding atop the rickety contraption, the bloated corpse following unceremoniously behind – and dig the grave himself, in some undisclosed spot. The German's possessions – with the exception of the identity cards and letters, which Travere said were evidence – were divided among the staff to use, or barter with, or sell on the black market in the nearest big town. And, after Travere returned, handing the shovel back to Giorgio and heading upstairs to wash off the dirt, the only physical sign that Adler had ever visited the estate was the half-dozen missing figurines on Signora's mantlepiece, the spaces between crystal satyr and nymph left empty in memory of where they had once danced.

That was the only physical sign Adler had been there. But there were other ways he had left his mark, the most notable of which was the change in Bugari. After Travere had finished his interviews, Bugari took to her room, delegating all decision-making to her housekeeper. She made no appearances downstairs after that time, neither to eat nor to oversee the reordering of her house. Giuliana herself prepared and brought up meals that remained largely untouched when she returned, hours later, to clear them away. Diana asked to see her employer but was turned away by Giuliana as she came out of Bugari's suite one day, carrying yet another tray of uneaten food. No, Signora was not well enough to receive her. No, she did not desire a doctor to be called. No, she did not want a nurse, either. Diana had followed Giuliana downstairs, insisting in broken Italian that she at least be told the nature of Bugari's ailment, when Travere emerged from the cellar into the kitchen where the two women were arguing.

'Excuse me, but I have a permission to ask of Signora.'

Giuliana scowled at the man. Diana thought it was at least partly due to his forgetting to address the housekeeper in her own language but, to Diana's amazement, Giuliana responded in English.

'Signora cannot be disturbed, at this time. What is it you wish?'

'You understood English, all along?' Diana demanded, incredulous. Giuliana's only response was a blank stare, before turning back to Travere.

'I . . . I was going through the items downstairs,' the man continued, glancing from one glaring woman to the other. 'From everyone's accounts, that is where Adler was focusing the energies of his search, before his death. That he had exhausted the rest of the house and was only concentrating there.'

Giuliana remained impassive.

'He had catalogued some of it already,' Travere went on. 'But much more of it remains. As you know, the item Adler was searching for may shed direct light on who his murderer was. It is very important I find that item, to find who killed him. But, as I said, there is still much to go through. Very much. I would not believe so much could be contained there.'

At last Giuliana spoke, setting the heavy silver tray down with a bang.

'This house is vast, and the cellar large, and Signora has led a full life and has many beautiful possessions to show for that.'

She began taking the items off the tray, one by one, handling them carefully, almost reverently.

'And I am a busy woman, *signore*. Signora Bugari has given me some authority during her illness. What is it you would ask permission for?'

Travere looked tentatively again from Giuliana to Diana. Ever since the change she had seen in him that first day – when he had seemed to switch from a solicitous companion to a driven detective – the relationship between Diana and

Travere had been strained. Her interview with him in the sitting room had been a formal reiteration of the facts she had already volunteered during their long walk together. He had barely looked at her throughout the brief interrogation, staring instead at the identity card Diana had handed Signora on her first day of employment. Travere had turned the card over and over again in his hands, as if searching for secret lettering, or the key to a code for what was happening, reading and rereading her name. Since then, Diana had seen little of the inspector, occupying herself with Paolo. But the boy was growing stronger and more independent, running outside, preferring the company of Sarina and Dorothea, and especially of Francesca who smothered the skinny boy with huge, motherly hugs that were no longer for her lost sons but for Paolo himself. So, with time on her hands, with the last of the housecleaning winding down and the extra staff preparing to return to the village, Diana would run into Travere on the steps, outside on the terrace, once by the reflecting pool itself. Their eyes would meet awkwardly, looking away almost instantly, a murmured *buon giorno* or *buona sera* before they moved off in different directions. That is how Diana felt. As if the two of them had been companions going in the same direction on that hot, sunny day, his courteous words and solicitude for her well-being a balm after the harshness of war (he would help her reunite with her army, he had told her – promised her – that). And then he had seen Adler's body in the reflecting pool and their paths had diverted. Something in him had snapped, becoming someone else entirely. An interrogator who upset the staff – Diana thought again of the woman covering her mouth with her apron, of Alfredo hurrying down the hallway, his woolen cap left behind him in the sitting room, forgotten. And Bugari. Shortly after her interview, Bugari had taken to her room, refusing to see anyone but Giuliana, withdrawing from her own home. What had happened behind those closed doors to make so strong a woman seem to lose the very will to live? What had Travere said to her?

Travere swallowed hard before speaking.

'As I mentioned, there is yet a great deal to catalogue in my search. I was unsuccessful in obtaining help from the local police – they have no interest in this matter. I therefore would ask permission for someone from this household to assist me, in an official capacity.'

Giuliana finished polishing the last of the silverware on the tray.

'I cannot help you, *signore.* I am overworked as it is and very soon I will again be in charge of this great household, by myself.' Giuliana's voice seemed to tremble slightly, but she went on in a stronger and more menacing tone. 'And do not think you can ask my husband for help; he is an old man and will have the rest of the harvest to bring in, on his own.'

Travere took a deep breath.

'I would not dream of interfering with your work, or the work of your husband. But you must see it from the official point of view, as well. There has been a death here, under unusual circumstances. I must resolve what is behind it so I may leave and return you to normalcy as promptly as is possible. This is what we all want, I am sure.'

He looked up at Diana, who could not turn her eyes away in time. She had seen the searching look he gave her.

'I would ask Miss Bolsena to assist me, just until the work is done and I can make my report. I promise, I will not stay one day beyond what is absolutely necessary.'

Giuliana shrugged her shoulders, hoisting the heavy tray again with a little wince of pain.

'This you do not need permission for. *Signorina* is employed here. If she can accomplish her assigned tasks, what she chooses to do with her free time is her own affair.' Giuliana trudged out of the room, yelling at a cat that had snuck in through the side door and gotten underfoot.

Travere looked at Diana, the first time they had held each other's gaze since the day they met. He took a step towards her.

'I know I get caught up in my work . . .' he began softly, then stopped. Diana wondered that he knew the English phrase, that he could make the words sound warm and appealing now when, so often, even on their walk together, his expressions had come across as stiff and wooden.

'I get caught up in my work, but that's only because I feel

so strongly about what I'm doing. I . . . I don't mean to . . .'
Here he ran his fingers through his hair. 'How do you
Americans call it? I don't mean to be a jerk.'

He smiled, a wide, winning grin.

'What I mean to say is, I'd like to start again with you, if
I can. This time, on the right foot. And I could really use your
help, if you'd be willing.'

Diana didn't respond. She still held his gaze, but as the
seconds passed without her responding, the smile disappeared
from Travere's face and he stepped away from her, resuming
his formal manner.

'The sooner I can complete my report here, the sooner I
leave you all in peace.'

Still Diana didn't speak. She didn't know what to make of
Travere, of his changing demeanor and fluctuating moods. One
moment, he was smiling – flashing his surprisingly white,
perfectly formed teeth – using expressions that should make
any American girl give a guy another chance. The next he was
buttoned-up, closed in on himself. Cut off. Hidden. She did
not fully trust this detective who did not always act like a
detective – she thought again of his stepping through the
puddles that first day, compromising the scene of the crime,
turning out the man's pockets like a common thief. She remembered Bugari's words, that maybe Travere was just what he
proposed himself to be – a man gathering information. He had
waved his hand in the direction of Adler's dead body when
he said it, and Diana had supposed that he meant information
about Adler's killer. But what if he meant he had come to
gather information not about the person who had killed Adler
but about Adler himself. The mysterious man Diana had first
met strangling her employer. Who had destroyed the idyllic
nature of her home. Who had torn the place apart looking for
something so valuable he was delaying his own escape at the
end of a war he had lost; that was so valuable Signora had
seemed willing to let him destroy her home if it meant she
could keep him from discovering it. Diana might not trust
Travere, might not know what to think of him. But she knew,
without a doubt, what she had thought of Adler. She thought
again of his fingers around Signora's throat, of the way his

thumb had tapped against her own wrist, of his hand holding out sweet candies to the boy on the lane, and she knew the man had been evil. The man had been evil in life and, the thought came to her suddenly, perhaps he had left something behind that could continue his evil, even after his death. If Diana's helping now could stop that, could help find that evil – if it existed – and destroy it, it would be worth whatever risk she ran with Travere. But she couldn't raise the detective's suspicions as to her real motives. She would have to make it seem that she was helping him for her own reasons. That she didn't suspect he was only there to uncover Adler's secret. That she wasn't only there to destroy it when they found it together. Thinking quickly, she held out her hand.

'You offered once to take me to my army, after you were finished here. Well, it looks like the quickest way back home for me is to help you now.'

Travere looked surprised, almost disappointed, frowning for a moment. Then his smile reappeared as he pumped her hand up and down and led her to the top of the cellar steps.

Diana started down a long flight of wooden stairs. They creaked and groaned loudly under her feet. At the bottom, she found herself in a basement crowded with boxes, crates, and steamer trunks of all sorts and sizes. The ceiling was arched and high, but exposed lightbulbs hung from a wire at eye level. The boxes were crammed so close together she could not make out how far the rows extended in each direction, but they seemed to go on forever. She reached out her hand and ran it over a nearby trunk covered with old packing labels. Her fingers left a trail in dust that had not been disturbed in years. She looked more closely and could just make out the faded lettering on some of the labels. Milan. Paris. Vienna. The brass hinges on the trunk were corroded and beginning to crumble. A thin layer of green mold covered the dark leather, a brown water stain near the bottom the only thing to show where labels had peeled off years earlier. Diana looked from the trunk to the rows of boxes behind it, and then back at Travere, who had joined her at the foot of the stairs.

'There's so much. How could anyone ever get through it

all? Do you really think the thing Adler was looking for is in there?'

Diana crouched down low, trying to peer between boxes. She could see for about ten or twelve feet by the light of the naked bulbs before everything disappeared into darkness.

'You can see why I was eager for help.'

Travere pushed his way through a narrow aisle that had been formed between boxes, motioning for Diana to follow.

'As far as I can make out, Adler started at the far wall and was working his way back here. You can tell from the dust. The boxes nearest the stairs haven't been touched.'

Diana rubbed the fine dust from the packing trunk between her fingers, as she pressed forward. Travere picked up a flashlight from one of the crates and handed it to her.

'The lights only go so far.'

Diana switched it on. The crates were piled two or three high and hemmed them in on both sides. The glow from her flashlight seemed to grow brighter as she played it against old lampstands and forgotten hat boxes crumbling with age.

'Here we are,' Travere announced, as he stepped aside. In front of them rose a stone wall against which boxes had been stacked high to make a small clearing. In the open space sat a low stool with several boxes arranged in front of it. Papers were scattered over the floor.

'This is where Adler was looking,' Diana said, bending down and picking up one of the papers. She ran her flashlight over it. It seemed to be a receipt of some sort, handwritten, the paper old and brittle.

'Yes. These boxes against the wall, I believe, he has already searched. The papers inside are disarranged, and he has marked each box with a small x.'

Diana played her light over the dozens of boxes and crates and could just make out a faint mark on each.

'OK, so it's one yard down, nine to go,' she whispered, exhaling, then shook her head. 'No, never mind. It's just an expression. But what are we looking for? There must be hundreds of boxes to go through, but I'm not sure I'll be much help if I have no idea what I'm looking for.'

Travere was silent. Diana replayed her last sentence in her

head, wondering if she had used an obscure word, or if he could still be trying to figure out her allusion to football. She looked at his face in the dim light, expecting to see a puzzled expression, but he was looking intently at her.

'Diana, I have a theory. Don't ask me to explain it all right now. But . . . you're a nurse.'

'Yes?' Diana wondered where his train of thought was going.

'You took science and math classes, I mean, as part of your training?'

'Sure. I mean, it was mostly practical training but, early on, to weed us out, yes.'

'Then look for anything like that. Mathematical figures. Scientific equations. Anything with numbers or formulae or variables. Things like x and y—'

'Yes, I remember what variables are,' she replied, a little shortly.

'Yes, forgive me, I get excited when I think I am on the correct path. So, you and I, we will look for those things.'

'And if your theory is wrong? What if he was just looking for something simple like, I don't know, hidden treasure, or gold or something?'

'I do not believe I am wrong. I could be, but I, personally, do not believe in it. A man like Adler does not remain in enemy lands after his army has lost just to gain wealth. Unless . . .' Travere paused, placing his own torch upright and prying the lid off one of the untouched crates. 'Unless that wealth is immense, and the item he has come for is small enough to carry off with him.'

Travere moved the stool closer to Diana, holding it formally for her as if seating her at a table. She sat down. Then he pulled over the open crate and knelt down next to her on the hard stone floor.

'So we look for the papers, yes. But also, as you suggest, for the treasures. Anything Adler might think worth dying for. Or, for the murderer, anything worth killing for.'

Diana picked up the first item in the trunk, a cast-iron statuette of a horse in full gallop. Its black painted body was still smooth to the touch, but the base of the statue had begun to rust, the gritty powder coming off in her hands. *This will take forever*, she thought despairingly, putting down the horse and reaching for a music box with carefully inlaid panels. As if she had spoken her thought aloud, Travere said cheerfully, 'Take heart. A trouble shared is a troubled halved.'

Diana sighed and reached for the next item.

Their search went on for days with no appreciable results, besides several bruised shins and a splinter that had to be carefully prized out. Every time Diana emerged into the bright light of the kitchen she would squint and blink after the long hours spent underground. When she went outside for a breath of fresh air, the summer weather seemed oppressive, as if she had become accustomed to a different, cooler, climate. She made time to play with Paolo, but the boy would fidget restlessly through a round or two of cards before begging for permission to go outside to play with his friends. Diana watched from an upstairs window as the threesome ran off to play in their fort, lunging at each other with sticks, mimicking fencing maneuvers and yelling gleefully.

Diana was passing through the hallway one afternoon when she heard Giuliana cry out. Diana turned just in time to see the large frame of Francesca reach up and support Giuliana as the old woman teetered at the top of a stepladder. She had been trying to replace a decorative china bowl on a high shelf when she lost her balance. Giuliana got down from the step-stool, visibly shaken. Mumbling angrily, she thrust the bowl into Francesca's hands and stormed off towards the back of the house. Francesca repositioned the ladder carefully before ascending, slowly and deliberately replacing the bowl. Diana was about to follow after Giuliana, but she turned instead and ran lightly up the stairs. She walked quickly towards Signora Bugari's bedroom, her footsteps silenced by the thick runner, and knocked quietly. There was a faint response from within, the words indistinguishable. Diana opened the door.

Bugari lay in an enormous four-poster bed, the opaque silk hangings moving gently in the breeze from the opened window. She looked small and shriveled in the center of the eiderdown mattress, propped up on overstuffed pillows edged in embroidery and lace. Diana stepped towards the bed as Bugari's voice, low and gravelly, came from behind the curtains.

'Where is Giuliana?'

'It is about Giuliana that I've come to speak to you, Signora. But, first, is there anything I can do for you?'

Bugari was silent for a moment, as if the effort to speak cost her greatly.

'Water. On the side table.' Then, drawing a deep breath and exhaling, 'If you would be so kind.'

Diana filled the crystal goblet and pulled back the thin fabric. Bugari reached for the glass, but her hands were trembling so much Diana placed a supportive hand behind her head and held the glass to her lips.

'Thank you.'

The old woman sunk back into her pillows and lay motionless with her eyes closed. Diana thought she had fallen asleep but, after a few moments, Bugari asked, 'Giuliana – what was it you wanted to speak to me about her?'

'Signora, I don't wish to trouble you in your current state. I have tried seeing you many times before, to see if I could help you in any way—'

'Yes, yes, I know. I told Giuliana not to let you in. Not to let anyone in. Go on.'

'You must let me help you, Signora.'

Getting no response, she went on.

'OK, you won't talk about yourself right now, but we will speak of Giuliana. I am concerned about her. She nearly fell just now. Taking care of this great house, by herself, I think it's becoming too much for her.'

Bugari did not move, breathing shallowly. After a moment, she opened her eyes and asked, 'And am I wrong to assume you would not bring this up now if you did not also have a solution in mind?'

Diana paused, then smiled, encouraged by Bugari's show of spirit.

'Yes, I *was* thinking of a solution. To Giuliana's problem, of course – but also to the problems of other people I've come to care for in this house. I was thinking of Francesca and her daughters. Francesca is an excellent cook. She handles nearly all the housework already. She is strong and capable and—'

'Yes, yes, you would have me keep this woman on, after the others leave. She and her children.'

'And not only for Giuliana's sake. But for Paolo's. He has come to love the family. The girls are his playmates, and Francesca is like a mother to him, the mother he never—' Diana failed to stop herself in time.

'You can say it. The mother he never had. The mother figure I never was to him.'

'No, Signora. I would never say that—'

'But you should. It would be true. And one should always speak the truth, when one can. The opportunity presents itself so rarely.'

Bugari tried pushing herself up to a seated position, her arms trembling with the effort, before she slumped back.

'Yes, tell them the woman can stay. As housekeeper under Giuliana. Giuliana will still have final say. You have to give her that much. We old women hold on fiercely to what power we have.'

'Thank you, Signora. Thank you for keeping on Francesca. There is not much food in the village. She and the girls will be safer here.'

Diana had thought she would have to fight harder to get Bugari to comply. She was worried now at how easily she had acquiesced.

Bugari nodded weakly, closing her eyes again.

'It was a selfish thing I did, taking on Paolo. I know that now.'

'No, Signora . . .'

'You are trying to comfort me, like a good nurse. But I know my own business better than you, my own intentions. Allowing this family to stay on will not undo my wrong. But at least I will not make it worse by sending them away now that the boy has found a little happiness.'

'Not just a little happiness, Signora. A great deal. A very great deal.'

Diana took the old woman's withered hand and, to her surprise, Bugari did not pull away. She had lost weight, her cheek bones standing out sharply on her drawn face, deep hollows under her eyes.

'There are other things I need to ask you, Signora. About your illness. About ways I can help you before I leave. About . . . about Adler . . .' Diana felt the limp fingers stiffen in her hand, and went on quickly. 'But not now. I can see how tired you are. How much you need to rest.'

Bugari's hand relaxed as her breathing became more regular, rhythmic, the soft white lace at her throat rising and falling with each breath. Diana stroked the iron-grey of Bugari's hair, caught between her own curiosity – about Adler, about what he had been looking for, about Bugari's own closely guarded secrets – and her desire to comfort an ailing patient, a failing friend.

'Rest now, Signora,' Diana said softly, still stroking her hair, a tear falling noiselessly on to the coverlet and disappearing from sight.

'I'm done with this one,' Diana said, throwing in the last of her items.

The system she and Travere had come up with was to open a new box, carefully go through its contents, and place them into a second waiting box, which they would then stack against the wall when full. Sometimes they worked separately, but the lighting was so poor that Diana and Travere often worked together, huddled close over an opened crate with an upturned flashlight to see by, rifling through pages, turning objects over and over again in their hands in the half-light. At first, Diana had tried to take an interest in what she was doing to make the time go by, guessing at the significance of this or that particular piece, trying to fathom why Bugari had chosen to store it away. She had found entire crates of Venetian masks, ornate and carefully painted, their feathers sticking out at odd angles. There were grocery receipts from some fifty years before, bundled up in twine, a bloody thumbprint from a butcher still visible on one in the upper right-hand corner. She had unearthed countless bolts of fabric – usually of an intricate, almost Moorish design – still intact after long years of storage, but repulsive now due to the overwhelming smell of mothballs.

(Diana would slam the lid back on, coughing, shoving the box out of her way, and start on another one.) She had tried to find a common theme to tie everything together. Souvenirs from the basilica of San Marco, traditional double candles from San Geremia in the shape of Saint Lucy's eyes, the carnival masks themselves, all these pointed to Venice, but there the trail grew cold. There were too many incongruous items thrown in with them – tortoiseshell hair combs, silver button hooks, correspondence in yellowing envelopes, dressmakers' dummies spilling their sawdust guts on to the floor – for Diana to make any sense of it except that these objects had once held meaning to Bugari but now rotted away in the bowels of her home, forgotten but still ominous, and crushing in their weight.

Travere dragged the crate away, hoisting it with a grunt on to the top of a stack and returning with another box. They had been at it for over a week, the monotony broken only by their brief sojourns in the upper world. Travere pried off the lid and placed it to one side.

'Oh, great,' Diana complained, 'more papers. I think I hate these the most.'

'More than the mothballs?'

'Well, maybe a close second to those. But I hate going through these. I tell myself maybe *this* one will hold the secret we're looking for, but it always ends up being recipes, or blueprints, or charcoal sketches. God, I hope I never end up having half this much junk to save.'

'Yes, you can't take it with you,' Travere quipped, chuckling, tossing aside a handwritten budget from 1912.

Diana paused.

'Just how do you know phrases like that?'

'*Ché?* I mean, what?'

'Phrases like "you can't take it with you." You seem to know a lot of our expressions. "Bottom dollar," "holy mackerel," "moxie." Where did you learn English, anyway?'

'You have been keeping track of what I say?' Travere stood very still.

'No. I mean, yes. I mean, we sit down here for hours each day and you start to notice stuff. Like, Giuliana speaks English, too, apparently, but if I told her she cracks me up, she wouldn't understand me. You would.'

Travere stood still for another second, then sat down and smiled broadly.

'I am so pleased. I do not wish to aggrandize myself, but my instructors always told me I was too formal, too careful in my pronunciation and the selection of words to pass as a native speaker. But the war did it for me, I suppose. Coming together with – no, hanging out with – your American GIs. They . . . wait – *come si dice?* how do you say it?' He closed his eyes, pressing his palm to his forehead. 'Oh, yes, I remember now – they give it to you straight.'

Diana laughed, tilting her armload of papers into the waiting bin.

'That's amazing. I've been in Italy nearly two years and all I can do is stumble around in the present tense. And curse, of course.'

'*Ma certo*, of course. Everyone knows how to do that.'

'But your command of English is really commendable. I mean, it's great.'

'No, no, I understood you with *commendable*. But perhaps' – he glanced up at Diana, then quickly back at his hands – 'you deserve some of the credit. Maybe it is because I feel so . . . so comfortable with you that I can find the words.'

A silence fell between them, interrupted only by the occasional shuffle of papers.

'I don't understand you, Inspector.'

'If you are going to not be understanding me, at least you could call me Giacomo, no?'

Diana smiled.

'All right, Giacomo. I don't understand you.'

'What is there that confuses you? It is my speaking? But you said I was good.'

'No, it's not that. Maybe in the beginning, but the words you say, I can understand them just fine now.'

'Then, what?'

Diana opened her mouth to speak, then closed it.

'No, never mind. It's none of my business.'

She stretched out her hand for more papers, but Travere reached out and lightly caught hold of her wrist.

'Please, finish what you were going to say. Do not come close and then fly away again. Like a little bird.'

'I . . . I mean, I just don't get it. What makes you tick. Sometimes you seem so straightforward – sweet, even, if you don't mind my saying it.'

'I do not mind it.'

Travere still held on to her hand.

'I've seen you with the children, with Paolo and the girls, giving them rides on your back. You are kind to them. You are kind, even, to Giuliana and Giorgio, and they can be . . . well, they can be—'

'Wet blankets?'

'There you go with the slang, again. I was going to say off-putting but, yes, wet blanket gets the point across, too. But you're still good to them.'

'They are good people. They deserve some goodness in their lives, Diana.'

He seemed to savor the syllables of her Christian name as he said them for the first time. Gently, he took hold of her other hand.

'And you, Diana. Am I kind to you?'

It was absolutely silent in the stone cellar, cut off from the rest of the house, from the rest of the world.

'It matters to me, what you think of me, Diana. I never thought it could matter so much, but it does.'

Diana struggled not to look up, but he seemed to draw her gaze, despite herself. She looked into his eyes and again saw him carrying in bundles of kindling for a winded Giorgio. Standing patiently as Giuliana piled him with woolen blankets to be carried up to the attic. Pumping the well handle so quickly the water smacked into the stonework and splashed up again as tiny crystals of light, the children running up to the living stream of water, reaching in their fingers, their toes, laughing and screaming under the noonday sun.

Diana wanted to say yes, that he was kind, that he was good. She wanted to admit the truth to him that she spent long hours awake on her bed, in the moonlight, the curtains flowing freely in the breeze of the open window, thinking of him when she thought that part of her had been switched off by the war. But then she remembered how quickly he had seemed to change. Going through Adler's pockets. Lining up the servants. The housemaid covering her face. The old man scurrying down the corridor like a dog with its tail between its legs.

Diana shifted her weight on the stool, knocking over the jug of water they brought down with them each morning. Travere smiled good-naturedly, letting go of her hands to pick up the papers in the water's path. He turned to put them into a waiting bin when Diana cried out.

'Giacomo, look!'

Still smiling, he turned back to her.

'What is it? You want me to see how clever you were, spilling the water and breaking my magic spell? I will not let you get away from me so easily,' he laughed, reaching out for her again.

'No, I'm serious, Giacomo,' she said, pushing him away and forcibly turning him to face the wet stone floor.

'Don't you see it?'

'What? There is nothing. Spilt water. But I have picked up the papers already. There is nothing more to see.'

'Isn't there?'

Diana had stepped forward quickly and was shoving with all her might against a stack of boxes piled four high.

'Help me move these, they're heavy.'

'I applaud your enthusiasm—' he began, but she cut him off.

'No, Giacomo. Think. That water jug, we refilled it after *pranzo*, no?'

'Yes, but—'

'So it should have been full. It should have made a mess, spreading out all over the floor.'

Travere didn't say anything, but he was frowning now in concentration. Diana rushed on.

'So where is the water? Look, after only a foot or two – as soon as it gets to this particular stack of boxes – it disappears. See?'

The two of them succeeded in pushing the boxes back a

few feet. The dark stain of water stopped abruptly where the boxes had stood a moment before.

'The water. It's gone,' Travere said, crouching down.

'And water always finds its own level, so . . .'

'So,' Travere interrupted, excitedly, 'there is another level, below this one, and—'

'And,' Diana finished for him, grabbing the flashlight and kneeling down next to Travere on the hard stone floor, 'I think we just found what Adler was looking for.'

'What's down there?'

'I'd say it's a tomb.'

Diana swung around and looked at Travere by the flashlight that mimicked candlelight, or the flame of a single, sickly lantern. Her skin began to prickle, the hair on the back of her neck standing up.

'A tomb?' she asked.

'Yes, they are common here. Etruscan tombs. The people who lived here before the Romans. You could call it ancient *ancient* history.'

Diana looked down again at the stone stairs disappearing into blackness. She had used her slender fingertips to feel all around the edges of the trapdoor skillfully hidden in the floor where the water had disappeared. With Travere's help, they had pulled on the brass ring – carefully concealed, and flush with the stonework – until the heavy slab had shifted. With the use of a crowbar, they had finally managed to open the trapdoor, and now stood – disheveled and panting for breath – looking down into the inky darkness.

'And they're buried right here, under the house?'

'Under the houses, under the little shops in town. They make handy-dandy bomb shelters, that is for certain. You've been walking over their graves ever since you came to Tuscany. But the people buried in them don't mind. They're not angry. Only dead. Should I go first?' he added in a helpful tone.

Diana nodded her head. Travere took the flashlight from her hand and started down the stone steps. Not wanting to be left behind, she quickly followed.

At first, it was like walking down any flight of stairs. She placed her fingers on the walls on either side of her for guidance in the half-light. The passage seemed to grow narrower as she descended, the walls close by on either side of her. By the fifth stair, whatever light had been filtering down from the strung bulbs seemed to disappear, the only light now coming from the dancing flashlight ahead of her. All of a sudden, her legs felt icily cool. She kept going, following the light; she stopped counting stairs when she got to thirty. At the bottom of the hewn-rock staircase, the coldness was all around her. She had never felt anything like that before – it seemed as if the coldness had seeped out of nowhere and engulfed her completely. For a minute, she worried that she was having another one of her hallucinations, that in another moment she would hear the baby wailing and see the village on fire. Her breathing came faster, until Travere stuck the flashlight into a small hole in the wall, angling it upward as the torches that had been designed to fit into that same crevice had done millennia before.

Diana looked around her. The room they found themselves in was small, no more than twenty feet square. On the wall to their right were three alcoves carved into the stone, big enough for a person to crouch down inside. To their left was a smooth wall, with a dark, square opening at eye level, just big enough to put in your hand. Littered in the corners of the room and ranged along narrow stone shelves were elegantly formed water pitchers, oil jars, bowls, and even a small candlestick holder, still upright and unmarred, its wax candle having disintegrated into the fine dust that covered everything. On the far wall from where she stood was another alcove, much bigger than the others, its base an oblong of stone big enough for a man to lie down on. She took a step towards the burial site, but it was lost to sight as Travere grabbed the flashlight and trained it on a corner of the room that had been in darkness until now. She inhaled sharply and stood motionless at what she saw. Arranged along the ancient stone wall that had been carved out by hand eons ago stood large, modern wooden boxes, piled nearly to the ceiling. The dust on the floor in front of them was disturbed, several sets of footprints crisscrossing each other. In the half-light, Diana could not make out the carefully typed labels on each box, but she could see the small silver eagles, each holding on to a laurel wreath encircling a small, shining swastika.

Travere opened a box and knelt in front of it, rifling through the pages.

'What is all this?' Diana asked, sinking to her knees next to him.

The stone floor – covered with a thick layer of dust three thousand years old – was unexpectedly soft against her bare knees. Travere didn't answer. He held a sheaf of papers up to his face, studying them carefully. The pages made a rustling noise as his hands trembled.

'Giacomo?' Diana prompted again when he did not answer.

As if coming back to her from a long way off – as if he had forgotten he was not alone in the dark tomb – he reluctantly lifted his eyes to meet hers.

'Oh, this?' he began, hesitating, almost guiltily, forcing a casualness into his voice that sounded unnatural to Diana. 'As you said, this might be what we've been looking for.'

He smiled, but Diana noticed he was now holding the papers tightly to himself, his arms crossed protectively over them.

'What are they? What was Adler hiding down here?'

'I don't think Adler put them here, or he would have known where to find them. Someone else moved them. Just look at those footprints. My money's on Bugari. I wouldn't put anything past her.'

Diana thought again of that morning, when she had returned from the fields and everyone had been frantically searching the house. Had Bugari scattered the contents of these boxes over several more accessible hiding places on the estate, only later to retrieve and hide them all down here, when she learned Adler was returning? Travere stood up quickly, awkwardly, disturbing fine particles of dust that danced in the light. He placed the papers back in the box and began to quickly finger through some other files.

'But what are they?' Diana persisted, getting to her feet. 'What was so important that someone hid them down here to keep them from Adler?'

Travere's only response was an angry sound, like someone flipping quickly through the pages of a book, as Travere shuffled through the papers. Diana reached out and gently took hold of his arm. She could feel the muscles of his forearm stiffen beneath her touch.

'Giacomo.' She breathed the word now. 'Please. We've been down here, side by side, for weeks now. You can tell me what this is. You can trust me.'

Travere dropped the papers back into the box. He turned towards her slowly, placing a hand on each of her shoulders and looking down into her eyes. He searched her face.

'Can I?' he asked quietly, and the way he said the words made Diana feel he was not questioning her, but himself. 'Can I really trust you?'

Diana reached up and took hold of his hands. Once again, she was overcome by the silence all around them. An ancient silence. *Silent as the grave.*

Travere's breath was coming quick and shallow. They held on to each other as, almost imperceptively, they moved closer to one another.

'You can't trust anyone, Diana. That's the first thing they teach you.'

'I used to think so, too. But that's wrong, dead wrong. You've got to trust somebody.'

They were so close now that Diana was surprised when the skin on her upper lip tingled.

'I know, Diana, but they say . . . they say . . .' Travere whispered hoarsely, his shoulders taut and hunched. In another moment, he straightened up, stepping sharply backward while still holding on to her shoulders, keeping her at arm's length. When he spoke again, he was in control of a voice that seemed too loud for the dark, secluded room. Whatever the spell had been between them, it was broken.

'I'll tell you what I can when I can. But we've got a lot of work to do first.'

Then, seeing the look on her face, his body posture softened, his voice low and smooth.

'And I need your help, Diana. I need you.'

FIVE

Diana sat by the old hand pump, near the little path where she had last seen Adler alive. She could feel the hot sun on her bare shins, feel it burning the bridge of her nose. Spring was turning into summer and the air was heavy with the scent of flowers, adding a feeling of drowsiness to the exhaustion she already felt. It had been three days since she and Travere had discovered the tomb and nearly every hour since then had been spent in organizing and cataloguing the papers they had found there. Diana couldn't read German, but her companion seemed surprisingly adept at the language, quickly running his eye down a page of tightly spaced, typed words before handing it to her to put in this or that pile. There were no diagrams on the pages she received from him in the half-light, no recognizable graphs or equations. But each was stamped in red, in the fancy gothic font the Nazis loved to use, and it didn't take long for her to learn that the word she kept seeing, *geheim*, could have but one meaning. Secret.

Diana shifted her weight on the dry, faded lawn, aching all over. She rubbed her back, tight and sore after hours spent crouching in close quarters. Travere had refused to answer any of her questions about the cache they had uncovered, except to say that it was important, that it was directly related to Adler, and that by going through it as they were and presenting it to the proper authorities, Diana would be substantially helping the war effort.

She knew he was lying to her when it came to Adler. Certainly, the discovery of German documents pointed to the German corpse they had found head-down in a reflecting pool. But he no longer spoke about finding Adler's killer or solving any crime. Travere's sole focus now was on extracting documents, and the only justification he gave for Diana continuing to help him was a vague invocation of patriotism and doing one's duty. Diana was sure of her own sense of duty to 'the war effort,' at least as she understood it. But she was far from certain about his. Travere also seemed to have forgotten about his promise to take her back to the Americans, and she let him, for the time being. She was becoming more and more suspicious that whatever they had unearthed together might be just as important as her rejoining her ranks. Maybe more important. And she wanted to stick around a little longer, to make sure.

Now she slowly, almost absently, traced her finger down her V-neck collar towards the tiny, pearlized buttons that ran neatly down her front. She heard a noise and turned quickly, her hand frozen in place, as Travere stalked across the lawn towards her.

'There you are. Playing truant?'

He was smiling again, but Diana set her face and did not answer. He sat down a little apart from her in the grass, splaying his long legs in front of him. When she still didn't speak, he went on, placatingly.

'Hey, I know. It's long and tedious work down there. And who wouldn't want to be out in this glorious weather?' He leaned back, lacing his fingers behind his head and closing his eyes against the bright sun, sighing heavily as he stretched out to his full length. Through her peripheral vision, Diana could still see the rise and fall of his powerful chest, the lean line of his muscles under the cotton and wool of his civilian clothing. After a few moments, he peeked at her out of the corner of one eye.

'But we should really go back to work, Diana. In another couple of days, we'll be through, and I can get these documents into the right hands—'

'Into whose hands?' Diana asked sharply, her sense of lethargy leaving her, all at once. Travere scrambled to a half-seated, half-kneeling position in front of her.

'What do you mean by that?' he asked levelly.

'It's not that hard a question, and you're a clever man. Very clever. You can speak Italian and English and German now, too. Is there anything you can't do, Inspector?'

'I thought we'd settled all that. That you would call me Giacomo.'

'I will call you Giacomo again when I can trust you. If I ever trust you.'

Diana looked down at the grass that was not really grass, but a million little low-lying plants that could go a long time without water, hardy and tenacious, determined to survive. She looked up.

'But I don't trust you. You gave up solving Adler's murder – if you were ever interested in doing that – the minute you got here. You have been almost as flagrant as he was that you were only here to find something, and now that you think you've got it, you don't care what you do or who you step on to pack it up and ship it out. But ship it out to whom? That's what I'd like to know, Inspector.' She spat the last word at him, her dark eyes boring into his.

'Is that what you think? Is that what you think of me?' Travere sat back on his haunches, as if she had just slapped him.

'I'm funny that way,' Diana went on, the steadiness of her own voice surprising her. 'I like to know when I am aiding and abetting the enemy. Am I?'

The heavy noonday silence fell over them. Even the swallows that chirped cheerfully at morning and sunset were quiet now, resting out of sight in the overhanging branches. Travere's face had gone very white, while Diana could feel her face burn hot but, this time, not from the sun. Her pulse sounded in her ears as she waited for his reply.

'You think I'm the enemy?' he asked very slowly and quietly, as if a single word might tip some gigantic scale. 'Because I speak German and Italian, the Axis languages, you think I'm – what? An Axis agent?'

Diana did not move, as if she, too, felt an enormous weight hanging in the balance, ready to shift at the slightest provocation. This was not the best place to confront a potential enemy spy, she told herself too late, isolated as they were at the back of the house while everyone drowsed inside after their heavy midday meal. But she couldn't stop herself.

'Are you?' she insisted.

The pulsing in her ears stopped, and Travere's blanched lips quivered for a moment before he spoke. He closed his eyes as if struggling to retain control.

'Diana, I've told you before. What you think of me matters. It matters very much. Maybe too much. Maybe enough for me to do things I swore I would never do . . .' and the way he left the last phrase hanging in the air, in the small space that separated them, gave her no idea if he had sworn a promise to himself or to some outside power. He went on.

'I . . . I didn't know you felt this way, Diana. About me. I guess I thought, I hoped, at least, that you were coming to care for me the way I have – the way I am – hopelessly . . .'

She heard the catch in his voice, saw the raised vein on the side of his neck as he wrestled with himself, as he began to lose the battle. The sun was hot, oppressively hot. Burning into Diana's body with an intensity she had only dreamed of that whole last winter, the coldest on European record. A winter where she had huddled, shivering, against a half-frozen patient she was trying to keep alive with her body heat, a boy with blue lips from Las Cruces, New Mexico, whose last words had been to lie, and write home to his mom that he hadn't suffered at all. Diana was shivering again now, in the merciless sun, in the heat of a garden heavy with lilac and gardenia, but shivering with an undefinable excitement. With a sense of power that startled her. Because this strong man was crumbling at her feet, about to give in, about to give her everything she wanted. A shadow of a smile curled her lip as he moved inexorably towards her, their faces almost touching, his short, rapid breath hot on her neck, his eyes closed in defeat or submission or delight. This was not love, she knew that; she told herself that. But, after the abstinence and emptiness of war, she was surprised at her response to him. Surprised that she could feel again. That she could want again, want anything as strongly and as foolishly as she wanted this, right now. But, at the last moment, Travere's eyes opened, and he jolted back and away from her, his voice leaden, his face an expression of misery.

'I am not working for the enemy. You saw my identity card. I am an Italian, and we work with your army now, whatever we may have done in the past. So that makes me Allied forces, just like you.'

He staggered to his feet. He could not look at her, he was staring at the hand pump, at the rusty pin that held the handle in place.

'I came here for Adler, yes, but if I uncovered something in my investigation that was more important than him – more important than you or me' – his voice threatened to crack again, and he hurried on – 'then I am duty-bound to go through with that, to follow that, no matter where it leads. I thought you understood, that you felt the same way about your country.'

He was wiping unconsciously at his knees, as if expecting clippings and grass stains, but the drab ground covering left no mark on the light-colored material.

'I'm going back down. To finish. I can certainly use your help, if you can see clear to give it to me. But whether you help me or not, Diana, I am finishing. I am doing my duty here and then handing what we found over to the authorities, to the *Allied* authorities, no matter what you think of me. That's what I'm going to do. Get these documents packed and labeled and then get the hell out of this place.'

His voice betrayed him at the end, distorted and strange as he hurried off towards the house, slamming the door behind him before disappearing into its depths.

Diana sat for another minute, thinking about what Travere had said, strangely calm and cool now that he was gone, now that whatever that had been had passed. Automatically, her hand went back to her collar, to the little buttons, and reached inside her brassiere, pulling out the small Moroccan-bound journal she had hidden there when she found it that morning, fallen behind one of the boxes in the tomb. She ran her fingers over the rich, mahogany-colored leather that held the well-worn shininess of decades of use. She had not shown it to Travere, although her first instinct had been to tell him, to call out that she had found something other than the neat paper files, all stamped *secret* in red or blue ink. But the gold embossed *B* on the lower right-hand corner had made her pause, made her turn to the flyleaf and read the inscription there, still angry and resentful after so many years.

April, 1912. I will write in English. The stupid peasants here cannot read even their own language. English will be an indecipherable code to them. I have no one to write to, no one to speak to, any longer. No one to dedicate this small volume to. So I dedicate it to myself, to 'Signora Bugari,' to the only one I can rely on. The only one left whom I can trust.

Diana had hastily slipped the thin journal into her bodice then, as Travere called to her a second time to take the stack of files from his arms and place them in a wooden packing box. She had decided instinctively – in the second between hearing his voice and her reading the line about the author trusting no one but herself – to keep the book from him. She had taken the papers from him obediently and packed the files tight against the others already crammed into the box and then walked up the stone stairs and out into the light, sitting down in the sun beside the well until Travere came up to look for her and they had said the words to each other that still rang in Diana's ears. *I hoped, at least, that you were coming to care for me the way I have – the way I am – hopelessly* . . . Diana had heard his voice give way: a strangled, desperate sound, a man fighting and losing a battle against himself. She had been sure in the moment he was about to reveal himself. The exquisite agony in his voice. The feel of his breath against her skin. He had been slipping, and if he had only kept going, only let her in and let her see him as he was, she might have, she would have . . .

Diana roused herself, giving herself a little shake and standing up quickly. No use falling for this man. This wasn't love, she reminded herself. Love was predicated on trust, and he was the last person she would trust on the estate. Besides, he had said he was leaving, getting the hell out of this place, and he was right. Diana had her duty to do, same as him. Strangely, she had believed him when he told her he was on her side, *Allied forces, just like you.* His hurt had seemed genuine, the pain in his eyes when he realized her suspicions. But, whatever his feelings for her, he had pulled away at the last moment, shutting her out (despite the pain in his face), and spoke only of duty. And he was right, Diana told herself again.

The war was not over, not in the Pacific, and she was duty-bound to leave with Travere, get to a port city, and go where the fighting was, where the killing was, even if it took another year, another five, another ten years to win this war, or die trying. She said these things to herself, as she stood in the sun that was burning the side-part in her hair, the exposed backs of her ears. She tried giving herself the kind of speech that used to move her, that should have spurred her into action. The kind of speech that had made her walk out of Oswego Hospital that cold December day nearly four years ago and join the army. Words of patriotism that had made her heart lurch with excitement, that had made her mother cry, that had pushed a strawberry-rhubarb pie into her hands as Diana waved over her shoulder and ran into the unknown. But the words now were flat, were meaningless except for the hard truth they revealed. That there was nothing for her now, at the end of one war and the beginning of the next. That she would never again have her youth, or her beauty, or her life as it once was, as she once imagined it could be. That she would never have love with this enigmatic Italian, not with any man, maybe, unless it was the cold, hard, brittle love of loving a man for a few minutes only, pretending to love him as he bled out between your fingers, before you could get him into surgery, before he stopped breathing in front of you in post-op. A boy cuddled up close to you under the blankets, his strong, lifeless arms still wrapped around you, his blue lips smiling as he imagined another life with another girl under another blanket, as he saw again, in that last instant, the face of his mother, sad but smiling, and rested in the peace of the lies you would tell her.

Duty called to Diana, but it was no longer a battle cry, no longer a star-spangled anthem with trumpets blasting. She would help Travere. Not because he was in love with her, not because she liked to imagine she could fall in love with him, but because he was transportation to the next town, to the next boat; he would be a stepping stone for her to cross the Atlantic. She would get back home – for a day, for a week, for a two-week pass – but she would never see him again, lost as she would become in a Japanese jungle, in a Philippine prison camp. She would most likely die and this Italian man she did not know would most likely die, and the war would end, or it would go on forever, like the Hundred Years War. But, whatever happened, first she'd make sure these boxes got to her superiors, and then she'd never look back. She walked towards the door that had swung open again after Travere slammed it, swaying slowly on its hinges. She would go back to help him, for a few days, for a few hours more. She would do what he said, and accept the lies he told her, if it got her her ticket home. *But*, she thought defiantly, smoothing down her bodice to hide the slight bulge beneath the fabric, *the journal stays mine.*

The *bad house* had been a safe house for the Nazis. Travere told her that, when she came back down again, when she entered the icy coldness of their shared tomb, as if he was proffering the information as a peace offering. He could not tell her what the documents said, what they were, exactly. But the files she was helping him collect had been theirs, he told her, and the Nazis had lived and worked with impunity, it seemed, from behind the brocade wallpapered walls of the estate house. Diana nodded without speaking, as if she had always known it. She knelt down to pack the papers Travere had piled high in her absence, trying to imagine Giuliana's face, Giorgio's expression as they had waited on the enemy – bringing them brandy, clearing away their plates, polishing their tall, black boots. Would the elderly couple have remained outwardly submissive, eyes downcast, enduring the occupation of their mistress's home as best they could, only to curse at them as they left the room, as Giorgio saw to their cars, or Giuliana wrung out their wash? And Bugari – where would she have been through all this, as radio transceivers were set up in her kitchen, or large-scale maps spread out messily on her dining-room table? Would she have taken to her room, as she had done now? Would she have flitted, like a ghost, from room to room, avoiding the intruders below stairs, keeping to the unused portions of her home like a small, scared animal, trying to avoid snares set by an enemy?

Diana struggled to close the packing lid, hammering in nails along its edge and sucking hard on her thumb after a nail slipped. The pain cleared her head for a moment and, suddenly, a different picture filled her mind's eye. Instead of a thin, frail woman cowering in some attic bedroom, she saw Bugari in all her glory, ringed and bejeweled, regally descending her own grand staircase to greet her guests, reaching out her rheumatic fingers to be kissed in greeting. She saw the aged woman nod imperially as she was escorted into the dining room on the arm of a senior officer, no maps littering its surface but laid instead with her best china, Giuliana and Giorgio standing respectfully behind the rows of highbacked chairs and the officers standing at attention, the amber liquid swirling in her best crystal goblets as the glasses were raised in unison in honor of their hostess.

Diana stopped sucking on her thumb and put down her hammer. She thought of Bugari, and her untouched home, her pristine estate, and knew beyond a doubt this second scenario had been the real one. It was the only explanation for her home being spared the ravages of a retreating army, the only reason she could still be so cash-rich. The woman who wrote that journal, who had had such disdain for the inhabitants of the small village nearby, would not have thought twice about betraying them if it meant she and her house of secrets would live on. Diana envisioned it as if she had been there herself, as if she could hear the hearty German thanks, the voices raised in song to *Frau* Bugari and the assistance she offered them in exchange for protection and exemption from the madness of war. Where Adler fit in, why his files had been hidden from him, Diana was not sure; it did not matter to her, really, in comparison to the revelation Travere had just made. Bugari had run a safe house for the German army, for the Nazis themselves, for Diana's country's sworn enemies. Whatever Bugari's past, whatever good she may have done – for Paolo, for Giorgio and Giuliana, even for Diana herself – paled now in comparison to the evil of collaboration, of betraying her countrymen at the end of a war to save her own skin. Diana thought of the young woman of her dreams, a Signora beautiful but sad, weeping into her own hands, running in terror across a dark *piazza*. Diana remembered again the icy grip of the beast that pursued her, its corpse-like hand that had crushed her own. Diana thought of the young girl, of the ancient woman, caught in the grip of that monster, and knew it had beaten her, it had devoured her, it had left her her home but ripped out whatever heart she had once possessed in payment for it.

'*Signora, signora . . .*' Diana whispered aloud, covering her face with the fingers of one hand.

'Did you speak?' Travere asked distractedly, glancing up from his papers, his brow still furled in concentration.

'No,' Diana answered in a defeated voice. 'I was just praying.'

Diana came across Giorgio one day, at the bottom of the kitchen stairs, poking with his leather shoe at some of the debris that had fallen out of the boxes in the cellar. Travere was down in the crypt, underground and a dozen yards away from them, the trapdoor open but obscured from their sight. Diana looked back towards the tomb, then at Giorgio. But the old man seemed lost in thought at something he had found, with no intention of searching the basement further.

'What is it, Giorgio?'

It seemed to take a long while for her voice to reach him.

'It is nothing. And everything.'

Diana tried to discern what Giorgio was looking at so intently. To her, the scraps of paper littered across the stone floor all seemed the same. He bent down and picked up what might have been the corner of an old photograph or, perhaps, the edge of a yellowed map. Giorgio sighed.

'You have been in the war, even though you are but a girl. So you will understand.'

'Understand what, Giorgio?'

Diana felt a kindliness towards the old man she had not known was there. She had seen him with Paolo, with Signora, she knew his devotion and dedication to both. But here, for the first time, she saw a little of the man, a younger man, looking back at her from the past through a snippet of paper. He held it out towards Diana.

'When you are old, little things, like this, they can transport you back. Suddenly, and without you wishing it.'

He dropped his hand to his side.

'You have been in the war so you will understand what war is really like, not what they tell you in school. And you are a girl, so you will know war is no place for women.'

Diana felt her anger rising at what she took as an insult to her calling, to her wartime service, but he spoke again, quickly.

'I see I make you mad. Let me try again. What you do, the nurses, that is all right. That is good. You help the men and, hopefully, no one kills you because you do not carry a gun and everyone knows you are valuable, you have a skill, like a doctor. But, other women, in wartime, men do not see them that way. They are – how do you call it? They are a bounty, no, a spoil of war. Something to be used and thrown away. Hurting them is just another way to hurt the men you are fighting.'

'And that picture . . .' Diana began.

'It reminds me, nothing more. It reminds me of a time when war stopped being war and became something else.'

Diana thought he had finished speaking, but the old man went on, no longer staring at the image in his hand but at the darkness beyond the small patch of light showing on the floor from the kitchen above.

'In the last war, the Great War, there was a captain. Not a bad man at first, but the war did things to his head until he was not fit to command. I was too old to fight, but the army let me in anyway – what did they care? I could still carry a gun, carry messages. And we were held down in a little carved-out place under the earth, somewhere people used to keep their vegetables, but the food was gone. They had called the retreat, but we couldn't get to the transports, there was too much shelling. And some women had taken refuge with us, the French troops had brought them along with them for comfort, but now they were just lost, like us. And we were all trapped down there when the captain, the man I told you about, who is not right in the head, they tell him the Ottomans are coming, we are outnumbered ten, twenty to one. So he turns to us – there are not many, just a dozen men, and the women. They are cold in their thin dresses. And the captain turns towards one of them, the one who would have been the prettiest but now she is just cold and dirty and wet, like the rest of us. And he asks her her name. It was Artemis. I remember because she had always been my favorite of the old myths, the goddesses, although in Italy we call her Diana. Your name.'

Giorgio looked up for a minute, as if the realization the two women shared the same name struck him. He shook his head, slightly, continuing in a low voice Diana strained to hear.

'The man was not right in the head. That is what I tell myself now. It is the only reason I can think of. Because he says to us – most of us only boys – he says to us to take the girls outside and shoot them, once, in the back of the head. That that will be better than what the Ottomans will do to them. Nobody moved, for a second. I remember someone was sick. And then the captain drew his pistol on us and started to shout and a few of us grabbed the girls and dragged them outside. I grabbed Artemis.'

The paper fell from Giorgio's hand, making graceful pendulum turns in the air until it fell silently on to the stone floor. Diana stretched out her hand, tentatively, to touch Giorgio's arm, then drew it back quickly. He was beyond her reach.

'It was a wasteland out there,' Giorgio went on, seeing the scene again with his old eyes. 'Everything destroyed, and the shells still coming down. The girls were crying and some of the boys were crying, too, but they were also biting their lips and pushing the girls around roughly, trying to prove they were men and could follow orders, a direct order, like this. They were too young to know sometimes an order is wrong. The girls knelt down, like they were praying, and one girl made the sign of the cross, just like she was beginning her rosary in church. A shell hit close by, killing a few of us, one of the girls, too, I think. But the stupid boys that were left kept following orders, kept yelling at the girls who were not dead yet to be still, to close their eyes, because they were cowards and didn't want to see them looking up at them when they were dead. I shouted at them to let the girls go, to not do this thing, but they were all mad by now, like the captain. I heard the first shot go off and the girl fell on her face, and then another. Artemis was in front of me, kneeling, but her head was not down like the others, she held it high, like she wanted to leave this world looking at the sky. I pull her up and push her towards the treeline, far away, there was no way she could make it there, alive, not with the shelling, and the enemy coming. But she began to run and I watched her. I just stood there in the middle of all that shelling and I watched her until I was hit and fell. But the last thing I saw was Artemis running across the field, like a goddess, heading for the trees.'

Diana surveyed the rows of tightly packed wooden boxes, their outsides marked hastily with paint Travere had taken from the garage, *A-145, C-24, H-9*. They were nearly finished, she and Travere, only a day or two to go. There had been some delay when Travere had come across encoded files – slowly cross-referencing them with a typed card he produced from his vest pocket that she could only assume was a key – but now they, too, were packed and labeled, their box receiving the special designation of a trident, underscored and painted on thick so as not to be missed. Diana turned her back on the boxes, walking past the stacks of recently rifled snowshoes, equestrian riding costumes, silver spoons, and broken cuckoo clocks. She switched off the cellar lights and headed up the stairs into the kitchen, blinking, as always, in the unexpected brightness, walking to the enormous stove and reaching out her hand to see if the coffee pot was still warm. Francesca always kept it on for her, the black cast iron holding the heat that rose from the banked fire below it. She poured herself a glass and drank the strong, dark liquid, closing her eyes as if to shut out everything that had happened to her since the bomb exploded and she ended up in this forgotten outpost. The coffee warmed and revived her, just as it had done on countless occasions during the war, her and the other nurses' blistered hands reaching out to receive the tin cups that would help keep them going. It was strange now for Diana, after the obscenity of war, after the mutilation and humiliation their patients had suffered, to remember how worldly the nurses had once thought they were, how wise and knowing they had thought themselves, as twenty-two-year-old girls. As nurses going into a war they were sure they were ready for, that could throw them no curve ball they had not already been prepared for by two years of stateside work. How rebellious the young women had seemed to their families, to their mothers' bridge partners. How risqué, even indecent their chosen profession. 'No daughter of mine would go into nursing,' they had heard murmured behind closed doors, or said right to their faces, and the girls had laughed and run their fingers defiantly down their noses. The young nurses knew what they were doing, and they loved what they were doing. But they had also known nursing in peacetime was not encouraged by 'respectable' folks, by the old ladies at church, that it worried their godmothers because it reduced their marriageability, tainted them and made them a less eligible match. 'Women and children are one thing,' her great-aunt Minerva had said once at a cousin's wedding, when the old woman had had too much punch and her sharp tongue was wagging more freely than usual. 'But men, mind you. They see men in their drawers or' – her voice had dropped as she inclined her head to her nearest companion at table – '*without* their drawers, even.' And she had nodded knowingly, one eyebrow raised, her listener blushing and mumbling feebly in dismay, as if the nurses were mere voyeurs at a carnival peep show, looking at their naked patients for pleasure, as if surgery could be hygienically conducted with a man's long underwear and boots in place. Diana remembered Beth, a promising nursing student with her back home in New York, whose parents had showed up one afternoon and packed up Beth's belongings, dragging the crying girl into an idling car without even allowing her to say goodbye to her friends, or explain her hasty departure to the head sister. Beth had been married off that same fall and now, years later, Diana remembered Aunt Minerva talking about the wedding to Diana's mother, looking darkly at her niece as she put on her hat and set out for evening rounds at the hospital, shaking her head and saying ominously in a voice purposely loud enough for Diana to hear, 'Mark my words. It's just not decent for your girl to go on like this. That path leads nowhere but corruption.'

Diana finished her cup of coffee and placed it down in the

kitchen sink, letting the water from the tap run over it on to her hands. Without knowing what she was saying, her aunt had been right. Not that the human body was somehow impure, or that the men and women and children she cared for as a nurse at their local hospital, or within their own homes, were somehow a contagion to her, unworthy of her respect and care. But the road Diana had followed – and she could see it now as a straight line, starting where she had flounced past her disapproving aunt out into the night air, and ending in her digging a lifeless baby out of the rubble of an air attack – had led her to corruption and indecency. But the corruption and indecency of war. Without even trying, she saw again the maimed limbs of her patients, the bloody bandages covering stumps where hands or feet should be, the missing eyes, the sheared-off ears, young boys retching from the after-effects of anesthesia, bursting their stitches and having to be wheeled right back into surgery again. War was not what she had once imagined. There were no clear-cut battle plans, like she and the other students had learned about in history class, or seen depicted on their Senior trip to the Metropolitan Museum of Art. There was no glorious general sitting astride a white horse, his gold braid catching the last light of the sunset. There was no recognizable plan of attack chalked out neatly on the blackboard, with x's and o's denoting famous battles, brilliant counterattacks, sorties and flankings so clever they were studied and revered centuries afterward. In the field, it was death. The point of war was death. And her point, as a nurse, had been to stop death. And so she had been thrust into a hopeless fight against a world war, with its crushing inevitability – no matter what side won – of defeating her and all those who stood in its way. Death – as she had seen it sometimes, back home, in the quiet Dutch sign maker's one-room house, the elderly man resting quietly under his eiderdown quilt, his white-haired wife sitting silently by his side – could be noble, could be beautiful, even. But not in war. She had seen men die screaming, and seen men die crying. Men cut off mid-curse, railing against God, against man, against their enemy sometimes but, more often than not, against the sheer injustice of it all, against the inhumanity of being cut down after only eighteen years of life. Calling out for vengeance, for another chance, to see their girl just one more time, for the right to live in a world hell-bent on death. Nursing had brought her to this place, to a world that was indecent and corrupt. Aunt Minerva had been right, despite herself.

Travere had gone into town. Before he left, he had told Diana to start packing her belongings. When he returned, they would load up whatever conveyance he could requisition – a car, most likely, but maybe a work van, or a truck, or even a horse cart – and make their way to the nearest American outpost. Giorgio had warned him there were no working vehicles left in the village – the Germans had taken everything with them in their retreat – and that it would be days until he could find anything. Undaunted, Travere had replied that he would walk as far as necessary – 'to Chianciano, or Siena, or Florence itself' – to get what he needed. Giorgio had grunted dismissively as he stalked away, as if the younger man's enthusiasm was merely tiresome. Now that Adler's secret had been uncovered, neither Giorgio, nor Giuliana, nor Signora herself had seemed much interested in its fate, as if their only objective had been to keep the files from Adler, and with him out of the picture, they no longer cared what happened to them. Diana wondered at their complacency. Surely, once it came to light that they had colluded with the enemy, they would face serious repercussions from the occupying Allies. But the elderly couple went about their daily tasks – bringing in the harvest with the help of the little girls and Paolo, yelling good-naturedly at Francesca whose help they relied on more and more each day, carrying trays of food upstairs to tempt their mistress – as if they were impervious to any outside threat. Even Signora had seemed to rally a little, sitting up in an enormous wicker chair on her balcony some mornings, before the heat of the day drove her back to the retreat of her four-poster bed. Diana could not understand it. Either they held yet more secrets they could exchange for amnesty later on, or (and Diana thought this a much more likely hypothesis) they were so relieved to have the threat of Adler removed from their lives that they were dismissive of lesser, or at least less imminent, dangers.

Diana thought whoever had held the struggling German's head underwater had done the old people a great favor and, as a result, they had become nearly giddy at their own good fortune.

It had not taken Diana long to pack up her meager possessions. Her olive-drab jumpsuit had had to be cut off her body by the farmwife who treated her wounds, so all Diana had were the items she had sewn herself, and the green dress she had stolen from Donna Lucia's washroom. She packed them now into a great carpetbag she had found upturned in the cellar, along with her pay in crinkly American dollars, and a sketch Paolo had done for her during her first week on the estate. Hoisting the bag on to the foot of her bed, she smoothed down her long coils of hair and started along the passageway towards Signora's bedroom, where a strangely familiar voice Diana could not place co-mingled with Bugari's nearly inaudible one. She had gotten into the habit of checking in, before going down to *pranzo*. Sometimes she was allowed to adjust a pillow, or move a glass of water infinitesimally closer to the edge of the nightstand. Now Diana knocked as a formality only, stepping quickly across the threshold as she called out quietly, 'I am just heading down now, Signora, is there anything I can . . .' but her words died on her lips as she stood, transfixed.

Signora Bugari was dressed. Diana could not remember the last time she had seen her employer out of her silk nightshift and kimono robe. The elderly woman sat upright before the empty fireplace, in her best black taffeta. The dress was too large for her now, and Diana was immediately reminded of her dream of the young Bugari running across the piazza, encumbered by her long, ill-fitting dress. Bugari's hair was pulled back unevenly, grey strands stretched tight against her shiny scalp, a tortoiseshell clip attached at an odd angle. In fact, everything about Bugari's appearance seemed rushed and haphazard – she had on some of her rings, but not on the usual fingers, and she was busy moving them from finger to finger, twisting them around compulsively. Some, but not all, of her buttons were done up. Diana could see she had started on the wrong buttonhole, and the whole of her bodice looked awkward as a result. Diana couldn't tell if the old woman was even wearing shoes. She had caught a glimpse of what looked like the brown leather of her bedroom slippers peeping out from beneath the voluminous black skirts. But, despite Bugari's unkempt appearance, despite her having unaccountably left her soft bed to dress herself and sit uncomfortably on an uncushioned chair, Diana's eyes were drawn instead to her employer's unlikely companion. Donna Lucia.

Diana stood stock still, her hand frozen on the door handle, her mouth agape. Wedged into the light-blue upholstered wingback opposite Bugari sat her old employer. In the confines of the narrow chair, Lucia seemed larger than she ever had before. Her arms were crossed against her enormous bosom, as if trying to compress her girth. She had on her best 'going to church dress' which had made her laugh when she told Diana about it, as Lucia never went to church. It was the dress she wore when she went into town to hire new girls. Both women had turned at Diana's entrance. Signora's expression was inscrutable, but Lucia smiled leeringly as she shifted her great weight and rubbed her hands together.

'*La fuggitiva ritorna*,' she began in her deep man's voice, but Signora cut her off.

'We will conduct this interview in English, for Miss Bolsena's benefit.'

Signora's voice held all the imperiousness it had on Diana's first day at the estate, although now her hauteur was directed at the woman seated next to her. She had stopped fiddling with her rings, her hands clasped motionless in her lap.

'We will conduct this interview in English,' she repeated, carefully pronouncing each syllable, as if speaking to a little child. 'If that will be a possibility for you, madam?'

Bugari's voice was ice that visibly burned Lucia. Her face flushed red, but she managed to respond, a little too loudly to be mistaken for civility.

'It is all the same to me.'

The two women glared at one another for another moment before Signora spoke.

'Miss Bolsena, please come in and close the door.'

Diana didn't know which was less accountable: seeing Donna Lucia ensconced in this sunny upstairs bedroom or hearing again the command in Bugari's voice. Knowing how weak the old woman had become in recent weeks, Diana could only imagine the exertion all this was requiring. Diana closed the door softly behind her and took a few steps into the room.

'We were just discussing you, Miss Bolsena. This . . . this person says she has some prior claim on your services.'

Donna Lucia turned from Bugari and fastened her gaze on Diana. Diana stood in the middle of the floor and felt again the shame at their first meeting, the feeling of being mentally undressed, clinically evaluated and found wanting.

'Yes, I pull this helpless wench out of the gutter and how does she repay me? With stealing from me, yes, *stealing*. I do not forget. The clothes, the food, the money I pay you, and what? You run off in the night and never come back? You think you can do that to Lucia?'

The woman's voice had started in a low grumble but escalated to a full-throated yell. Diana could hear her heart pounding in her own ears. This was all happening so quickly, so unexpectedly. It had been months since she had last seen Lucia, since she had put on the green dress and made her long way to Signora Bugari's estate, to another life. She was not ashamed of the work she had done for Lucia, for the help she had offered the girls. But seeing her again now, after all this time, after so much had happened, after so many people – Giorgio and Giuliana and Paolo and the girls and Francesca and Travere and Adler – had come and gone from her life, was too much. She felt her head spinning, as if she were a character dropped into the wrong book. Diana opened her mouth to speak, but the deafening laughter that had greeted her that first day was rattling around in her head, drowning out rational thought. She was grateful when Bugari spoke.

'Miss Bolsena is many things,' the old woman's cat-eyes found Diana's and seemed to hold them, to will her to stand a little taller, 'but "helpless wench" is certainly not one of them.'

Lucia frowned, recalcitrantly thrusting her head down into her multiple chins. Bugari continued, her iron face belying her polite words.

'If you would please state what you believe to be your claim, quickly and succinctly, we would be most thankful.'

Lucia shifted her weight again, this time noisily moving the chair a few inches across the parquet floor.

'My claim is this. This woman, this Diana' – she said the name in a mocking, singsong voice – 'comes to me when she has nothing, when she *is* nothing. And, out of the goodness of my heart, I help her. I give to her many things. Clothing and food and a job, which is what she asks. She would be dead without me, without what I give her. You tell her,' Lucia demanded, turning towards Diana, and pointing furiously from her to Bugari, 'you tell her Lucia is no liar.'

Diana looked into Bugari's unblinking eyes and seemed to be speaking only to her.

'Yes, that is true. Part of that is true, anyway. I was separated from my unit, as I told you when I came here. I was hungry. As hungry as I'd ever been. And I had recently been injured. I was weak from that, and I could not find work – any other work – in the village.'

Diana's eyes had fallen, and Bugari's steady voice seemed to be coming from a long way off when she replied.

'Yes, I remember you telling me this much upon your arrival. You did not tell me you had previously worked at this person's establishment—'

Donna Lucia cut her off, laughing loudly and slapping her thigh.

'Hah! She does not tell you, no. She does not. See, she keeps that from you. Now, who is the liar?'

'As I was about to say, before I was interrupted . . .' The frost in Bugari's voice was withering, one of her thin, grey eyebrows rising independently as she continued. 'As I had been about to say, you did not tell me, Miss Bolsena. But, even if you had, it would not have mattered. I would have hired you, anyway.'

Diana's eyes shot up, looking incredulously into Bugari's face.

'You are a competent woman, Miss Bolsena – if I may say so, a resilient woman. It takes a certain caliber of character to reinvent yourself, as you had to do, faced with that particular set of circumstances, as you were. Not many women could have done that. Not one in a hundred. Believe me, I know from experience. And I would be the last person to hold that against you.'

Diana took a deep breath, as if she had been underwater for a long time, struggling to surface, and had come out suddenly, into the clear light of day.

'And you,' Bugari continued in her most businesslike manner, turning back to Lucia, 'I can only assume that you requested to meet with me privately in the hope of . . . what? Extracting blackmail, perhaps? Of silencing the fact that I had one of your previous employees living in my home?'

Lucia opened her mouth to speak, then shut it quickly.

'I know you may not have noticed,' Bugari went on, her hands curling around the arms of her chair and pushing herself up even straighter, 'these things are always such a boon for businesses like your own, but there has been a *war*, madam. And some of us have had to do things – and take confederates – we would not otherwise have chosen.'

For a moment, Bugari's face held a far-off look, and Diana could not help but remember the image of her as a gracious hostess, happily welcoming Germans into her home, and wondered if she could have been mistaken in her judgment of Bugari, and of the reasons for the confederates she had taken.

'But your blackmail and your threats will not work here, so you can forget them. If you have no other business—'

'But I do have other business, business with *her*.' She spat the word out at Diana. 'If you do not honor your debt to me, what you owe me for my kindness, I know your language. I know what you want.'

From the recesses of a black handbag that had been jammed next to Lucia in her chair, she pulled out two thick wads of cash.

'American dollars,' she proclaimed triumphantly. 'Good American dollars. You do not see these, I know, in a long time.'

Diana did not bother to contradict her, her eyes flicking for a moment towards Bugari.

'I want you should come back. Some of the girls, they are stupid and are pregnant now. They do not use the prophyl . . . the prophyl—'

'The prophylaxis,' Diana offered.

'Yes, *that* they do not use correctly. The medicine you tell me to buy—'

'The antibiotics. To protect them from disease.'

'Yes, those pills are expensive on the black market. I want to stop them.'

'If you stop them for girls who are already infected, they will infect others. Their babies will be sick, born blind—'

'You think I care what happens to their bastard children? You think I even bother to save the boy babies, who are useless to me?'

Diana thought she was going to be sick, struggling to shut out the vision of Lucia snatching an infant out of the arms of a weakened mother, dealing with it as she would an unwanted litter of kittens. Diana shut her eyes and pushed down the nausea, telling herself, *Lucia has no heart, talk to her only on terms she can understand. For the girls. This is the only way you can help them.* Diana swallowed hard and opened her eyes.

'Lucia, you don't need to give the medicine to everyone, all the time. But once they show signs of infection, you must buy this for them. The girls know now when they are sick, they can tell you and you can give it to them then. If you don't, remember, the men they will not pay. Your girls will not be able to hide the signs from them, and the men will go somewhere else, with clean girls right off the farms. You will have lost a great amount of money just because you were afraid to spend a small amount of money. Of course, you can do whatever you want.' Diana managed a weak, ingratiating smile that turned her own stomach. 'But, to me, that just does not sound like you.'

Donna Lucia scowled again but, this time, as if she were calculating numbers in her head. Diana pressed her advantage.

'And the same thing with the prophylaxis, with the condoms. You spend a little money for them now, you spend a little money to get the word out that your girls are clean, one hundred percent, they all use rubbers, they cannot harbor disease. And then, just think of the money you can make. These boys, the

American GIs, are going home. They do not want to bring back sickness to their wives and girlfriends. They are leaving soon but it will take some time, and some will surely stay on, for six months, for a year, to keep the peace. Think of what you can make in a year, Lucia.'

The woman clearly was thinking of it, an expression of rapture spreading out over her face. She was beaming from ear to ear as she brought her fist decisively down into the palm of her other hand.

'Yes, you are right. It is modern. American. No one else in the whorehouses will do it, would dream of doing it, even in Rome. And we will put them all out of business. You come back with me now, you take this money.' She flung the tied packets of money at Diana's feet, as she stood up abruptly. 'I give you more. As much as you like. You see to all this, you manage this for me—'

'I cannot work for you any longer.'

'Nonsense, ridiculous, of course you will. You will not stay in this asylum for the dying, this home of the pensioners. With me, you will become rich and you can do anything you like.'

'I cannot do anything I like. Not yet. There is still a war on.'

'The war is ended—'

'Here, perhaps. But my country still fights in Japan and I have to go.'

'Nonsense,' Lucia said again, snapping her purse shut and smoothing down the front of her skirts. 'Tell them you are dead. No one looks for you. If anyone does, I pay them off. You are worth that much to me.'

Diana smiled wryly at her change in valuation in Lucia's eyes, and also at her own change of loyalties. Diana remembered a time not so long ago when she had been ready to board one of Lucia's trucks and run away from the war, from any obligations she felt towards her army. But then the boy had come, telling her Adler was dead, and she had met Travere – Giacomo – and so much had happened to her here, since then, that now she felt she was running again. But not from the war. Towards it.

'Lucia, I *am* leaving, in just a few days. Maybe less. To

meet my army. But I will come up to the village, one last time. To see to the girls before I go and make sure they have the supplies they need, that they know how to get more when they run out, and know how to use them.' Turning deferentially towards Bugari. 'If I have your permission, Signora.'

Diana didn't know why she added that. She had already discussed her leaving with Bugari, and the rest of the household, that she would be going with Travere when he returned. She felt, perhaps, she said it now in thanks for the way the frail woman had stood up for Diana before she could find her own voice, the way Bugari had seemed to pull her back from the brink.

'Of course, you are free to go where you will. But' – here Bugari got shakily to her feet, taking a step forward until she stood toe to toe with the towering frame of Lucia – '*never* come back here again. I was not raised to even acknowledge the existence of persons like yourself, let alone deign to speak to one.'

Lucia started, her face blanching and then flushing unevenly as if she had just been struck. Bugari stepped back and slumped into her chair, as if the effort had taken the last of her strength. Momentarily stunned, Lucia squatted down slowly to retrieve the wads of cash from the floor, before following Diana into the passageway. Suddenly, Lucia stopped and hurried back into the room, bringing her massive face within inches of Bugari's.

'You dried, shriveled-up old goat, you damn woman. What do you know of me? Of any of us? What do you know of how I was raised? If I could, I would tear you down, you and everyone who judges me like you do. Why do you think I do this? How do you imagine I became like this . . .'

And then, catching herself, as if she were about to reveal something no one, not even Donna Lucia herself could know, she turned on her thick, hobnailed shoe and slammed the door behind her, the delicate crystal chandelier shivering in her wake.

Diana was patting the soft down of *bambola*'s head as she sat in the kitchen with the little girl's mother. They had been discussing Diana's imminent departure – 'as soon as Travere returns' – although it had now been two days without word from him. Diana had told the grateful woman that she and her small family would stay on permanently at the estate, that they would be safe and well fed and appreciated here. Suddenly, the quiet morning conversation was shattered as Paolo, Sarina, and Dorothea – the 'Three Musketeers,' as Diana had christened them – came barging into the kitchen. In a moment, all was a confusion of kisses, scoldings, stolen treats, slapped wrists, and laughter. Diana looked approvingly at the scene, at the strong and summer-bronzed young children who would see no more of death, who had found not only safety but true, abiding friendship in one another. Paolo especially had blossomed, surrounded by love and acceptance. He had been initially sad when Diana had told him she would be leaving soon, immediately asking in a quavering voice, 'And Mama Francesca, too? My friends, too?' When Diana had reassured him, no, they would be staying on 'for good,' as she translated the words, they had struck her as doubly true. It *was* a goodness that these people had found and held on to each other, despite the chaos of war, and Diana was proud that she had helped them. Paolo had walked up to her then, and pulled down her head to kiss her forehead, saying simply as he pointed to his chest, '*Va bene, puoi andare, ma il tuo cuore rimarrà proprio qui.*' OK, you can go but your heart will stay right here.

Now Paolo suggested to his friends, in between enormous bites of sweet roll dipped in honey, that they go downstairs and see if *il ispettore*, the inspector, had brought back any candy with him. Diana began to correct him, that Travere had still not returned, but Francesca confirmed what the boy said.

'*Molto presto stamattina, mentre era ancora buio.*' Very early this morning, while it was still dark.

'He's here?' Diana asked disbelievingly, passing baby Evangelina off to her mother and heading for the cellar steps. The children went to follow her, but Francesca called them back, sensing that Diana wanted to be alone. Why hadn't Travere come to see her when he got back? It was nearly nine o'clock. If he had returned while it was still dark out, he must have been in the cellar now for nearly four hours. What had he been doing all this time? And had he found a vehicle? She had not heard anything that morning, and her open bedroom windows gave on to the drive. Surely, she would have heard something, even the steady clip of a horse's hooves, if it had passed that way. She switched on the cellar lights, which flicked brightly for a moment before shorting out. She exhaled in frustration, feeling for the flashlight they usually kept at the bottom of the steps. It was gone. Maybe Travere had taken it. No matter. She would feel her way down the long aisles of hoarded, useless junk; she knew her way well enough by now. She would just be careful when she got near the trapdoor. She did not relish the idea of falling down thirty-odd stone steps. As she walked, she ran her fingers lightly over the stacks on either side of her for guidance. Eventually, the pitch blackness seemed to lighten a little in front of her, taking on a dark grey rectangular shape. The opening to the tomb. She reached her arms out, like a child playing blind man's bluff, and then began to descend the staircase, the light below her becoming brighter with each step. Her foot made no sound as it touched down on the stone floor of the tomb, the silt – thousands of years old – muffling her step.

Travere had not noticed her arrival. He sat, motionless, on one of the packing boxes with his back towards her, a hurricane lamp and several folders arrayed in front of him on another crate. His elbows were on his knees and his hands were in his thick hair. As Diana drew closer to the frozen figure, she could see his hands were balled up into fists, as if he had been trying to pull out his hair by the roots right before he was turned to stone.

'Giacomo?'

She had barely whispered the word, but he jumped up as if a shot had just been fired. His face was twisted in an expression that was neither rage nor confusion but something more. In another moment, Diana recognized it for what it was – sheer terror. He glared at her as if seeing a monster, a ghost, even, one of the Etruscans come back to haunt him for disturbing her rest.

'Giacomo, it's me.'

She reached out her hand in an assuring gesture, but he flinched reflexively, stepping back from her and bumping into the wood of the crate.

'Shh, shh, now,' she coaxed, as she used to for her shell-shock patients, for young boys shaking violently, lashing out suddenly at enemies only they could see. 'Hey, now, darling, come on, baby,' and now she was using the voice she had used back home, on pediatric patients putting up a fight against a cast or a hypodermic needle. He seemed to recognize her then, his face starting to crumple, as if he wanted her, badly, but also wanted her as far away as possible from whatever nightmare he was trapped in.

'Francesca said you came back this morning,' she started very slowly, taking a tentative step forward, relieved he did not jerk away. 'Why didn't you tell me?'

He looked confused, as if she was asking him the wrong question. Diana went on.

'Were you able to find a car, or a truck?'

'A car?'

'Yes, Giacomo. You left two days ago, to get something to move all this out.' She made a sweeping motion with her arm. Surely, he remembered that, could remember that. He shook his head, although to Diana it did not seem to be in response to her question so much as his trying to erase something from his memory. Diana took a step, and then another. She was close enough to reach her hand out, to try to take his arm.

'You didn't find a car, then?'

He rubbed his face roughly, as though trying to wake himself up. He squinted hard as if concentrating was physically painful.

'A car is coming. I mean, a truck. Maybe two. Tomorrow, or the day after.'

He put out his hand as if to steady himself, but Diana took hold of it and held it firm.

'Giacomo?'

When there was no response, she repeated, 'Giacomo. Look at me.'

Her voice was very low, but commanding, and he obeyed.

'What on earth happened?'

He looked down at her now, with pity in his eyes, but not

pity for her. He opened his mouth as if to speak, but only a tortured, animal sound came out. The next instant, he was kissing her hard, his free hand supporting the back of her neck, his soft moans continuing as he kissed her, again and again. Diana seemed to see white lights exploding in her head, to feel – despite herself – something rise within her to join him in his agony and ecstasy. But he pulled away too soon, before she could find him, wherever he was. He released her, his head bowed low, panting hard. Diana still held on to the wrist she had taken hold of when he had seemed about to stagger. They were only inches apart.

'I'm sorry, Diana,' he murmured, his eyes shut, burying his face in her hair. 'I needed to do that.'

He was shaking, his body now trembling against hers.

'I needed to know there was still something warm and human left on this earth.'

SIX

Diana and Travere sat in the open field where Diana had come to find herself, a lifetime ago, the morning before Adler arrived and turned her world upside down. She had held on to Travere's wrist after their kiss, tugging at him, leading him like a chastened child, and he had followed her, obediently. They had emerged from the dark of the cellar into the bright kitchen, out of the side door, over the patch of grey-green by the well where they had quarreled, across the dusty farmer's lane where Adler had called her his prey, out into the fields ready for harvest. It had been slow going, the dry grass up to their waists, hard seeds filling their shoes, trudging through it like explorers in a trackless land. Diana had stopped in the middle of the largest field, up on a hill, its golden expanse falling down and away from them into the valley. They were utterly alone, no one near, nothing to mark their presence but the squiggly line of bent stalks they had left in their wake that was already beginning to disappear in the freshening wind. Diana inhaled sharply, the sweet, malty smell of grain all around them. The wisps that escaped from her tight braids showed the same deep copper as the highlights that played over the ripening field. She pulled him down and they sat opposite each other, his crossed legs making him seem even more like a little boy. She took his other hand in hers and looked into his face, although he kept his eyes averted. She felt strangely, completely, in control.

'Giacomo, tell me what happened.'

He didn't respond, except to mechanically pluck at the blades of grass under his fingers. Diana persisted.

'To make you feel like that, to . . . to make you kiss me like that, to see if the world was really rotten? What happened? What did you find this morning?'

Giacomo's hand froze for a minute, although he continued to stare at the ground.

'I can't tell you, Diana. You know that.'

'Fuck that.'

His eyes shot up in surprise and met hers.

'Giacomo, I know you're not supposed to tell people about your work. About your secrets. But I'm a US Army nurse, not some secret agent you met in Paris. I know you take oaths and promises when you sign up – just like we do, for that matter – and I'm sure that's probably a good idea, in most cases. But not in this case.'

Her grip tightened on his wrists.

'I can see that what you found down there, whatever you found this morning, is eating you alive. You looked like you had seen a ghost. You looked as if you'd seen Death himself.'

'I had.'

The passion in his voice startled her, like the animal cry he had made earlier.

'Then *tell* me, Giacomo. I won't tell anyone else – who could I tell, anyway? I'm still military, even if I am a non-combatant, I wouldn't be allowed to. And I know if you go carrying this around inside of you, it will eat you up. I've seen it too many times before.'

Her voice trailed off for a moment, as she saw again all the deathbed scenes with all the dying boys who had unburdened themselves to her – and all those who had died before they could.

'And . . . and . . .' she continued, surprised when her own voice began to falter. 'We'll be leaving here soon, and then we won't see each other again. So tell me – tell someone safe – while you still have the chance.'

The waves of grass around them bent in the wind, undulating like a golden sea. Travere seemed lost in thought for a long while, before the shadow of a smile flickered across his lips.

'So, I'm to whisper my secret to you, like in King Midas?'

Diana took heart at the connection he was making between himself and the ancient Greek barber who had gone out into a field very much like this one, and dug a hole, and whispered into it his secret that the king had ass's ears.

Diana smiled encouragingly.

'Yes, something like that.'

Travere paused for another moment, his face once again taking on its lost expression.

'I can't tell you all of it. I can't tell you most of it, Diana.'

She held the silence for him.

'But, if my plan works out, it won't matter so much if I tell you, just a little bit of it, anyway . . .'

To Diana, this aside seemed more for his benefit than for hers. He went on.

'But it might help if I say some of it aloud, if only so we can see how right we were, in this war, I mean. How right we were to fight them, those damn Nazis.'

Travere shifted quickly to his knees, bringing both of Diana's hands up to his chest. He seemed filled now with a kind of nervous energy, as if he had to tell her quickly before someone – before he – stopped himself.

'Remember how I told you this was a safe house during the war? Well, it seems like Adler was a regular here. Those files, downstairs, a few of them are from different offices and departments, but most of them are signed by Adler himself. My guess is that, as the war was ending over here, he saw which way the wind was blowing and hedged his bets by storing important files here, rather than at some government office where they would be destroyed before the Allies – or he – could get to them.'

Diana nodded, as he rushed on.

'Well, from what you and everyone told me when I got here, Adler came back to collect something and leave. That told me whatever it was *was* important. If a German officer has made it out of Allied-held territory, he does not lightly come back into it. Not unless the thing he wants is something he values as much as his life. More than his life, actually.'

'But Signora beat him to it, and collected the files and hid them in a tomb Adler didn't know anything about?' Diana offered.

'Right.'

Travere closed his eyes and was so still Diana felt he had said everything he was going to, until he spoke again.

'Do you love me, Diana?'

The question took her by surprise.

'Giacomo, I don't . . . I mean, we haven't known each other . . .' She stumbled over her words, embarrassed that her body was still pulling her towards him while her mind was pushing her away.

'Because it will matter, Diana. If you love me. If I can trust you not to repeat what I'm about to tell you.'

Good, she thought. *I can get out of this without answering him directly.*

Aloud, she said, 'I've already told you, Giacomo, yes. You can trust me.'

Loose strands of hair whipped her eyes as the wind picked up, and she blinked away the tears.

'Adler was a scientist. Those files down there are the results of years of research. He wanted to take them with him before he left Europe.'

'He was going to take all of that? There are hundreds of files.'

'No, I don't think he was going to take all of them. Just the encoded ones, the ones you need a key for.'

Diana remembered how he had marked the box with a trident, sloshing on the black paint.

'The studies were done for the advancement of science, and medicine, and if they proved successful, they would benefit the whole world.'

Travere's voice sounded odd and mechanical as he said the words.

'I went into town, not this village but three, four villages over. Found someone who could find someone to get word to the Americans that I had something and would need help moving it out. The officer I eventually met with told me to come back here and secure it, that they'd send a truck in a day or two. One of the major roads is blocked but they would clear it by then.'

There has to be more, Diana thought. None of this was enough for his wild-eyed look she had seen earlier.

'The American officer – I can't tell you what branch – he seemed to know about Adler. At least, he had heard of his work. He was especially interested in Adler's work with the Luftwaffe, research into reviving pilots who had crashed into the English Channel during winter. I remembered seeing those words when I was decoding the files – *pilot* and *channel* and *freezing* – but a lot of it, even when decoded, hadn't made sense, at the time. So, this morning when I got back, I went straight downstairs and pulled those files. And, this time, I understood.'

Travere let go of Diana's hands.

'Their doctors wanted to know if you could bring back a pilot who had frozen.'

'You mean, if you could resuscitate someone with hypothermia,' Diana corrected, but Travere shook his head.

'No, Diana. Not that. I mean just what I said. Can you bring a man back to life, after he has frozen to death?'

Diana recoiled, not from Travere, but from the implication of what he was saying. She put up both hands, as if to stop him.

'No, Giacomo, no.'

But he didn't seem to hear her any longer, didn't even seem to know she was there.

'They took prisoners from their concentration centers – death camps, it turns out, is what they were – and they tested their hypothesis. Held men down in tubs filled with water and blocks of ice and killed them.'

There was silence between them.

'I hadn't understood it, before, because the code words they were using for their test subjects were *cow* and *horse* and *adult pig*. But the Germans documented everything: body temperature, ounces of alcohol given as stimulants, the exact volume of water and dimension of each tub. And that's when I figured it out. There is no way a large animal could have fit into those containers, not even a full-grown pig. The only thing that could fit was a man, with his knees drawn up, sitting up to his neck in ice water.'

Silent tears were streaming down Diana's face.

'After that, it was easy. Everywhere I looked. Some experiments Adler had overseen in Poland, on *rabbits*, tests in which incisions were made in the subject's right leg, and bones removed, or bacteria cultures and bits of wood and dirty glass inserted to cause infection. But rabbits have four legs, not two, not just a *right* and a *left*. And these *rabbits* were always referred to as *she* and *her*, and then I realized that camp was only for women.'

Travere swallowed hard.

'They were using human beings in their experiments like we use mice and rabbits and guinea pigs in ours, but they even called them that. They saw them like that. And there was more,' he went on, staring into space. 'Adler was fascinated with mind control, if you could achieve that with drugs, and deprivation, and a combination of those and hypnosis.'

Diana remembered the feel of Adler's fingers on her wrist, the swirling amber cordial picking up the light, the power that had seemed to emanate from the man's eyes.

The sun poured down on the two figures crouched in a field, dark figures oblivious to the beauty of summer all around them, transported to concrete cells splashed with ice water and blood, listening to the echo of screams that still carried across Europe.

Diana was the first to recover, wiping her eyes on her sleeve.

'Thank God we found it. Thank God the Americans will take it now and destroy it. And thank God we stopped these madmen.'

Travere looked up, his face haggard, his eyes rimmed with red. He struggled to his feet.

'Thank you for listening to me, Diana,' he said, but his voice was flat and lifeless. Diana had thought talking about it would help him, help release him from his torture, but Travere seemed more defeated than ever.

'Don't go,' Diana said, reaching out her hand towards him, saying again the words that had brought comfort to so many desperate men. 'You're not alone.'

Travere looked down on her, sadly, for another moment, before striding away quickly across the field.

'I wish to God I was.'

Diana walked up the long hill back into town, one last time. Halfway up, she passed the shrine to Saint Anne, where she had slept while Adler was being murdered, past the home with the chickens and the girl in pink, where Diana had knelt in the dust and forgave herself for the loss of another child. When Diana reached the *piazza* in town, she saw a knot of old men and small children crowded around the tobacconist's shop. She knew the town had run out of tobacco months earlier, and wandered over to see what the attraction was. The old men were talking loudly over each other, gesticulating at a newspaper that was being snatched from one hand to the next. Diana caught the image of a battleship, and Japanese men in incongruous top hats and tails standing alongside American servicemen in khakis, and then she saw the words in thick, block print. *Il Giappone si arrende.* Japan surrenders.

Diana stood motionless in the square, as the men argued and the children ran in and out among them, laughing and trying to steal packs of stale gum from the distracted shopkeeper. It was over. It was really over. All the death and the destruction, all the countless lives lost around the globe, and it was finally over. She stepped back from the little group, walking towards the side street that would take her to Lucia's. She moved like someone in a dream, looking down at the shiny, slate-grey cobblestones beneath her to make sure her feet were really touching them. Japan seemed a world away, the men standing at attention on that deck as far from her as the sun or the moon. But they were real men who had stood there and said words and signed papers that would change the course of the world – of Diana's world – because now the war was over. She had been ready to go back to the army, to serve in the Pacific and, most likely, die in the Pacific, but now no one would be going because the war was over. She kept repeating those words to herself like a mantra, like a prayer she could not yet believe had been answered because she had stopped daring to ask for it. She wanted to feel elation inside – to whoop and holler as she was sure people were doing back home, stopping work and throwing up their hands, kissing friends and strangers alike, holding on to their young boys who had just been called up but would not have to go. She wanted to do and feel these things, but she couldn't, not yet, wandering as she was down a Tuscan side street that had remained unchanged for half a millennium, through a sleepy, sun-drenched town that had just survived its own war, which would see to its own healing before turning its attention to the Orient. Diana was unable to take in the enormity of what had just happened; it was too much, coming from too far away, leaving her numb inside. But she knew, someday soon, that elation would come.

Diana stopped walking and found she was in the same dark alleyway, in front of the same gaping portico that had swallowed her up only a few months before, when she had been desperate enough to sell her soul, only to have it flung back in her face by a bunch of laughing women. But back then, they had been faceless, nameless entities, throwing back their heads and baring white teeth. Now Diana knew them as people, as young girls, as innocents caught in the crosshairs of war. Diana smiled when she realized – despite their differences in age, and education, and even nationality – they were more alike than different. That she would be glad to call any one of these young women her friend.

She spent the day with them. Blessedly, Lucia was out, and Diana and the girls could speak freely. She asked after their rations, their treatment by the men in the towns, if Lucia was good to them. Two of the girls were pregnant. There had been three, they explained, but one girl had miscarried after visiting *strega glicine*, the witch of the wisteria vines, an old woman who lived outside the city gates by the church of Saint Agnes, whose small home had become almost completely overgrown by the creeping, purple flowers. The two girls proudly presented their firm, round bellies for Diana's inspection, laughing and rubbing the small of their backs. Diana checked on the other girls – out of the whole household, half a dozen were showing the first signs of venereal infection and needed antibiotics, and one girl – who had been struck during a bar fight – needed three stitches above her left eye. But Diana did more than just administer first aid during her visit. Emboldened by Lucia's absence, she did in the open what she had only tried clandestinely during her earliest days with them. She encouraged the girls to seek other employment, to carve out new lives for themselves, on their own terms. Even to the girls who had been sold as children, who had grown up in Lucia's house and knew no other life, Diana preached heresy, urging them to seek out work as scullery maids, nannies, and even, eventually, students when the schools opened up again, just as the posters back home in her high school cafeteria had encouraged her to seek out her own career.

'But, *signorina*, no one hire us,' they said in the halting English they were picking up in the cities. 'They will no permit us in their schools. We are bad girls. We are fallen.'

'Fuck that,' Diana laughed brazenly, the girls laughing along with her, surprised to hear the word that needed no translation.

'Who knows that?' Diana asked, impassioned. 'Just the people who live here, in this small town. The next town over – in Pienza, Chianciano, Acquaviva – no one knows that. No one knows *you*. You do not deserve to be here, to be bought and sold. You work hard. But you could work hard at something else, and keep your own money, rather than have Lucia take it all.'

Diana gave them her address back home, spelled out her rank and full name carefully for them, even the middle name she hated, and had them memorize it in case Lucia came upon the small slip of paper and destroyed it. Diana would be their patron, their reference, an American Army officer who would vouch for them, *Dear sir or madam, Angelina is the perfect cook, Rosaria an honest housemaid, of course Benedicta can be trusted with your children, I would trust her with my life.*

As the rest of the girls stood around giggling or strutted about with sheets draped over their shoulders imitating ladies of leisure, Diana saw Gabriella frown and take up a basket of damp laundry. She followed the girl downstairs and out to their small, enclosed back yard, crisscrossed with half a dozen clotheslines.

'You did not like what I said?' Diana asked as she came up alongside the titian-haired girl and helped her hang up a printed sheet. Remembering Gabriella had spoken no English at all when she had arrived, Diana tried to translate the question she had just asked.

'*Non – non ti è piaciuto quello che ho detto?*'

To Diana's surprise, the girl answered her in English.

'Is OK. I know small English now. I understand what you say to us.'

'But you do not like it?'

Diana snapped out a pillowcase to get rid of the wrinkles before securing it with an ancient clothespin. Gabriella shook both hands in a placating manner.

'Is no that. Is no I no like. Is only . . . what is the word in English? Is no *nice*? No, maybe, is no *thanks*?'

The pretty girl closed her eyes and squinted hard.

'Ah, is difficult, in your language. The word for me is *grato*.'

'*Grateful?*' Diana asked, translating quickly. 'You do not think it is *grateful*, what I suggest? Grateful to who?'

The sun burned down on the girl's hair, turning it to strawberry gold. She smiled.

'To Donna Lucia, of course.'

The horror showed in Diana's face.

'To that woman? That horrible, horrible woman? How can you, Gabriella, how can you say a thing like that?'

Gabriella turned a placid face towards Diana.

'I owe it her. I belong to her.'

Diana took the long nightdress from Gabriella's hands and tossed it back in the basket, taking the girl by both hands and speaking very slowly.

'You do not belong in this place. You are beautiful inside, like an angel—'

Gabriella smiled, as if she were placating a tiresome child.

'Your English. It is *difficile*, difficult. I no mean I belong here, to this place. I belong to Lucia. She owns me. She bought me.'

Diana stared, incredulous. Suddenly, a loud voice from behind them made Diana jump.

'That is right. The girl is right. She is stupid as the *agnelli*, the little lambs who trust everyone, even the farmer when he cuts their throats. But she knows her place. She belongs to me.'

Donna Lucia strode across the lawn, towards the pair. Gabriella dropped her eyes meekly and turned to finish putting up the laundry. Diana kicked the basket over and snatched the wet clothing from the girl's hands.

'No, Gabriella. Listen to me. Donna Lucia is wrong. You do not owe her anything. You do not belong to her.'

Lucia laughed, menacingly.

'Ah, the pretty American with her pretty ways. Maybe for you, with your fine manners and your money, maybe for you, you are free. Although do not forget when you come to me, hungry. You are willing that day to do things you are ashamed to admit now.'

'I am not ashamed.' Diana was yelling now, she was almost screaming. 'I was hungry. These girls were hungry, that is the only reason anyone comes to you, to be yelled at, and kicked, and treated worse than dogs.'

There was a whoosh and a rush in Diana's ears. Gabriella's angel face looked scared as she held out her white arms, separating the women from each other.

'Do not fight. Is no worth it. I no worth it. I belong to her, this is true. She paid money for me, she tells me this. It is simple. Oh, do not fight!'

The slender girl looked fragile, swaying between them as the sheets whipped in the wind, but Diana had become a fury.

'I will fight, Gabriella. I'll fight for you, even if you won't.'

'Stop your nonsense,' Lucia roared. 'The girl is right. I tell her I buy her, and I do, for the price of a train ticket. Her mother work for me, and becomes *incinta*, pregnant, and when this stupid child is born, her mother come to me, weeping. Say she is in love, with someone she first meet in the last war, a German, no, maybe an American soldier – I don't know which, they all fuck the same.'

Diana saw Gabriella flinch a little at Lucia's brutality. She realized the girl was hearing these details about her parents for the first time.

'She sells me the child, says she will be beautiful, like she is, but please, she must go to the man and she needs the ticket. So, I buy her and she leaves and that is why this *capretta*, this kid goat who bleats and blahs and trusts the world like an idiot is mine.'

Gabriella was crying. Her hands were by her side and her head was bent and she was crying like a lost child. Donna Lucia cursed and walked up to her, her hand raised to strike the girl across her face, but Diana stepped between them.

'How much?' Diana asked.

Lucia was stunned for a moment, her hand still poised in the air.

'You interfering American. What do you mean? How much do I buy her for? The price of a ticket, twenty years ago. I have told that already.'

'No,' and Diana's voice was suddenly devoid of emotion. It had become cold and hard and businesslike. 'How much to buy her off you, now?'

Both women stared at Diana, their mouths open.

'I have saved up my pay at the bad house. Whatever you pay for these girls on the open market, I am prepared to meet that.'

'But—' Gabriella began.

'But,' Lucia interrupted, pushing the young girl aside, 'what will you *do* with her?'

And, for a moment, Lucia's eyes narrowed, as if seeing Diana for the first time, trying to discern if there was some aspect of her she had misjudged, some proclivity or persuasion she had not considered before.

'I will not use her, and barter with her, as you do. That's all you need to know. Name your price.'

So the two women haggled and negotiated, as Gabriella – from sheer force of habit – slowly picked up the scattered garments and hung them neatly on the line. In the end, they settled on a price, Lucia laughing and making crude gestures, Diana calmly telling the girl to get her bag, she would be leaving this place and never coming back.

'I belong to you, now?' the girl asked flatly, expecting no more from life than to be bought and sold, as Lucia had done, as her own mother had done.

'No, you blessed girl.' Diana's face was beaming. 'Now you belong to yourself.'

Diana knocked on Bugari's door and waited for a response. It came, very low, and if Diana had not had her ear pressed to the door, she would not have heard it. As soon as Diana saw the old woman – back in her own bed now, blankets pulled up to her chin, despite the heat – she knew Bugari was dying. The hands that rested atop the white bedding were motionless and nearly translucent, the thick blue veins showing through the papery skin. Her face looked slumped, uneven, and Diana immediately thought of stroke. Bugari's dinner tray lay untasted on the side table, the glass of water left that afternoon still full. Diana lifted the cup to the old woman's lips, supporting her head as she took a sip.

'Take another,' Diana coaxed, but the old woman frowned, shaking her head almost imperceptibly. Diana replaced the glass and sat down gently on the edge of the bed.

'Signora, I am leaving. Going back to America. I have come to say goodbye.'

The old woman looked at Diana for a long while, her dark eyes inscrutable.

'But, before I go, Signora, I found something I want to return to you.'

Diana pulled the small leather volume from her pocket and slipped it on to the bed. The old woman ran her fingers over the smooth cover for a moment, before slowly bringing the journal up to her chest.

'I know what I have said here.'

'I found it, Signora, down below. Where you had Adler's papers concealed.'

Bugari closed and opened her eyes again slowly.

'Yes, I lost it around that time. I did not know where I had left it. It makes sense, now, that it would be there. Secrets buried with secrets.'

Diana smoothed back some iron-grey hairs that had gotten in the woman's eyes.

'Travere does not know. I did not tell him I found it. I read only the inscription myself.'

'Yes,' Bugari smiled weakly, closing her eyes. 'A man would not understand what is in here. What I have said.'

The room was absolutely quiet except for the ticking of an ornate mantle clock, loud and rhythmic. Diana thought Bugari had fallen asleep until she spoke with an unexpected vigor.

'I am dying. And I surprise myself that, at the end, I do want to speak. So much of my life has been lived in silence or, when I spoke, I was lying. I would like to tell the truth, for once, now that it does not matter any longer.'

Bugari opened her eyes and stared hard at Diana.

'I have kept so many secrets and, now, there is no time to recount them all. If there were, I would tell you of my sister, my little *fagiola*. I loved her more than life, I realize that now, but I lost her, while we were young. And I had to take work, work without honor, as you did. And then I had a chance and I did something bad, for which I am not sorry.'

Bugari's expression was set, remorseless.

'I switched places with a rich woman who had died, a woman my own age, a woman who was coming to live in this house for the first time, where no one would know I was not her. Those were happy times, or the only happy times I knew after *fagiola*, because I was young and I was in love with a man I thought loved me, too. But he only loved my money.'

Bugari's voice trailed off for a moment, before rallying.

'Or he loved mostly my money and only a little bit me. But when he died, too, and left me with my baby daughter, that hurt me as now I cannot even imagine hurting, but I felt it then. It hurts so much when you are young.'

Diana felt Bugari was revealing so much of her past, so much of herself that Diana could not take it all in. The color was draining quickly from Bugari's face and Diana tried giving her water again, but she waved it away, impatiently.

'No, there is not time. Not for that. Not for me to tell you how lost I felt, how empty. And then, it is not important how, but I was introduced to work I was good at, during the Great War. Work I continued, even until now. Even until Adler.'

Bugari's lined face darkened as she said the man's name.

'That man you call a detective, the man you brought back from the village that day, he has found Adler's papers, I know. And that is all right, because he will simply do for me what I planned to do all along but am too weak now to finish.'

Diana interrupted.

'What do you mean, Signora? Travere is handing the files over to the Americans.'

'Exactly.'

And the old woman looked deep into Diana's eyes, as if willing her to make the connections.

'You want the Americans to find them? You were not working with the Germans, all along?'

Bugari shook her head slowly from side to side.

'Do you not still see? Yes, I offered to the Germans what they thought was safety, here, during the war. They trusted me. And so I learned things I could pass on to the Allies. Eventually, the Germans started leaving things in my safe-keeping, important things. But Adler came back before I could arrange to have his documents moved. And then he told me something – something that changed everything – and then the files did not matter any longer.'

The door opened and Giuliana came in. She scowled at the untouched dinner tray and then began to shoo Diana out of the sick room.

'*No, no, tranquillo, tranquillo,*' Bugari urged, motioning weakly with her hands. 'Be calm, old friend. It is the end now, and I tell the girl what we did.'

'*L'uomo era una bestia*—' The man was a beast— Giuliana began viciously, but Diana cut her off.

'What *you* did? What you did, to Adler?'

Diana looked at the waif in front of her, the spindly arms and legs stretched beneath the thin blankets, and remembered again Adler's height, his girth, his pink, healthy flesh bulging above his celluloid collar.

Giuliana came and sat down heavily on the other side of the bed and silently took Bugari's hand.

'Giorgio and Giuliana are my oldest friends,' Bugari went on, a sad smile on her face. 'No, they are my only friends. But they were also my confederates, in my work, in this war and in the last one. They helped keep my secrets. And my daughter – who, when she grew up, chose a life like our own – she was our biggest secret of all. Until Adler found her.'

Bugari's voice cracked, and Giuliana continued, at first in a rapid Italian and then switching quickly to English for Diana's sake.

'He killed her. His army had her killed. She was so beautiful, so smart, she work in the *resistenza*, not here but in *Francia*. And when he discover she is from this town, he become suspicious of Signora – a woman he has always trusted, a woman who has always been a powerful ally – and he hurries here, unsure if his secrets are safe. Luckily, he does not know about a daughter, so he cannot be sure. But his documents are missing, and he does not fully believe Signora when she tells him German soldiers come and take them away a month before. So he searches the house, and he nearly finds them. He was near to finding them the night he died.'

Bugari raised her hand to interject.

'I am the one who is dying, Giuliana,' she chided gently, the other woman pressing her hand to her lips in apology.

'Miss Bolsena, my two faithful companions will try to tell you we are all equally responsible for Herr Adler's death, but it is not so. By the time I called them into my room, I had already given him the draft that should have killed him. But he had an unnatural strength, he was only stupefied by the drug. Between the three of us, we got him outside, and held his head underwater until he died. Even so, he put up a tremendous struggle.'

Diana shook her head, as if erasing the image Bugari's words conjured up in her head.

'And when you sent the boy into town, you were expecting the local police, someone to accept Adler's death without question.' Diana smiled wryly. 'And I brought back a detective inspector.'

'Did you?' Bugari asked pointedly.

Diana remembered Bugari saying Travere behaved as no inspector she had ever met, as someone not interested in solving a crime. She recalled how readily Travere had given up his search for a murderer as soon as he got close to Adler's secret. She remembered Travere pushing her away when she was sure he had been about to open up to her, saying there were things he could not tell her yet.

'What do you mean, Signora?'

But by now Giuliana was supporting Bugari's back as the old woman coughed into a lace handkerchief, a rattling noise sounding in her throat. Giuliana brushed away Diana's attempts to help.

'Go, now, there is nothing you can do. This is death and we know how to meet him. But go to your *ispettore* now, if you have any more questions. If he is even still here,' and, as Giuliana said these last words Diana, too, could hear the rumble of a truck engine outside the window, and the sound of men calling loudly to one another.

'There you are,' Travere said distractedly, in between breaths, struggling to hoist one of the boxes into the back of the idling truck. The driver, a young man in civilian clothing, was helping him. Diana looked at the interior of the truck, which was nearly filled with the boxes Travere had labeled.

'I asked Giorgio if he had seen you, but the old man was pretty closed-lipped with me. I offered to help him with that' – Travere gestured with his chin – 'but he said he had it under control.'

Diana looked towards the garage where Giorgio was struggling with a burn pile that was beginning to get out of hand. The old fencing and broken furniture had caught fire and now the flames leapt ten feet into the air. Giorgio poked at it with his rake, trying to topple the stack and decrease the height of the flames that were threatening to ignite the overhanging branches.

With a grunt, the two men got the box on to the truck bed.

'You've got your stuff?' Travere asked Diana. 'Ready to move out in a few minutes?'

He wiped his brow with a linen handkerchief, dark patches showing on his shirtfront.

'What are you going to do with all these?' Diana asked, her quiet voice belying the emotion she felt. She didn't want to believe what Bugari had implied – that he was just finishing her work for her. That he was not a detective inspector at all. That he was not what he appeared to be.

'We've gone over all this already,' Travere answered, frowning, as he passed the last box up to the other man in the truck. 'I'm handing this in at the nearest Allied outpost—'

'Why?'

Diana's voice was sharp, and for the first time Travere looked up and seemed to notice her. He smiled tentatively, his voice light and playful.

'That's a funny question. What would you like me to do with them? Give them back to the Germans?'

Diana did not return his smile.

'Why are you giving these to the Allies? What will they do with them?'

Travere smiled again but shot a sidelong glance at the driver, who was looking now with interest at the American lady.

'*Cibo in cucina*.' Food in the kitchen.

Travere nodded in the direction of the house. The driver looked at Diana and then back at Travere. He shrugged, jumped down from the truck bed, and sauntered away.

Travere walked over to Diana and took her by the arm, leading her over to a nearby cluster of olive trees.

'In answer to your first question, it's my duty to hand these over. And, as to the second,' his voice rising in annoyance, 'how the hell do I know what they'll use them for?'

'But you do believe they will *use* them for something?'

'What are you talking about?' Travere looked lost.

'I mean,' Diana continued, enunciating every word, 'you think they will use this stuff, as opposed to destroying it?'

'That's not for me to say . . .' Travere began, but he released her and would not meet her eyes. Diana took hold of his hand.

'Giacomo, remember how you felt when you read those files for the first time, when you felt the whole world had gone rotten?'

'It's not all rotten, Diana, I was wrong. It's just the Germans, they did these things, horrible things for sure, and it threw me there for a minute. But the world is still good. We are still good.'

'We're still the good guys, Giacomo?'

Diana's voice was soft and low, and, again, he misread her meaning.

'Exactly.' He sighed in relief. 'You see what I mean. The Germans were wrong to do these things, absolutely wrong. But now that they've gone and done it, well, it'd be a waste to just throw it all away. We could learn a lot from them, from . . . from what they did. We can take what they started and make the world a better place.'

Diana's dark eyes bored into his.

'By becoming like them. By continuing their experiments. Are we going to freeze men, too, Giacomo? Are we going to use human guinea pigs, too?'

Travere cursed, stamping his foot and twisting his wrist out of her grasp.

'Now you're just being childish, Diana. You're just being a stupid kid. The world's a nasty place, you'd better learn that if you haven't already. And the Soviets, well, we don't want them getting their hands on this stuff before we do. It's America or them, after this war. One of us is going to come out on top, and I'll be damned if it's those commies.'

'You're not sounding much like an Italian, right now, Giacomo.'

Travere looked quickly towards the house, as if making sure they hadn't been overheard. He snatched the keys from the ignition, glanced in the direction of the isolated maze garden, and pulled her along with him until they stood alone at its entrance.

'OK, kid, here goes,' he began, running the fingers of his free hand through his bushy hair. 'You're US Army, so you can't repeat anything I tell you. If you do, I'll just say you're lying, so don't even try.'

He seemed to notice he still had a tight grip on her upper arm. He released it, rubbing her sleeve gently, as if erasing the mark of his fingers beneath the bold stripe print.

'Some of the things I told you before – well, they weren't true,' he began. Diana shot him a scornful look and seemed about to speak, but he hurried on.

'No, wait, let me finish. I wasn't *allowed* to tell you the truth. About me, or what I was really doing here. When you came into town to report the death of one German, I had to see if that German was the one I had been sent to find. So I used one of my backstories – I have a couple – and Detective Inspector Travere was born.'

He paused for breath.

'Is that even your real name, Giacomo?'

'Yes, actually. But it's Captain Giacomo Travere, US Army. The guys just call me Jack.'

Diana stood still for a moment, taking in what he had said.

'And the way you spoke, when you first got here. Your difficulty with English . . .?'

'That was easy to do. I spoke Italian back home, in Brooklyn, before I spoke English. I just remembered what it was like for me, in school, trying out my twenty-five-cent words to impress everyone, only to have the other kids laugh, and the nuns say I would never pass as a real American. You don't forget that stuff.'

Travere looked at the maze without seeing it.

'But that's one of the reasons I was chosen for this assignment, Diana. Italian and English I already had, and German was my major in college before I joined up. I was at the front line, pinned down by a bombardment, when this jeep pulls up and some bigwig asks if I'm Lieutenant Travere, and next thing I know I'm being driven to divisional HQ and given new papers and a new rank and a new job. To find German scientists who were hoofing it out of the country and persuade them to come work for us.'

'Persuade?' Diana asked, the suspicion sounding in her voice.

'Yes, *persuade.* OK, a couple were ornery and I had them detained, but I can tell you most of them were only too eager to cut a deal with Uncle Sam. They agreed, right off the bat. They had had enough of Hitler or, at least, enough of their laboratories being bombed out, never enough supplies for their experiments, or enough food to go round. They cut deals for themselves, and their families, and some of their staff, even. I had to turn people away.'

Diana was silent for another moment before speaking.

'If this is all so hush-hush, why are you telling me, now?'

Travere stepped forward eagerly, slipping his hand around her waist and pulling her gently towards him. 'Because I love you, you idiot.'

His face broke out in a smile, his perfect teeth flashing.

'I love you and I want to start telling you the truth. It doesn't go well if you build a relationship on lies. I've had to lie, for my job, and I'd be in a hell of a lot of trouble if anyone ever found out what I've told you already – if they found out I let you help me with those files, even. But that won't matter, now. We'll drop this stuff off. Once we do that, it's out of our hands, it's not our responsibility any longer. And' – Travere's free hand caressed her cheek – 'there's another advantage to getting back to base. We can get the chaplain there to marry us – today even.'

'You're asking me to marry you?' Diana asked in disbelief.

Travere slipped to his knees in front of her.

'Will you marry me, Diana Bolsena?'

She didn't move. She didn't even seem to breathe. When she didn't respond, he pulled her close, resting his head against her abdomen, and, against her will, something turned over inside her. On some level, some part of her wanted him, but still that small voice, that tiny undercurrent pulling towards the shore, even as she was in danger of being swept out to sea.

'And the papers, Giacomo. All those papers. You'll be able to give them to our army and never think about it again? It won't keep you up at night?'

'You're the only thing that will keep me up at night, I hope,' and his hand started at the back of her ankle and slowly began to move its way up her bare leg.

'Giacomo, it's wrong,' she nearly moaned.

'Don't be a prude, darling. You'll be my wife this time tomorrow.'

She pushed him away.

'Not this.' Her voice was angry, exasperated. 'What you're doing, with those files. Continuing that work. It's unconscionable, Giacomo. It's wrong.'

Travere knelt for another moment, his face perplexed, before springing to his feet.

'You know,' he began, shaking his head and laughing bitterly, 'you're a really sweet kid, the kind of girl I'd like to marry. Hell, the girl I'm *going* to marry. But you've got to grow up. Not everything is Florence Nightingale shit.'

Diana felt as if she had just been slapped, the prelude to an all-out fight. But she suddenly realized it was a fight she was ready for.

'Giacomo, we fought these guys for a reason. What they did – to innocent people, to prisoners of war, to women, to their own countrymen – that was inhuman. You can call it the march of science, you can say they did it to make the world a better place. But I'll call it by its real name. Murder.'

Giacomo scowled at her, wiping the back of his hand across his mouth. When he spoke, his voice was low and gravelly.

'If we don't do this, Diana, some other country will.'

'Then let them,' she nearly screamed. 'At least it won't be us. At least we will not be doing the exact same thing these butchers did to the weak and the helpless. If we do these things, don't you see, we *become* them. We will be no better than them. And we will have no more right to stay in power than they did.'

'You shut your mouth, Diana. I will not have you say that. I will not have you speak against your country like that—'

'Against my country? I am speaking against Nazi scientists and the terrible things they did, and I am fighting to stop you from bringing that filth back home. You can't do it, Giacomo.'

'I warned you. Shut up. I will not have my—' but he didn't stop himself in time.

'Your what? Your wife, Giacomo? But I'm not your wife yet, am I?'

A thought seemed to dawn on her, and she continued in a hushed voice.

'Is that your big rush to get married?'

Travere opened his mouth, but she cut him off.

'As your wife, I couldn't tell on you, legally, tell them what you told me, what you showed me. You don't love me at all, do you? You were just using me, from the first, to get what you wanted. And now you're in a scrape, you'll even go so far as to marry me to get out of it. No wonder you want to bring this stuff home. You're no better than Adler.'

He struck her, then. It was so fast she hadn't seen it coming, it was just pain – a stunning, disorienting pain, like when the shells would go off too close to the medical tents and the concussion knocked the girls over sideways. She could see his lips moving, see his white face looking scared at what he had done, his hands reaching out towards her. But she was too fast for him. She was running, into the maze, between the tall, green walls four feet thick, running with the distorted sound of his voice coming to her as if she were underwater, breaking the surface for a moment and the sound coming clear before diving back down again. She had never been in the maze before, it had always seemed ominous and foreboding to her, something men like Adler would use to hide their evil deeds. But here was another man, ostensibly not like Adler, ostensibly her countryman, so much more beautiful, so much more attractive than Adler had ever been. Even through her pain, she felt again his face pressed up against the small pleats of her dress and her body cried out for that, wanting to feel again the lurching, the desire, the magnetism. The mesmerism. And then she felt again the pressure of Adler's thumb, she looked down at her wrist even as she twisted and turned down one green alleyway after another, heedless of where she was going, heading towards the center of this wicked place. She felt that tapping on her wrist, her body remembering the energy that had seemed to emanate from Adler, pulling her towards himself, a darkness that had threatened to engulf her completely, that she had been only too eager to throw herself into. And she knew the two were the same. Adler's thumb against her wrist, Travere's face against her belly. They were one and the same. They were neither of them love, they were neither of them even a longing for her, but a desire to entrap her. An attempt to ensnare her. A man laying a careful trap for her and then asking her, willing her to step into it.

Diana shook her head, and first one ear cleared, and then the other. She could hear Travere calling for her now – saying he was sorry, saying he loved her, saying anything to stop her from running – but he was much farther away than she had thought, nearly on the other side of the green. Without warning, she found herself back at the entrance. The topiary walls were so high she had had no idea of where she was. She stumbled out of the maze on to the white pebbled walkway. And then she was running again, gasping for breath, heading for the truck.

There was no one in the courtyard when she returned, the driver still enjoying Francesca's generosity. Next to the garage, Giorgio was still cursing at the junk pile, the blaze still too high, kicking at its edges as it threatened to creep closer to the wooden structures. She jumped into the back of the truck, scanning the boxes quickly, running her fingers over them,

looking for one in particular. She knew she would have only
one chance. She seized the box marked with the trident, it was
heavy and she strained to get it out from where it was wedged
beneath two others. She prized off its lid and, as she staggered
down from the truck, she saw Travere emerge from the maze,
no longer shouting but staring at her coldly. She was calling
to Giorgio as she ran, the old man taking in the scene, the
young girl running with the heavy box, the young man maybe
only fifty yards behind her. Giorgio threw down his rake, but
as Diana readied to throw the box into the fire, Giorgio stopped
her.

'*Aspetta*.' Wait, he said, grabbing her around the arms. 'What
are you doing?'

'There's no time, Giorgio.' Diana struggled, surprised at the
iron of the old man's grip. 'Let me burn these, please. Let me
go before he gets here.'

She shot a look over her shoulder and saw Travere was
closing the gap, he would be upon them in a moment.

'These belonged to Signora,' Giorgio said calmly. 'She had
me hide them, to keep them safe for the Allies. This man' –
his eyes glanced up at Travere, who was running towards them
like a sprinter – 'he is Allies. He will take them there.'

Diana stopped struggling, realizing she could not free herself
by force. She knew, given enough time, she could reason with
Giorgio, make him understand that the papers his employer
had hidden without knowing their content would not be something she, or he, or any reasonable human would want to be
saved, recipes as they were for the destruction of the world.
She knew she could make him see all this, if she had time.
But her time was running out. She could hear Travere's breath
coming in short bursts as his shoes crunched against the stones.

'Artemis,' Diana said, looking Giorgio square in the eyes.
'Remember Artemis.'

The old man's eyes opened wide, and a second later he
released her. Diana wasted no time, dumping the paper files
into the very heart of the blaze. She heard Travere yell, felt
him push her violently aside a moment later. From her
position on the hard ground, she saw Travere grab the rake,
plunging it deep into the fire, trying to pull out the paper that

was quickly curling into black ribbon. The wind shifted, and the living, breathing flame suddenly bent towards Travere. The air between them rippled and Diana heard him scream as the heat beat him back, singeing his hands as he dropped the rake. The fire made a rushing sound as it righted itself, an enormous orange column, reaching up, blackening the twigs of the yew branches high above. Diana looked and saw the papers destroyed, lost in the heat and light that twisted into itself, writhing and alive, dying down only to rise again, like a phoenix.

Travere stared, open-mouthed, at the flames, then kicked the stones angrily in his rage.

'*Puttana del cazzo*,' he screamed, his voice high and hoarse. Giorgio silently helped Diana to her feet, standing close by her as Travere approached.

'You fucking bitch,' he repeated, pointing at the fire. 'Do you know what you've done? Years . . . *years* of research, gone,' and he stared at the fire for another moment as a few of the larger items – an old cabinet, half of an upholstered settee – shifted and crumbled in the blaze, giving off sparks as the flames lost some of their height and settled down into a steady burn. Diana's temple throbbed from where he had hit her. She didn't respond, only looked at him blankly, as if he resembled someone she had once known but could no longer remember clearly.

'You will go now.'

It was Giorgio speaking, without emphasis or emotion.

'You will take your truck and go, now. And you will not come back.'

For a moment, Travere glared at the old man. Then he laughed, a caustic laugh that distorted his features.

'All right, pops, I'm going. I'm taking what's in that truck and I'll be damned if there's not something in there we can still use. And don't worry, Diana,' he jeered, still trembling with anger, 'don't think you've actually accomplished anything, here.' He motioned to the fire, to the flying sparks. 'There's more where that came from. Killing one man and burning one box of papers won't stop us. We are the greatest nation in the world, and these bastards are going to help guarantee it stays that way. And no stupid, Pollyanna, little idiot like yourself can get in the way of that. Hell, you never even had a chance.' He looked almost pityingly into her eyes as he spoke. 'We have a thousand Adlers.'

Travere turned on his heel, stalking back to the truck. The driver had emerged from the kitchen at the sound of the shouting, a folded *panino* still clutched in one hand. Travere barked at him, and the young man broke into a trot, getting into the cab as Travere joined him, the truck starting up a moment later and rattling down the stone drive and out through the open gates. Giacomo picked up the handles of a nearby wheelbarrow, wheeling it close to the flames. Slowly, he bent to pick up the discarded rake and methodically pitched clumps of wet leaves and sodden hay on to the fire. A white, billowing smoke emerged as the fire damped down, smoldering under the weight and moisture. The wind lessened and, soon, the fire was manageable again, a simple burn pile to eliminate unwanted debris, and no longer the holocaust it had been only minutes before. Giorgio was leaning with both hands atop the handle of his rake, his chin resting on his hands as he surveyed the flames, when Diana came up beside him.

'Thank you, Giorgio. I would have explained if I had had more time. That was the only thing I could think of to make you understand. He was following orders, but those papers, they were—'

He cut her off.

'No, *signorina*. Do not tell me what they were. I know already too much of evil. I know how quick men are to get into bed with a new wickedness when they find it.'

They stood together in silence for another moment. Diana was surprised when Giorgio placed a hand gently on her shoulder, his eyes still fixed on the glowing fire.

'Things hurt when you are young. And the heart can be the worst of all. But do not worry. Something like that' – he jutted his chin towards the front gate, making a grunting sound – 'it burns up in a day. You will find something more, later on.'

Diana looked at the lines that crossed the old man's face, wondering at his own loves and losses, hoping against hope that what he said was true – that she would find happiness, one day. The old man smiled, as if sensing her eyes upon him, and turned to meet her gaze.

'The American Army, they are in *Firenze* now. A few trains are running again, from Chianciano, it is not too far. I will walk with you to the train station tomorrow, and you can go back to your world, Diana.'

He had never used her Christian name before, and they both smiled at the realization. 'But that is tomorrow. *Adesso*, now' – he pointed at the ground beneath their feet for emphasis – 'we go back to the house. There are people there who love you and will need to say goodbye.'

EPILOGUE

No one lives in the old house now. On Tuesdays and Thursdays, and every other Saturday, a bus runs from town and day trippers tour the gardens Giorgio no longer tends, walk the hallways Giuliana no longer keeps clean. Outside, the estate remains very much the same – the white gravel still reflects the light of the Tuscan sun, the lawn remains neatly edged. Padlocks secure the doors to the garage, ensuring no idle boy breaks in, but the cars are gone, sold long ago. The steep stone steps are kept swept and clean, although they no longer lead to the hedge maze. That great span of shrubbery had seemed too gloomy for the new owners who had had it cut down and replaced with grass tennis courts. The owners after them had thought the courts too plebeian and attempted a formal Grecian garden before running out of money. Now the great expanse has gone back to nature, tall grasses swaying in the wind, brightly dotted with poppies, corn marigold, and valerian. For a time, the reflecting pool in the drive had been drained, exposing its chipped, ceramic tiles. No one seemed to remember the story about a man who had died there and, long after the wild grape vines had grown thick over Adler's unmarked grave, the pool was refilled and now, once again, reflects the clouds floating tranquilly on its surface. The perennials that surround the house still come up, year after year, growing a little taller, spreading a little farther with each season, the work of Giorgio's hands living on after him. They stand as a testament to the people who had the faith to plant them because – no matter how many new hands prune, and dig up, and cut back – they always return, unable to die because, despite the sorrow of life, they still love it, they still reach for the sun.

Inside, the kitchen, the sitting room, and the main hallway are kept as they were, fully furnished, the grandfather clock still ticking out the seconds for the visitors as they pass. The tour does not go upstairs, where the rooms are bare except for the sheets that cover the glass chandeliers. The cavernous basement stands empty, devoid of its hoarded plunder sold at auction. Here, tourists hold hands nervously in the half-light before they are ushered towards a gaping hole in the floor, incongruous velvet ropes and brass stanchions setting it off like the entrance to a movie theatre. Ticket holders are allowed down into the tomb, two at a time – three, if they accompany a young child – to enjoy its coolness, and take flash photographs, but emerge disappointed at its small dimensions. There are better tombs in the village, in nearby Chianciano, Orvieto has an entire underground city.

The rest of the week, the house stands empty, regal and beautiful and timeless, but alone. The one-eyed Madonna still dotes on her son, a few more flakes of gold falling silently from the stone wall each year, but no one notices them now. In the beginning, Gabriella had liked to look up at the pair, smiling that the baby's mother loved him, still held on to him after all these years. She worked at the *bad house* for a few weeks only, quickly finding work with a rich family passing through the village, relocating to Lake Como in the north and in need of a helper for their six small children. Gabriella had taken to them right away, and the family had found in her a childlike innocence inexplicable after a war. Diana's reference had secured her position.

Once a week, or once every other, a girl comes in from town to dust the downstairs rooms, nothing more, there is nothing else to do in that great, shut-up house, no children running through its corridors, laughing and disarranging as they go. Dorothea, and Sarina, and even Evangelina Augusta Victoria – who did, eventually, grow into her name – are grown women, with children of their own. Women who stood, silently, as their friend Paolo was laid to rest in the cemetery – between his beloved Giorgio and Giuliana, close by the shrine of Saint Anne – succumbing to an illness that had cut the man off in the middle of a life made rich by love. Francesca had followed soon after – the loss of three boys being too much for her kind, old heart – and her daughters had married and moved off, one as far as Chicago. To the country where their *Miss*

America had returned after the old woman died, and the handsome man who used to bring them candies had driven away without saying goodbye.

Diana never saw him again. She would think of him, on her long voyage home, lying awake in her sister's attic bedroom before she found an apartment of her own. But she used Travere – and, to a degree, she even used her memory of Adler – as a litmus test for the men she met. There were lots of men in post-war America already half in love with a woman in uniform, desperate to get that woman out of uniform. If a man made her insides turn over – if her skin, her lips tingled just being near him – she checked that off in the plus column. But if that man also made her feel like she was nothing, like she was speck that was falling into the black of his void, if he wanted her – not because he loved her or cared for her, but because he was nothingness, and he wanted to cram her into himself to try to fill up what could never be filled by another – she would smile coyly. Put down her drink. Make some wisecrack as the other guys laughed and slapped each other on the back at the woman's moxie. And she would walk away from what could never work, from what had never worked with Travere.

She thought of him the first time she made love to the man who would become her husband. There was that same connection, that magnetism, that pull, as if this was where she had always belonged and always wanted to be. But, unlike how it had felt with Travere, she was still herself. No matter the ecstasy – and, thankfully, there was ecstasy, Giorgio had been right, she did find something more – no matter the heights they now achieved together, they achieved them together, and not at the expense of one another. Not in an attempt to block out the world, or its evil, or even themselves, but in a way that said *I love you and you are still fully you, you love me and I am still fully me.*

In the end, Travere became a memory, an incidental, something she had experienced during the war, like long stretches without rations, or without breaks in between surgeries, or even without proper baths. But while Travere receded in her mind, she noticed with growing concern the effect what he had brought back with him seemed to be having all around her. Man reached the moon, but the man who helped design the rocket that got him there was the same German who had rained down his invention – the deadly V2 rockets – on tens of thousands of terrified civilians. She stayed on in nursing, even after her babies came, and the innovations she saw in surgery, in pharmacology, even the way they neatly pinned and plated broken bones now instead of slathering them in pounds of plaster, made her wonder how much of this was due to the other files – and the other Adlers – Travere and others like him had brought home with them.

Diana was conflicted. The advances in science and medicine were phenomenal, and really did save the lives of those in danger and improve the quality of life for nearly everyone else. But even as a middle-aged woman and then, later, as an old woman stepping back from a long and fulfilling career as both a nurse and a mother, she felt as strongly as she had on the day Travere struck her, that the ends do not justify the means. And the millions – the countless millions of people who had suffered, who had been tortured and killed and discarded like so much rubbish – more and more, she felt herself somehow channeling them, channeling their rage, their righteous anger. What Travere – what her country – had capitalized on, in the name of science, of medicine, of progress, was wrong. The German doctors and scientists who had escaped the gallows of Nuremburg had become some of America's most prestigious citizens. Diana railed against it, despite her advanced age, with all the fury and passion she had felt as a young girl throwing the box with the trident into Giorgio's fire.

The bus pulls to an abrupt stop in front of the gates, the driver slamming the long arm of the stick shift into neutral. The old woman is the only passenger, the heat being oppressive and pleasure seekers flocking instead to Lake Trasimeno. She shuffles down the aisle, passing the driver who wipes his forehead with a yellowing handkerchief.

'*Fa caldo oggi.*' It is hot today, the driver says, replacing his regulation cap over his wet hair. '*Come l'inferno di Dante.*' Like Dante's Inferno.

The old woman doesn't seem to hear him, holding both handrails tightly as she descends the steep steps of the bus and lands, with a little unsteady hop, on to the white gravel. The bus pulls away, its diesel engine rattling noisily, the grey smoke disappearing into the blue-violet sky. The woman crunches her way slowly over the stones, her orthopedic shoes leaving deep imprints behind her. She pauses, but only for a moment, in front of a reflecting pool that has small water lilies dotting its glassy surface. She looks at the fresco on the building to her right – a stately, empty house – but she just nods in the Madonna's direction and moves on. She has come a long way, and there is somewhere she needs to be. She follows the winding drive around the house, passing the empty garage and the tall yew that towers above it. She smiles absently at the perennial gardens, at the life that is still in them, but she is heading somewhere else and she does not stop to admire them. At the back of the house she steps up, almost reverently, to an old hand pump. She looks around her, like a naughty child, but there is no one to see the old lady struggle, sweating in the sun, fumbling with the handle, and then triumphant as the first cough comes, heralding the cold stream of water that has not splashed on to the stone below it in many years. Her hands – thick now, after years of work and service – run under the cool water, bathing her face, neck, and arms, cupping to bring some of the icy coolness to her lips. She leaves the pump, trying to push her way through the trees that line the road, but they have become enmeshed, growing into themselves without break or gap. In the end, she walks the long way around before gaining the farmer's lane, still dusty, still dappled with sunlight and shade and cut off from the rest of the world. She steps quickly now, not wanting to linger, forcing herself not to look back, not to see an outstretched hand, a face passing from sun into shadow, turning into a death mask. At the end of the lane, she turns sharply uphill. The field has been recently cut, and huge, round bales stand at odd intervals, the rest of the field a short, yellow stubble. She continues to climb, glad she has lived an active life, happy she can still walk and move and travel much as she has all her life. Still, by the top of the hill, she is breathless. She stands in the upper field, panting, looking down at the patchwork of beauty that is Tuscany, at green and brown and yellow patches far below, the wind whistling over the shorn field and pulling at her silver hair. She has come a long way to ask something here, in this place, but now she hesitates, the moment finally arriving. What will she say? She has not practiced the words, she told herself she would know them when she arrived, when she stood again on the spot, on the same spot she had before. She closes her eyes, seeing again her friends from the war, long gone, all of them. Her fellow nurses, the friends she made in this town, the old woman who had lived here and seemed so ancient to the young girl but had, in fact, been younger than she is now. She sees the laughing face of Paolo and the children, young and strong, sword-fighting in the sun; the sad, proud smiles of Giorgio and Giuliana; the beatific vision of Gabriella's face when she had been given back her freedom. Then she sees, with a start-ling clarity that had not come to her in decades, the face of the baby in her arms, looking up at her in wonder. But, this time, the fires from the village do not reflect in its eyes; this time it is the gold of the fields not cut short but waving freely in the sun. The baby laughs, a tiny sound, and it catches at the old woman's heart, and breaks it, and releases the words she has come so many thousands of miles to say.

'I could not save you all, I could not even save most of you. So many died, from the evil we did, and from the evil we fought. To those of you who died – alone and scared, hungry and cold and in pain, unsure of what had happened to your world, to human decency – I stand here now, to beg your forgiveness. No, not that, exactly, but something like that. I ask for your love, and I give you mine, because even though you died alone, I still believe my love can reach you, then and now. If love is outside time, I send my love back to you then so that, even for a minute, even for a second, you can know that someone loves you. That you are not alone. That this evil that threatens you now will pass away, and the world will become beautiful again. Shoots will spring up, the world will be renewed as long as there is love. I give you my love and I ask for yours, too. Because I have lived a long time, perhaps too long. But long enough for me to come back here and say what I needed to say before the end, because . . . because I am joining you soon.'

The woman opens her eyes. For a moment, she is not old, but young again, her feet bare in the grass and the fabric of the new dress she has just sewn whipping in the wind. Slowly, she raises her arms, stretching them out like she is on a cross. But what comes across the field towards her now is not the pain of youth, or the disappointment of middle age, or even the fear of obliteration at the end of life. What races towards her now is love, and she knows its voices, recognizes them in every tongue. They are coming for her, arms outstretched, full of joy and laughter and life. And Diana reaches out her arms and embraces them.

AFTERWORD

've only ever told two lies in my life.

The first was when I told my parents I had made Varsity (which was true) and that I was such an asset to the girls' basketball team they couldn't risk my getting injured by continuing to feed livestock (which was false). Despite the patent deception, however, my parents sold the troublesome goats the following week, and that positive reinforcement set me up for my next lie – some twenty years later – that would result in this book.

I lied and said there was an earlier flight out of Houston. Which was ridiculous (the common denominator of my lies being how obvious they are). Back then, anyone with dial-up internet could have logged into their home PC and confirmed, after only a twenty-minute search, that I was already booked on the first flight out of town. But my sister and I had had our first – and last – real argument. And I was immature, and eager to get back East, and said the first thing that popped into my head to make her drop me off early. My sister – being an actual grown-up – didn't even bother to call me out.

I stood at a lone kiosk in the bustling airport. I was checking in so early (as a result of my lie) that the computer was asking if I wanted to switch my seat for one that had just become available in the bulkhead. I typed in *2C* to accept the new seating assignment and sat down to await the boarding call, never imagining I had just changed the trajectory of my life.

They canceled every flight East, starting with Fort Lauderdale, moving up the coast through Savannah, Charleston, and Raleigh, an enormous storm rolling in off the Atlantic. By the time they canceled Washington, our small waiting area had accumulated stand-by passengers for the entire East Coast. A flight attendant stepped forward, announcing in clipped tones the flight for Philadelphia was still departing but would have to depart *now* to beat the storm. No carry-ons, no handheld items, no questions, and we filed in obediently.

We didn't beat the storm. The plane shook with turbulence nearly the whole way back, dropping and gaining altitude continually in an attempt to avoid the worst of it. When we finally landed (amid lightning that lit up the night), we had to stay seated, strapped in, on an active runway, for another three hours, amid the crying of babies and the despairing moans of nearly everyone else aboard.

And I just wanted it to go on forever.

My new seatmate and I had started out with shared interests (basketball figuring in prominently, a nice, karmic hat-tip, I feel, to my first lie), but moved on quickly to deeper topics, our love of medicine, our utter devotion to our families. By the time we hit 30,000 feet, we were recounting our childhoods, and by the time we reached our cruising altitude we were energetically debating ethics, and practicing the right way to pronounce our (very difficult) first names.

Once the captain turned off the seatbelt sign, we were quickly separated amid the rush to disembark. But we had memorized our email addresses (our phones being stowed away in the overhead compartment) and kept in touch over the years, sending good wishes at holidays and birthdays, condolences at the loss of a loved one. When he bought a villa in Tuscany, he lent it to my daughter and I with the graciousness – and casualness – with which one usually lends a friend a ballpoint pen. And the two summers my daughter and I spent studying Italian in Tuscany – in the medieval, hill-town of Montepulciano – became the foundation for this book.

For those wishing to see the places inhabited by my characters in *What We May Become*, they are all still there, waiting for you to discover them for yourself. The real-life Giorgio and Giuliana run the eco-friendly agroturismo *Raggio di Sole*, where you can lie in Diana's wrought-iron bed, or sneak over her balcony wall in the middle of the night. *La Foce* – the incredible gardens created by real-life World War II heroine, Iris Margaret Origo – form the basis for Bugari's lavish estate. The language school my daughter and I attended, *Il Sasso*, is housed in the old hospital, where Diana goes seeking work when she is first stranded in town. Directly across the street from the hospital, you can see the same Etruscan tomb Travere and Diana discover together, beneath a current-day gift shop. If they have not moved off to new adventures by now, the beautiful Benedicta and Gabriella will sell you the incomparable *vino nobile di Montepulciano*, the noble wine of the region, and hand-tooled leather journals and ornate quill pens. Although no restaurants would have existed in Diana's time, *Osteria Acquacheta* is not only one of the finest restaurants in Tuscany, but now among the best, anywhere; visitors stop there on their way to the shrine of Santa Anna with its dried flowers hung in tribute, or *il duomo*, the cathedral in the *piazza grande*, where the cats still sleep in the heat of the day.

One reason I wrote this story is because I am of Italian descent. Italian civilians suffered a great deal during the war, their government initially siding with the Axis, then with the Allies, with a year in-between in which they were relentlessly bombed by American and British airpower until they made up their mind. As Travere tells Diana, Italians had multiple governments during the war, with civilians being rounded up and shot as a result of both the occupying German armies, and the constant change in national loyalties. Italians who fled Mussolini by emigrating to America shortly before the war (like my own maternal grandparents, Giuseppe and Giuseppina Chiaramonte) faced difficulties of their own, many being conscripted by the United States to fight in Italy against uncles, cousins, and even brothers they had left behind only five years before.

But the main reason I wrote this story is because I am an American, haunted by Operation Paperclip and the deals we cut with high-ranking Nazi scientists at the end of the war.

Stephen Kinzer's *Poisoner in Chief: Sidney Gottlieb and the CIA Search for Mind Control* and – even more stunning in the depth of its research – Annie Jacobsen's *Operation Paperclip: The Secret Intelligence Program that Brought Nazi Scientists to America*, provided actual, horrific detail to add authenticity to my novel. But, even more than that, after reading those books I became convinced the only Nazi scientists hanged at Nuremburg were the ones nobody wanted anymore. All the 'good' ones were already working in American laboratories – and living in plush, American neighborhoods – and they never looked back.

I love my country. But the best way – the *only* way – to avoid repeating our country's mistakes is to remember what we did, the bad along with the good. Travere argues with Diana that what he is doing is expedient, is necessary, even, in light of the looming Cold War. And it's true that secret operatives from France, England, and the Soviet Union were scavenging Europe at the end of the war for scientists of their own. But I feel there is a fundamental difference between profiting from evil and *not* profiting from evil. Between realizing there is a potential benefit from utilizing techniques – and *technicians* – trained in inhuman practices, and simply walking away from both. The end does not justify the means, but the American government chose to profit from these techniques, and promote these technicians. And despite any advance in science, I feel we suffered a loss, morally, as a result. Those who think like Travere might rail, and curse, and call me a 'silly, stupid kid,' but I know what I would do, given Diana's choice. I would throw the whole lot into Giorgio's fire.

ACKNOWLEDGMENTS

I would like to thank my editor at Severn House, Carl Smith, for his vision and passion; my agent at Trident Media Group, Mark Gottlieb, for his tenacity and professionalism; my friends and mentors in the DeSales MFA program, Stephen Myers and Juilene Osborne-McKnight, to whom this book is dedicated; James Perano, for taking a chance and hiring me when no one else would; Elango Vinjirayer for sharing his friendship and his villa with me; my sister, Andrea Messineo, for her understanding, and for double-checking my Italian; the four loves of my life, Johnny, Grace, Nicholas, and Sophia; and my little grandbaby, Jack.